Rain Storm

2-24-09

Also by Vanessa Miller

Former Rain

Abundant Rain

Latter Rain

Rain Storm

Only Love Could Calm Her Raging Storm

A novel by

Vanessa Miller

URBAN CHRISTIAN

www.urbanchristianonline.net

URBAN CHRISTIAN is published by

Urban Books
10 Brennan Place
Deer Park, NY 11729

ISBN-13: 978-1-893196-96-4
ISBN-10: 1-893196-96-8

First Printing June 2007
Printed in the United States of America

10   9   8   7   6   5   4   3   2

This is a work of fiction. Any references or similarities to actual events, real people, living, or dead, or to real locales are intended to give the novel a sense of reality. Any similarity in other names, characters, places, and incidents is entirely coincidental.

Submit Wholesale Orders to:
Kensington Publishing Corp.
C/O Penguin Group (USA) Inc.
Attention: Order Processing
405 Murray Hill Parkway
East Rutherford, NJ 07073-2316
Phone: 1-800-526-0275
Fax: 1-800-227-9604

This book is dedicated to my loving daughter, Erin.
Thanks for being your mother's pride and JOY!

Acknowledgments

The years keep rolling by, and I am now on my fourth book. I still say there is none higher than God, no joy greater than what He brings into our lives, and therefore I must thank my Lord and Savior for the great things He has done in me and through me. My God is awesome and I shall meet Him face to face one fine day.

My family is wonderful. Since my first book was released in 2003, they have tirelessly traveled all over the United States with me, spreading the word about the Rain Series. So I'd like to say thank you to my mother, Patricia Harding, my daughter, Erin Miller, my nieces, Diamond Underwood and Jonae' Clark, my sister, Debra Clark, and my brother, Raymond Miller. A special thanks to my cousin, Lala Underwood, for housing me every time I come to Virginia, and to Dolly Hudgins-Moore for housing me in Baltimore.

I am so thankful for the pastors God has given me, Pastor Paul and Keisha Mitchell and Bishop Marva Mitchell, and for my church, Revival Center Ministries International, and all the people in it. Although I attend many different churches while I am on the road, there is still no place like home.

I would also like to thank my editor, Joylynn Jossel at Urban Books/Kensington, my publicist, Rhonda Bogan, and Jacqueline Thomas for all their encouragement and support. And don't get me started talking about my readers and the book clubs that have supported my books. You are #1 in my book.

Any acknowledgments page of mine would not be complete

before I give a big shout-out to my crew, **THE ANOINTED AUTHORS ON TOUR**, Kendra Norman Bellamy, Norma Jarrett, Vivi Monroe Congress, Michelle Stimpson, Shewanda Riley, and Tia McCollors. Thanks for traveling the world with me and spreading the good news about God's grace!

Prologue

And the Lord said to Hosea, Go take unto thee a wife of whoredoms and children of whoredoms: for the land hath committed great whoredom, departing from the Lord.
Hosea 1:2

Cynda was nine when she decided to hate her mother. Standing over the coffin that held the body of the woman who gave birth to her and watching her grandmother sob and fall apart, she whispered, "I hate you for leaving, for loving that man more than me."

"Hush, child," her grandmother said. "It's not right to speak so of the dead."

"It's true, Grammy. She was a whore. The kids at school said so. Her pimp killed her because she gave it to somebody for free."

The smack brought tears to Cynda's eyes and sent her scampering to sit down and "stay in a child's place" as Grammy instructed. Sitting in the back of the funeral home, Cynda listened as men and women openly discussed her mother.

"That Flora was some woman," an old, grey-haired man said.

Another man, his teeth so big, he looked like he should be chomping down on a carrot, said, "Prettiest thing this side of Georgia."

"That was before Romie turned her out," a portly woman dressed in a long black dress added.

"I don't care what Romie did to her. I still wanted to be with that beautiful woman. Something special about Flora, that's for sure," the carrot-chomper said.

"Well," a pretty woman with greenish-blue eyes said, "all the special done been beat out of her now."

A baldheaded man shook his head. "I hope they give that good-for-nothing the chair."

A mean-spirited laugh escaped the portly woman's mouth. "For killing a whore? Get real."

As Cynda got up, she wished that her grandmother could hear all her mother's so-called friends. Maybe she'd backhand each one of them.

The portly woman nudged the baldheaded man. "Hey, that's her kid."

"Look at the flawless amber skin tone and that long flowing hair," he said. "She's going to be more beautiful than Flora ever would have been."

The carrot-chomper's eyes danced over Cynda, his mouth watering in sweet anticipation. "I hope she likes older men."

The group laughed as though they were at a comedy club.

Cynda ran out of the funeral home when she noticed the man with the big teeth leering at her. She knew that look meant she had to get away before he wanted to touch her. She ran down the street, around the corner, and she kept on running until she couldn't remember where that awful place was.

She smiled at her escape, until common sense halted her

glee and caused her heart to pound. If she couldn't remember where the funeral home was, then she wouldn't be able to get back to her grandmother.

She sat down on the stoop of an abandoned house and began to cry. Cynda admitted the one thing she'd refused to accept since they told her that her mother was dead. She was afraid. Afraid to grow up without her mommy. Afraid to be lost.

A chill went through her when a shadow appeared in front of her. Cynda prayed that the man hadn't followed her. She tried to stop the tears. It wouldn't do to look like a big scared kid in front of a stranger, so she tried to wipe her eyes and look grown up. But the tears wouldn't stop rolling down her face. Without looking up, she asked, "Why are you bothering me? What do you want?"

"I came for you," the stranger said.

Cynda looked up. At first all she saw was a glow. No, more like a big burst of light. She blinked, and as the light dimmed, this huge man stood before her. Cynda liked the blinding light better. She blinked again. This man was too big, too scary. As she scooted back a little on the stoop, all she could say was, "Huh?"

"You are lost, are you not, little one?" the big, scary man said.

"Why do you want to know? Why are you bothering me?"

"The Good Shepherd sent me."

"The good *who*?"

The strange man sat down next to her. "The Good Shepherd. He sent me here to bring you safely home. You are lost, right?"

Cynda nodded. She saw no harm in admitting what a blind man could see. After all, she had been sitting on this stoop crying like she'd just gotten beat with three of Grammy's thickest switches.

He reached out his hand to her. "Well, come on, Cynda, your grandmother is frantic with worry."

For some reason Cynda didn't fear this man as she did those bad men who leered at her during the funeral. "How do you know my name?" she asked, putting her small hand in his humongous one.

"The Good Shepherd knows all."

They walked around the corner and up a few blocks. They walked around another corner, and then the strange man lifted his long arm and pointed. Cynda looked down the road and saw her grandmother, who was pacing and looking more mad than worried.

"Why'd this Good Shepherd guy care so much about me?"

"The Good Shepherd loves all that belongs to Him. And if one should get lost, He would leave all the others to go find that one and restore her to her rightful place," the man explained.

Okay, she didn't understand all that, but whatever. This nice man had brought her back to her grandmother. She opened her mouth to ask his name, but before she could get the words out her grandmother frantically screamed for her.

Flailing her arms in the air, Cynda yelled, "I'm right here, Grammy."

Grammy ran toward her. "Oh, thank You, Lord. Thank You." She picked Cynda off the ground and swung her around. "I was so worried about you, chile. Are you all right? How did you find your way back?"

"I'm okay, Grammy. I was lost, but this nice man helped me find my way back."

Her grandmother put her down and looked around. "What man, baby?"

Cynda looked around also. "I don't know, Grammy. He was right here. I promise."

She hugged her granddaughter again, and as tears streamed down her face, told Cynda, "Maybe that was one of God's angels protecting you." She looked to Heaven and prayed. "Lord, we let Flora get away, but if my precious Cynda should ever lose her way, please send another angel to lead her back to where she belongs."

1

Cynda sat on the edge of the bed, swinging her leg, impatiently waiting for her last customer to get his pants on and leave her alone.

"Woo-hoo, I tell you what, girl, the half has not been told about the wonders of your pot of gold," her customer said. His bloodshot eyes greedily devoured her as he lay on his side, a tattooed elbow propped under his thin body.

Great. A poet. Cynda smiled to herself and threw his blue jeans at him and glanced at her watch.

"Oh no, you don't. I paid for an hour and I'm getting my whole hour this time. I want to talk," he insisted.

Rolling her eyes and rubbing her temple usually helped Cynda's customers understand that they'd overstayed their welcome. But not the poet. This knucklehead thought his words could sway her, make her change her mind.

The Poet walked around the bed, got on his knees in front of Cynda, and put his hand on her leg. "I want us to be together, baby." Happy fingers traveled up her leg. "You don't have to be out on these streets. Why don't you let me get you a place?"

"You want your own personal whore, is that it?" Cynda tilted her head and smacked her lips.

His hand stopped. He stood and turned his back on her. "It wouldn't be like that, Cynda. I want to take care of you."

She got off the king-size bed, squeezed into her red leather skirt, and bent down to put on her stilettos. "What would your wife say about you taking care of me?"

"I done told you about bringing my wife into this."

Cynda stood and straightened her mini. "Look, I've got to go. Why don't you go home and spend some of this quality time with your family?"

The poet sucked his teeth. "Why you always gotta talk trash?"

"Why you always gotta act like a fool?" Cynda threw on her tank top and grabbed her purse. "Let me ask you this— How much money have you put aside for your son's college expenses while you're making plans to put me up?"

The poet put on his pants, grabbed his hat and keys, then opened the motel door and turned back to face Cynda. "You know something . . . beautiful outside and ugly inside is a horrible combination."

"Whatever, man. Don't overstay your welcome and you won't see the ugly side of me."

He rolled his eyes and then slammed the door behind him.

Cynda sat back on the bed and took the money out of her purse. Between her three customers she'd earned a hundred and fifty dollars. Three years ago a trick wouldn't have been able to look her way with fifty bucks. Back then she was raking in three to five hundred per trick. Back then she did her tricking at four- and five-star hotels. Today she received her callers at the Motel 6.

Someone knocked on her door.

Cynda quickly put her money back in her handbag and prayed that she wasn't about to get robbed. Not today. She had something important to do with that money. Something real important. "Who is it?" she asked.

"Girl, it's me, Jasmine. Open up this door."

Cynda smiled. Her girl Jasmine was cool people, big fun all the time. They'd gotten into some deep stuff that made them call on the name of Jesus. Well, Jasmine called on Jesus, but Cynda would rather ask for Satan's help. As far as she was concerned, Jesus hadn't done jack diddly for her, so why should she waste her breath?

Cynda opened the door, and Jasmine floated in, her boyfriend Cooper straggling behind. The two couldn't be a more awkward pair. Where Cooper was tall and lanky, Jasmine was short and well-fed. Cooper's cheeks were sunken in, and his face always bore a frown. Jasmine, on the other hand, could put life into the dullest party.

"Girl, I thought your last customer would never leave. Coop and I just finished selling our stuff and I had a little left over." Jasmine pulled a bag of weed out of one pocket and some rocks out of the other. "Let's get this party started."

Cooper rubbed his hands together. "Lay it out and let's get to it."

Cynda held up her hand. "I've got to go, Jasmine. I can't get into this right now."

"What you talking 'bout. Girls like us are always ready to party."

"I've gotta get to Spoony's. Today is Iona's birthday."

Jasmine looked at the watch on her chubby wrist. "That girl don't get out of school until three o'clock this afternoon. You've got at least an hour before you need to be over there." She put the bags of temptation against Cynda's nostrils and shook them. "What you gon' do?"

Cynda hesitated. With the bag still under her nose, she couldn't concentrate on what she had set her mind to accomplish that day. "Spread the stuff on the table," Cynda

ordered her friend. "I don't have all day. I've got to get
going."

The frown on Cooper's face reversed itself. "That's what
I'm talking about."

Jasmine shook her ample behind as she put the stuff out
on the table. As Cynda watched her friend she remembered
the time she'd asked her how come smoking crack didn't
cause her to lose weight like it did for most people. Jasmine
told her then, "Them crackheads get so high, they forget to
feed themselves. But I don't care what I'm doing, a dinner
bell always goes off inside my head."

Cynda walked out of Motel 6 at five o'clock with ten dollars to her name. The money she'd made earlier was supposed to go to Iona, her daughter, for a birthday present. Or
better yet, a hundred was for Spoony for benevolently
housing her child, for which he charged her a thousand dollars a week, and the other fifty was to take Iona out to eat
and pick up a doll for her. But the money went up in smoke
from her crack pipe.

Now she stood at Spoony's door, shaking like she was
headed to the electric chair. Spoony would kill her for blowing that money.

Spoony wasn't just her baby-sitter. Actually, he didn't
baby sit at all. His loser of a wife, Linda, did that. Spoony
was Cynda's pimp. Cynda had lived with Spoony and his
stupid, go-for-anything wife, until Spoony threw her out of
his house a year ago and then refused to let her take her
daughter with her. That way, even though he'd stopped
housing and clothing her, he was still able to pimp her because she had to bring him her money in order to see her
child.

Cynda reminded herself for the thousandth time how un-
wise it was to make a deal with the devil. She rang the door-

bell and waited. The devil's big, angry feet stomped toward the door and swung it open.

Spoony growled, "About time you got yourself here. This girl been waiting on you since she got out of school."

Cynda stepped past the crusty blue-black man who haunted the doorway and smiled at Iona. She was standing in the middle of the living room with one of them frilly white dresses that went out in the eighties. Linda tried her best, but the woman needed to get out more.

"Happy birthday, baby," Cynda said as she bent down in front of her daughter and hugged her real tight.

"What did you bring me, Mommy?"

Closing her eyes, Cynda wished for leeches to suck out her blood while a lion clawed her heart out. Horrible mothers deserved deaths like that, didn't they? She opened her eyes and forced herself to look at her daughter's innocent face. Iona's excited eyes always reminded her of someone else. Someone who didn't want anything to do with her. Someone she'd rather forget. But her daughter looked more like him with every passing day. That smooth chocolate skin and those deep dimples were a signature from the man Cynda refused to think about.

"That's what Mama needs to talk to you about." Cynda nervously rubbed Iona's arms. "See, Mama doesn't have any money right now. I was hoping we could celebrate your birthday this weekend. I'll be able to take you some place real nice then, okay?"

"You don't have a present for me, Mama?"

Cynda's heart ached as the excitement seeped out of her daughter's eyes. Where were those leeches? Why didn't her heart explode after she put her daughter's birthday money in a crack pipe? A tear trickled down her lovely face.

"Don't cry, Mommy." Iona wiped the tear from her mother's face. "Auntie Linda gave me lots of presents. Do you want to see them?"

Auntie Linda was always showing her up. "Not right now, baby. Why don't you get your hat and coat and let Mommy take you to get a slice of pizza?" It was only the eleventh of October but already windy in Chi-town.

Spoony grabbed Cynda by the back of her coat and pulled her up to face him. Snot drizzled from the hairs in his big black nose as he snarled at her. "Where's my money?"

Cynda turned to Iona. "Baby, go in the other room with Auntie Linda."

Iona didn't move.

"Where's my money?" Spoony asked, his fist looming down on her. "I'm not going to ask you again, Cynda."

"I didn't make any money today." Cynda braced herself for the blow she knew would knock her across the room.

The first lick caused blood to trickle from her lip and knocked her against the black cocktail table.

"Iona get out of here!" she screamed.

Spoony then took a handful of her hair, twisted it around his hand, and then yanked it as he punched her in the eye.

Iona ran out of the room whimpering for her aunt.

"You think I can't tell that you smoked up my money?" Spoony threw Cynda on the ground and kicked her with the pointy part of his boot. "It's in your eyes, liar. They're glassy."

Cynda grabbed her rib and forced herself not to cry. "I just want to take my daughter out for a slice of pizza, Spoony. Why do you have to do this on her birthday?"

"She ain't going nowhere with you."

"Let me have my kid, Spoony, please. That's all I want from you."

He opened the front door and dragged Cynda toward it, kicking her in the ribs as he threw her out. Just before slamming the door he told her, "Maybe I should call her daddy and get all that back child support he owes me."

Cynda wanted to spit on him as she lay on his porch

bruised and battered. He always threw that up in her face, reminding her of the secret they shared. Which was the reason she allowed herself to be pimped by this animal. She was tempted to just leave, never look back; just forget that Spoony the devil existed, but her daughter was still in there. And it was her birthday.

Cynda began to pound on the door and plead with Spoony to let Iona come with her, but her attempts fell on deaf ears. With tears streaming down her face, she stood and straightened her clothes. As she walked down the steps, a searing pain shot through her. She sat down and lifted her shirt. Her chest was black and blue. Spoony messed up everything. Didn't he know that birthdays were important to little girls? She still remembered the last birthday she'd spent with her mother. She'd been left outside knocking then too.

"Mama, please let me in." Knocking harder on the door, Cynda said, "Come on, you know it's my birthday." Footsteps thudded toward the door. "Do you hear me, Mama? I want to open my presents now."

Flora wiped the sleep from her light brown eyes as she inched the door open. "Hey, baby," she said to her then nine-year-old daughter, "you know I've got company right now."

"Are we going to have a party today?" Cynda asked, concerned only about her birthday and not the man her mother was entertaining inside.

Flora touched her daughter's smooth, young face. "No, baby. Mama has to work today."

"But we always have a party on my birthday. You always get me lots of presents."

Flora's head bowed low as Romie walked into the hallway. His big Jackson 5 afro swayed this way and that as he stalked toward them. "Are you bothering your mother?" he asked. "She's busy."

Cynda backed away from him, terrified of his cold black

eyes. Her mother made her call him Uncle Romie, but Cynda's Grammy told her that she'd never birthed no low-life animals, so he wasn't her uncle. "But it's my birthday," she whined.

Romie grabbed her arm. "Come with me, baby girl. I've got a present for you."

"No! No!" Cynda pulled away from him and barreled into her mother, pushing Flora backward into the bedroom. The smell of must wafted in the air. "Don't let him take me, Mama, please."

Flora's eyes widened as she looked from her daughter to Romie.

There was a man in Flora's bed. He sat up and pulled the cover over his naked body. "What's going on, Flora?" the man asked.

"Nothing, Ralph," Flora answered him. "Just go back to sleep."

Romie barked, "You don't have time to be fooling around with this child. You need to be making some money."

Flora reached into the pocket of her robe and pulled out several bills. She threw them in Romie's high-yellow face. "Is that enough money? Now can I please spend a few minutes with my daughter on her birthday?"

Fire flashed in Romie's eyes as he smacked Flora. He then grabbed a handful of her long black hair and pulled her close to him. "Don't make me beat you this morning."

Flora put her hands up. "Okay, b-baby. Calm down."

Romie grabbed Cynda's hand. "I *am* calm. You get back over there and handle Ralph. I'll take Cynda with me."

Birthdays stopped being special for Cynda when her mother failed to stand up for her. Today, she'd done the same to her daughter.

2

Keith Hosea Williams closed his Bible and then knelt down in front of his mammoth leather chair and prayed. He dubbed his office "the throne room," and this chair, "the throne of God." Keith bowed down before this chair whenever he prayed. He loved to be in this room. He loved to talk with God each day. He and his Heavenly Father met in the cool of the day, the dark of the night, and just about any time Keith needed to lean on the Lord. Like most new converts, Keith gave his life to God after some trying times. But, unlike most, it took murder to bring him to his knees. Sometimes, when he closed his eyes he could still see Ray-Ray falling to the ground, lying in a pool of blood. The night Ray-Ray died, Keith swore that he'd never touch another gun. The only problem with his declaration was that he made his living as Isaac Walker's enforcer. Simple job description— Shoot hustlers with attitudes.

When Nina told him about God's love and how He forgives sin, Keith knew he would spend the rest of his life safe in the arms of his Lord.

The Lord had blessed him to start a construction company that was well on its way to earning millions. Construction work suited Keith. Six-two and 220-pounds of rock-hard muscle, he was more than able to handle any job thrown his way. It was his baby face that caused people to do a double take. Teddy bear on steroids he'd once been called. He didn't care. He liked his face and thought it added a soft touch to an otherwise hard body.

All those years ago, Keith had learned to trust God. Twelve years later he still didn't doubt his Lord.

Well, he did have one problem. Keith's Lord and Savior, as he prayed, had just spoken into his heart, telling him the name of the woman he would marry. As far as Keith was concerned, it was the wrong name. In his heart he felt that he had already met the woman he was sure would be a wonderful helpmate. He hadn't heard God's word right, that's all. Somehow Satan had snuck into his throne room and was speaking into his ear.

Don't get him wrong, Keith had much love for Cynda Stephens, but it wasn't the I-wanna-be-your-baby's-daddy kind of love. Keith shook his head as he remembered the last time he'd seen her. Like a wild cat, she'd stormed into Isaac's wedding reception and told him and his new wife that they didn't mean nothing to her. As high as gas prices were, why would she drive from Chicago to Dayton if they didn't mean anything to her? It sure wasn't to throw rice at the departing couple. Salt, maybe, but not rice.

Then Cynda blurted out that she was the one who'd informed the cops about Isaac's drug run, causing him to do three years of federal time. The thought of that moment still sent sweat chills to Keith's forehead.

Cynda's declaration was a true test of Isaac's salvation. Where he and Isaac came from, snitches got shanked. Cynda should still be on her knees thanking God for Isaac's salvation. But right now she was probably on North Street selling her body.

Go see about her.

"What do you want me to see about her for?" He looked to Heaven and said, "I'm telling You right now, whether this is a call from God or from the Devil, I ain't about to turn no hooker into a housewife."

He waited on God to respond. Waited for God to tell him that Satan had been bound, gagged, and banished, and would never again be allowed near the throne of God, requesting to sift His people as wheat, but God didn't say a mumbling word.

He is the Almighty, Keith reasoned, and didn't have to speak if He didn't want to. So Keith backtracked. The last thing he'd heard from God was, *Go see about her.*

He could do that, right? No big deal, but marrying her would be another story. Standing, Keith put down his Bible and picked up the keys to his sonic blue Ford Ranger.

Driving down the streets of Chicago, he wondered, not for the first time, why he still lived here.

Since finally marrying Nina a year ago, Isaac was now a permanent resident of Dayton, Ohio. Truth be told, Keith wanted to be there, helping with his best friend's street ministry, but God kept his feet planted in Chicago. He left Bishop Sumler's church after Isaac and Nina married and was now attending a small church on the South Side. The pastor was a decent, honorable man, and Keith knew that he could grow spiritually at this church. Maybe he would talk with Pastor Norton about what God had to say about Cynda. Maybe he needed to see a doctor, get on medication or something.

Keith got off the highway in one of the hot spots and turned on Slumville. Or was it Trashville? *When did the trash man run around here?* He held his breath and rolled up the window as he parked. "I must be crazy," he said to himself.

Just as he was getting out of his truck, his phone rang.

Hopefully it was Jesus calling to change the plans for his life. He looked down at the caller ID. It was his boy, the Ike-man. Keith smiled as he hit the talk button. "What up, playa?"

"What's with all this playa stuff?" Isaac told him. "I'm a happily married man now."

Sometimes that fact slipped Keith's mind. He wasn't used to his boy being hooked up like that. He kept praying about it. Didn't know if it kept slipping because he was still in love with Nina, Isaac's wife, or because he was getting older. He chuckled. "Okay, I'll try to remember that."

"Do you have plans for next weekend?"

Keith glanced outside his truck window. A lot of people with nothing to do were leaning against walls or walking down the street like zombies. *Somebody should hand them some gloves and a trash bag.* "No. What's up?"

"You remember Spoony Davidson?"

A knock on the window caused Keith to jump. The man outside his window asked, "Hey, man, you looking to get your high on?"

Keith held up a hand to the snaggle-toothed brother. "Yeah, I remember ol' Spoony. Couldn't tell you the last time I saw him though."

"It's been about ten years for me. That's why I need to come down there. I'm really starting to feel bad about not reaching out to him since I got out of jail."

Spoony Davidson had been Isaac's mentor. As a twenty-seven-year-old pimp, Spoony taught the eleven-year-old to pick pockets, run women, sell drugs, and how to set up his own territory. Isaac thought it was high time he returned the favor. He wanted to teach Spoony a thing or two about his Lord and Savior, Jesus Christ.

"You sent him a couple of letters when you were in prison, right?"

"Yeah, but I haven't contacted him since."

"All right, man. I feel you. Come on down. Maybe I'll even go evangelizing with you."

"Like old times."

The pang of wanting to be with his friend to help in his street ministry stabbed at Keith. "Yeah . . . like old times."

After ending the call on that note, Keith got out of the truck to do a little evangelizing himself. Flesh and temptation were sold by the hour all day long on this street.

A woman in Daisy Dukes and an unbuttoned shirt exposing mounds of cleavage said to him, "Your wait is over, baby. I got what you need right here."

"No, thank you. I'm looking for someone," Keith kindly replied.

Twenty years ago he had walked these same streets looking for a woman. He had loved that woman with all his heart and just wished that she'd made better choices in life. Now God had sent him back to the same place to save another woman. He doubted that this was going to turn out any better.

Farther down the street an older woman pushed on her bra, exposing what the Good Lord endowed her with. "I'm right here, sugar," she cooed. "Come tell Mama what you need."

Keith shook his head and tried to walk past her.

She grabbed his arm. "What's a matter? 'Fraid I'll be too much woman for you?"

He removed her hand from his arm, his blood pressure rising. "I don't want what you're offering. I'm looking for someone."

"All I want is twenty bucks. I'm a lot cheaper than these other whores down here."

"Hey, why don't you leave him alone, Granny? Didn't he ask you to leave him alone?"

Keith recognized the voice. He closed his eyes to the reality of this place and turned to face Ms. Cynda Stephens. She'd been Isaac's lady over a decade ago. When Keith met her back then, she was one of the most beautiful women he'd ever seen. He wished then that he'd met her before Isaac did. Maybe her life would have turned out differently.

After all these years, even with her current lifestyle, she still took his breath away. Her type of beauty didn't fade easily. She had that J-Lo thing going on. But if P. Diddy saw her now, instead of falling all over himself to drop his model of the week, he'd probably loan her a bottle of Proactiv.

"Hey, Keith, what you doin' down here?" Cynda asked him.

He took note of the short skirt, stilettos, and the low-cut shirt showing bosom and belly. "Looking for you."

She laughed. "Wonder what your God would say about that?"

He studied her face and found her hazel eyes mesmerizing. He knew she'd purchased that eye color, because her natural eyes appeared coal black, but the hazel looked good with her amber skin tone.

What didn't look good on her was the fat lip and swollen cheek. Fire shot through his eyes as he speculated on how her wounds might have come about. Before he could think about it, his hands were caressing her face. "What happened?"

She averted her gaze and moved his hand from her face. "Just some black splotches."

"You know I'm not talking about the pimples and splotches on your face." He pointed at her swollen eye. "Who did that?"

"Man, you know what I do. It's just a hazard of the job."

He backed up, inhaling deeply to calm himself. "Do you have some time? I'd like to talk to you about something."

"Time is money."

"How much for an hour?"

"For an old friend like you, fifty bucks."

He pulled his wallet from his back pocket and gave her a hundred.

"What you want to do, man? I'm all yours . . . for the next hour anyway."

"Have you eaten?"

Cynda twirled her hair around her finger. "Not since yesterday."

"Can I take you to lunch?"

"If you want to waste money like that, I won't complain."

They walked hand in hand toward his car, the prostitute and the man of God, for God told him to take this woman to be his wife and to love her, so that he might know the magnitude of God's love for a world that continually whored after other gods.

3

Cynda tossed a few fries into her mouth. "So what's this free lunch all about?"

Cutting up his pork chop, Keith said, "I just wanted to check on you, see if you need anything." He took a bite, chewed, and then pointed his knife at her lip and cheek. "Looks like I came just in time."

"Please . . . I get a black eye about once a month." She touched her cheek. "This is nothing."

He clasped his hands together. "Well, I'm here to take you away from the nothing that keeps going upside your head."

As Cynda laughed, some chewed-up hamburger flew out of her mouth and onto the table. "Sorry," she said, picking up her discarded hamburger pieces.

"I'm serious. I've got a job offer for you. See, I just opened my own business about nine months ago, and I could use help with all the paperwork. You used to be a receptionist, didn't you?" Keith's current receptionist was Janet Price, but he planned on finding her something else to do.

"Look, Keith, for years I've watched you stare at me, so I know you think I'm attractive."

The acne splotches on Cynda's face was the only diminishing quality on her otherwise gorgeous face, which he figured would go away when she stopped using drugs. "You're not just attractive, Cynda, you're the most beautiful woman I know."

She held up her hand and cut her eyes. "Whatever. Look, all I'm saying is, if you want to get some, you don't have to dress it up with a job offer. Just show me the money and I'm good."

He looked to Heaven. *Did you hear her?* Then he turned to Cynda. "I'm not running game on you, and I'm not trying to get some. I'm here because I want to help you. Will you let me be a friend to you? It sure looks like you could use a friend right now."

Cynda took another bite of her hamburger and shoved a couple of fries in her mouth. "I've got to go, Keith." She attempted to stand. "It was nice seeing you again."

Keith raised his hand and pointed to his watch. "Not so fast. You still owe me time."

Cynda looked at her watch. "I'm like a psychiatrist. I give fifty-minute hours."

"But I paid for an extra hour. Remember?"

"Why don't we just consider the other fifty a tip? I've got things to do."

"A normal tip is about fifteen percent."

She slunk back in her seat. "Look, man, what do you want from me?"

Keith smiled. "I want to be your friend." He reached out and touched the back of her hand. He looked into her eyes. "I want to give you a hand up, get you off these streets."

She pulled her hand from his grasp. "How do you know I don't like what I do? Matter of fact, I love it." She leaned closer to him and seductively said, "I'm good at what I do,

Keith. If you want to know how good, we can go get it done right now."

He leaned back in his seat. "I'm not interested. Guess I just don't like to share."

Her face hardened. "It's your loss." She stood up. "I've got to get going, but this has been real fun. If you're on my side of town again, look me up, okay?"

Keith pulled out one of his business cards and handed it to her. "If you change your mind or need help, don't hesitate to call me. I mean it."

Cynda put his card in her purse and left without looking back. She stepped out of the restaurant and sashayed down the street.

As a car pulled up next to her, she bent over and leaned into the driver side window. Then she ran to the passenger side of the car and jumped in.

4

At the end of the day, Isaac liked to walk around his neighborhood and talk to God about his plans for the people God had given him. Of course he did his talking with his mouth closed. Wouldn't do to have the people he hoped to convert think he'd truly lost his mind for Jesus.

God had been good to him. He'd spared his life more times than Isaac could recount. Back when all the craziness was going on, Isaac didn't realize that God was watching out for him. He just thought he was a bad somebody. Little did he know, God had brought him out of a life of drug dealing, running women, and killing so that he could reach back and bring others out.

He used to own a crack house on the very street he now walked down. Broadway, and the surrounding streets, used to be his territory. And nobody messed with what belonged to Isaac Walker, because back then he'd kill to protect his turf. Money and power was what he craved, and he had plenty of both.

He, Keith, and Leonard spent many nights in that crack

house, counting money and distributing slow, intoxicating death—crank. Well, that was before he'd murdered Leonard.

The memory still stung and caused him to turn away from that house every time he went by. Isaac shook his head, trying to shake off the memory of the night he'd put a bullet in his one-time best friend, Leonard Pope. With every street hustler he brought to Christ, he tried to atone for what he did to Leonard.

A small-time thug by the name of Charlie Depree now owned the house. He'd introduced himself to Isaac a couple months back and told Isaac that he was going to be top dog around here from now on. Isaac sized him up and knew that if he didn't introduce Charlie to Jesus, the punk would be dead inside of a year.

Isaac had been king of the inner-city drug trade. Now he'd come back as a friend of the King of Kings. Together they would reclaim the streets.

"Hey, Pastor Walker," a woman who'd just gotten off the number three bus told him, "I enjoyed your sermon on Sunday. I'm going to bring my thick-in-the-head son next week."

The weariness in her face dimmed the light he'd once seen in her eyes. "Thank you, Sister Patty," Isaac said. "Bring him on in. You never know when the Lord will move on his heart."

"I sure hope so, Pastor. I sure hope so." She rolled her two-wheeler cart full of groceries toward her house.

Isaac continued down Broadway. This had always been a low-income kind of place. In fact, half the residents of the neighborhood didn't have automobiles and used the bus to get to work, church, and the grocery. The houses, however, had been well maintained, despite the retail and fry-cook incomes that sustained the owners, but the onslaught of crack had destroyed the community. Once proud homeowners, they were now too busy taking care of grandchildren left behind by crack-addicted parents, and had no time to mow the grass, plant flowers, or paint the garage. When Isaac came upon the park where his son had almost lost his life he stopped.

About a year and a half ago, Donavan and his mother, Nina had been gunned down on their porch, but the whole episode began when Donavan attempted to meet one of his friends at Broadway Park. Donavan's friend was dead, his killer standing over him when Donavan happened upon them in the park. Donavan had enough sense to run like Forest all the way home, but the maniac followed him; and when Nina stepped onto the porch she and Donavan both had been splattered with bullets.

At least once a month, when Isaac reached this park, he was compelled to walk on this land and pray that God would bring about a difference in the lives of the youth that inhabited this place. Because of the history he had with the area, and because Charlie Depree's crack house was right across the street, the Holy Spirit led Isaac to hold a tent revival at Broadway Park. The revival would be held in the spring, so he had five months to plan and pray.

He had almost completed one lap around the park when he heard a woman scream. He backtracked and headed toward the other end of the park.

"Didn't I tell you I need my money?" The man's left hand held on to the girl's bloodstained shirt collar, while the other swooped down on her face.

"Y-yes, Ch-Charlie."

Charlie smacked her. "Didn't I tell you what would happen if you didn't have it this time?"

Before Charlie could bring down his hand on the woman again, Isaac grabbed his raised arm and twisted it behind his back. "So you like beating on defenseless women?"

"Man, get your hands off me!"

Isaac tightened his grip. "Let her go."

Charlie let loose his victim.

Instead of running for her life, the girl fell backward onto the ground and cried.

"This is between me and Ebony, man," Charlie said. "Why don't you find somebody else to save?"

Isaac seemed destined to tangle with Charlie Depree, whose specialty was beating on women who owed him money for crack. At five-foot seven and one hundred seventy pounds, Charlie shrunk beneath Isaac's six-foot, two hundred-pound frame. Turning him around so they were eye to eye, Isaac told him, "This is my turf, young man, and I'm not going to let you take advantage of this girl." He extended his finger toward Ebony. "She is off-limits, and this area is off-limits to punks like you."

Fist clenched and neck jutting forward, Charlie said, "You can't ban me from a public place. You don't own this park."

Isaac shoved him. "Act like I own it. And act like you think I'll kill you the next time you step foot on my property."

Charlie backed away. He kept backing up until he reached the edge of the park and then turned toward Isaac. "This ain't over!" he shouted. "You gon' get yours. Ebony, I'll see you around."

Isaac heard Charlie's bold words, but he'd also seen the fear in Charlie's eyes when he pushed him. He prayed that God would forgive him for handling things in the manner he did before coming to Christ. He turned toward Ebony and held out his hand to her. She wiped her wet cheeks, and then grabbed hold of his hand. As he pulled her up, he got a good look at her young face. He wanted to chase Charlie down and give him a good beatdown.

"How old are you?"

Sniffing, she told him, "Eighteen."

Isaac gave her a stern look and raised a suspicious eyebrow. She lowered her head. "I'm fifteen."

Isaac shook his head. "What are you doing with a guy like that?"

Ebony kept her head low and began to cry again.

Isaac put his hands in his pocket and backed away. He needed Nina if he was going to help this young girl. "Stop crying, Ebony. Look, have you eaten anything?"

She shook her head.

"I live a couple blocks over. Let me take you home so my wife can fix you something to eat."

Sizing him up to be a perv, Ebony pursed her lips and crossed her arms.

Isaac put up his hands. "I'm a pastor. I'm not interested in taking advantage of you. When we get to my house, I'll have my wife come outside so you can talk with her, okay?"

Still plagued by her doctor's proclamation that she couldn't have any more children because of the damage done to her body by a gunshot wound, Nina spent the evening on her knees praying that God would heal her womb. Needless to say, Isaac bursting through her bedroom door threw her discussion with the Lord way off.

"Nina," Isaac said. He halted when he saw her on her knees. "Sorry to interrupt, babe, but I need your help."

She smiled, remembering the first time this magnificently sculpted man had invaded her world.

It was fifteen years ago, but Nina remembered walking into that Dayton nightclub on the west side like it was yesterday. Isaac's diamond bedecked hands glittered in the air as he sauntered toward her, smelling of money, his Armani suit jacket curved nicely over his muscles.

She ran her French-manicured fingers through her short-layered hair and turned slightly in his direction, putting out the welcome mat.

His pace quickened. Honey oozed out of his chocolate-coated mouth as he asked, "Have you been waiting long?"

She looked into those deep chestnut eyes, which seemed to read her every thought and intent. *Lord have mercy.* "Waiting for what?"

"A man," Isaac said. "Someone to take care of you, like you deserve."

His words were bold. Everything about him was bold and over the top. "So are you here to rescue me?" Nina asked, playing coy.

"Why don't we get to know each other a little better first?" He pulled up a seat next to her. "Then we'll see if you're worth rescuing." He flashed a dimpled smile.

Nina thought that his smile must have driven countless women wild, and she was no different. All these years later, those dimples still drove her wild.

"Nina, did you hear me? I need your help," Isaac repeated, snapping her back to reality.

She knew what that meant. A month ago Isaac needed her help with a five-year-old boy who'd been abandoned by his heroin-addicted mother. They'd found the woman, got her into rehab, and then turned the boy over to his grandmother.

Then two weeks ago Isaac brought a teenage gangbanger home. For a week straight, Isaac drilled the word of God into the young man's heart. One morning the boy woke up and said he was ready to go home. Isaac bought him a bus ticket and sent him on his way. Of course, a brand-new Bible was in his suitcase.

"Can you come downstairs with me?"

Nina stood up. "I'm nervous. What am I going to see when I go downstairs this time, Mr. Walker?"

He grabbed her hand. "Don't be scared," he joked. Then he became serious. "I need you, babe."

Following Isaac down the stairs, Nina recalled coming downstairs one week after their honeymoon to a kitchen full of drug dealers breaking bread and talking about turf wars.

Isaac walked over to her then and whispered in her ear, "God wants to save them, Nina. It's our job to help."

He opened the front door to introduce her to this woman-child in skintight leopard-print pants and a dingy white shirt with blood spots. "God wants to save her, Nina, I can feel it."

The bruises on the girl's young face made Nina's heart sink. "Come on in here, honey. Let me clean you up."

The girl hesitated at first, but Nina opened her arms and reached out to her. She didn't walk into Nina's arms, but she did go inside the house.

Nina frowned and looked to her husband. "Who did that to her face?" she mumbled.

"Some drug dealer. He pimps the women he supplies drugs to, so she could be into anything right about now."

Nina walked back into the house, shaking her head and mumbling to Jesus.

"She's hungry, babe. We need to feed her." Isaac directed them to the kitchen.

Donavan, Nina and Isaac's twelve-year-old son, was in the kitchen fixing a second helping of hamburger pizza. A mix between Isaac's chocolate and Nina's olive complexion, he had his mother's hazel eyes and his daddy's smile.

Nina took the plate out of his hand just as he'd put a healthy slice on it.

"Hey, that's mine," Donavan said.

"Cut yourself another slice, honey. I need to give this one to a guest."

Donavan looked at the girl his dad had just seated in one

of the leather-backed kitchen chairs. His mother put the hamburger pizza on the table in front of her. "Who's that?" he asked.

Nina smiled as she looked at her son. It was still hard for her to believe that she and her son had survived after being shot about a year and a half ago.

Before she and Isaac got married, Donavan and his friends had made some bad choices. His friends were dead now, and all she could say was thank You to Jesus for answering her prayers and saving her son's life. That episode was the reason her doctor didn't think she would be able to have any more children, but it was also the thing that had scared Donavan straight; sent him running to God.

That incident also helped to heal Nina and Isaac's relationship to the point where, after years of being apart, they decided to get married.

Nina prayed that this young woman at her kitchen table would soon find peace with God and a place to belong also.

5

"Come on, Spoony, open up!" Cynda yelled at the top of her lungs while banging on the door. She couldn't care less about disturbing the neighbors. They probably needed to get up and get a job anyway. She had worked all day and night making Spoony's money, so there was no way he was going to deny her the chance to spend time with her daughter today. She leaned on the buzzer. "I know y'all in there. Linda, please open the door. I just want to spend some time with Iona."

The door swung open, and Spoony stood in front of her with a rag tied around his big head. His eyes dilated as his crusted lips cursed her for waking him. Wouldn't you know it, while she was working her rear end off, he was partying and sleeping in late. She held out three hundred dollars to him. "Now, can I see my child, please?"

He was still half-buzzed and slurred his words. "You gon' have to do better than this," he said, taking the money from her.

Cynda brushed past him. Linda and Iona were seated on a black leather couch. Everything but the glass lamps and the cream-colored carpet was black in the living room. She should have known something was wrong with him when she saw his house years ago. Anyone whose favorite color was black needed therapy.

Linda puffed on her cancer stick. "I figured you would come see her today." She nudged Iona. "Stand up. Let your mother see how pretty you look today."

Iona was dressed in a Rocawear jogging suit and had ribbons around her perfect ponytails. She stood, twirled around and said, "You like my new jogging suit, Mama?"

Cynda glared at Linda. "Why didn't you let me in if you had her ready and waiting on me?"

Shoulders slumped, eyes downcast, Linda said, "I had to wait for Spoony to open the door."

Spoony snarled, "You got some more questions, detective?"

Cynda turned to face him. She knew she had to put up with his attitude before she could get her daughter out of this house. "Naw, I don't have any more questions."

He waved the money she gave him in her face. "Good. 'Cause ol' Spoony got some detective work to do." He closed in on her. "Now, you been out trickin' all night, right?"

She nodded, hating him for talking about business in front of her daughter.

Iona stomped her foot. "Mama, you didn't answer me. Do you like my jogging suit?"

Cynda turned toward Iona, but Spoony grabbed her chin and turned her head back in his direction. "Sit down, Iona. I'm talking to your mother right now." Some white flakes from the crust around his lips fell as he taunted her. "If you've been out trickin' all night, how come you only brought me three hundred dollars?"

Cynda wanted to call him a fool so bad, but she'd received her quota of fat lips for the week. "That's all I made. I can only take one customer at a time, you know."

He grabbed her arm and shoved her against the black wall. Three of the walls in the room were white, but the entry wall was midnight black.

"Stop!" Iona screamed. "Why can't you leave my mother alone?"

Linda grabbed Iona to prevent her from running any more interference and put her hand over her mouth.

Spoony ignored Iona as he patted Cynda down like the po-po would a robbery suspect. He finally finished his search and found that there was no more money on her. "Take your sorry self on out of here. And don't keep Iona out all night long, you hear me, Cynda? Don't make me come looking for you."

She rolled her eyes as she grabbed her daughter's hand and walked out of the house.

When they were down the street, Cynda took off her hat and pulled out the lining. She smiled as she showed Iona two hundred and fifty dollars. "This is for you, baby girl. Just tell me what you want. We're going to celebrate your birthday, just like I promised."

Biting her nails, Iona glanced over her shoulder.

Cynda stopped and stared at her daughter. "What's wrong, honey? Don't you want to celebrate your birthday?"

"Yes, Mama, but don't you think you should give that money to Uncle Spoony?"

Cynda smirked. "I've given him more than enough money to blow up his nose." Cynda grabbed Iona's arm to hurry her along as she resumed her pace.

Iona jerked away from her, with the same terrified look on her face. "But I don't want to work for Uncle Spoony."

Cynda turned. "What are you talking about, girl?" she asked, a puzzled look on her face.

"I can't tell you. Just give him that money, okay, Mama. I don't need presents. I swear I don't."

Cynda bent down in front of her daughter and looked into her innocent eyes. That's when she saw that Iona's eyes weren't so innocent anymore.

"You don't have to keep anything from me, baby. Tell Mama what's wrong."

A tear rolled down Iona's dark brown cheek. "I just don't want to work for Uncle Spoony."

Cynda frowned. "Work for Spoony? What are you talking about? Why would you think that you would ever have to do that?"

Tears streamed down Iona's face and mingled with the snot that dripped from her nose. "Uncle Spoony said that if you don't start making more money, I'm gon' have to take over for you." Iona couldn't look her mother in the eye. She knew what her mother did for a living and was ashamed of her.

Cynda felt like the dumbest mother in the world. It wasn't that she thought Spoony above child porn or even pimping a child, but she never thought he would do anything to harm this child. Not out of respect for her, but for Iona's dad. But Spoony had evidently stopped reminding himself of the good times he'd had with Iona's father. Her daughter was no longer safe in her pimp's house.

Cynda would rather die before Iona carried the whore legacy of the Stephens family one generation farther. She pulled Keith's business card out of her jacket pocket and put the numbers in her cell phone.

Janet was at her desk typing and taking calls when Keith walked into the office and took his hard hat off. His office was a one-story building just like his house. There was only room enough for Janet's reception area, his small office, a conference room to meet with clients or his four staff members, and a vending area where they could get coffee and donuts before going out on a job. It was small, but he loved all 965 square feet of it because he didn't earn it by selling poison on the streets. He'd scrimped and saved, and learned his craft the hard way, by working.

"Did any of our clients send their payments in today?" Keith asked Janet.

"Nope. But your suppliers are on time with their bills." Janet held up a pile of invoices and watched Keith frown. "No sense pickling up your face. Just thank God that we have enough money to get these bills paid."

"Yeah, you're right." He rushed to his office to look somewhere on his messy desk for the plans for the job they were on today.

Janet walked into his office as he was flipping papers over on his desk. "Looking for this?" she asked, holding out some sketches.

Keith shook his head. "I left them on your desk this morning?"

She nodded.

"I thought I left them on my desk." He took the papers out of her hand. "What would I do without you?"

As he was getting ready to rush back out of the office, Janet asked, "Did you like the curtains I hung in your living room last week?"

He stopped and looked at her for a moment. She was about five feet seven inches, always neatly dressed, hair not too long, but not too short either. She had a nice shape on her and a pretty face. But most of all, he'd met her at his church and knew that she was a godly woman.

Why not Janet, Lord? This is the one I want. "Did I forget to thank you for doing that? I'm sorry; I've had a few things going on lately. Anyway, the curtains are nice. Thank you."

She smiled. "I'm just glad you like them. I didn't think you were a big fan of olive green, but that color matched your living room best."

"Well, it goes good with the carpet, and you know I'm not planning on changing that carpet anytime soon."

"That's why I picked them out."

He put his hand in his pocket and shuffled his feet a bit. "Janet, I was wondering . . ."

"Yes?"

Maybe God needed his help with this one, Keith thought before he ran interference on God's word by posing a question to Janet. "We get along pretty good, and, well, I was just wondering if you'd like to go to dinner or to a movie with me some time."

She smiled, but as she opened her mouth to answer, Keith's cell phone rang.

He held up a finger. "Keith here," he said, answering his phone.

"I need you to come get me," the voice on the other end of the phone stated.

"Who is this?"

"You don't even know my voice? Thought you wanted to deliver me from the streets? Or do you take every wayward girl you meet out to lunch?"

He turned away from Janet. "Cynda? Oh, praise God. I was just praying for you last night. God is so good."

"Yeah, yeah. Save all that good-God stuff for the next church convention meeting, okay. Can you come get me or not?" Cynda said, getting right to the point.

Keith looked at his watch. He needed to be back at the job site, but he couldn't just turn his back on Cynda. "Tell me where you are and I'll be right there."

When Keith pulled up, Cynda opened the back door and deposited a little girl. She then opened the passenger door and jumped in. Keith couldn't take his gaze off the little girl. She reminded him of somebody. He reached out his hand to her. "Hello, my name is Keith."

Shaking his hand, the little girl said, "I'm Iona."

Cynda growled, "Are we going to sit here all day, or can we go?"

Without saying another word, Keith drove his two companions to his house. He took them inside and showed them around. "The towels are in the hall closet, and there's food in the fridge," Keith informed his houseguests as they stood in the living room surrounded by the olive curtains that Janet had hung the week before. He smiled as he thought of how right Janet was. Those curtains matched his carpet to perfection.

As if cutting into his thoughts, Cynda asked, "What's up with all the puke green you've got going on in this living room? I mean, even your couch has a green tint to it, for goodness' sake."

Keith wasn't about to discuss what Janet had done for him out of the kindness of her heart, so he changed the subject. "If you need anything while I'm out, give me a call and I'll pick it up on my way home."

"What? You just gon' leave us here?" Cynda asked, hands on hips.

"I have to go back to work, Cynda."

"Oh, yeah. I forgot that people do things like that."

"Cynda, what's going on? Why'd you need me to pick you up?"

She instructed Iona to go into the kitchen and see if she could find something to eat. When she and Keith were alone in the living room she said, "Look, I didn't mean to bring you my problems. It's just that when Iona told me that Spoony planned to turn her out, I freaked."

"Is Iona your daughter?"

"Yeah, man." She rubbed her eyes. "She's all I've got. I can't let Spoony turn her out like that."

Keith stood, mouth agape. He knew that Spoony was no

saint, but this? *Lord, is this why you wanted me to help her?* "Don't worry about it, Cynda. We'll work it out."

Keith left the house and got into his car. He drove away with something gnawing at him. He couldn't put his finger on the problem, but knew it had to do with the precious little girl he'd just met.

The construction site was calling his name though. Keith and his crew were on the most important job he'd been able to land all year. It still fascinated him that his bid was approved and that the CEO of a Fortune 500 company was now relying on him to handle the add-on to his seven-thousand-square-foot home. It wasn't the Sears Building, but it was a step in the right direction. He'd bring this job in on time and on the money. But even with the job on his mind, Keith couldn't stop thinking about that little girl. Something about her just didn't sit right with him.

Keith almost cut off his finger while using the drill, when a thought hit him. Throwing the drill down, he grabbed his cell phone and called Isaac. His voice got caught in his throat when Isaac picked up.

"Keith, are you there or what?" Isaac asked after not getting a response from his initial greeting. "Look, man, I've got caller ID, you know."

Keith cleared his throat. "I'm here."

"I was about to say, thought you were too old for prank calling."

All Keith could think about right then was getting home and talking to Cynda about his assumptions. "Sorry about that, man. I've got a lot on my mind right now. What's up?"

"Not a problem. Hey, I'm glad you called anyway. Do you think you can pick me up from the airport at noon tomorrow?"

"Pick you up from the airport? What's going on?"

"What's wrong with you? I told you I would be in Chi-town this weekend. Told you I needed to talk to Spoony, re-member?"

Keith smacked his forehead with the palm of his hand. "Ah, man, I forgot. Look, I got you, I got you. Don't even sweat it."

"Thanks, man."

Before Isaac could hang up, Keith called out, "Hey, man, let me ask you something." He hesitated. "How long has it been since you dealt with Cynda Stephens?"

Isaac only took a moment to answer. "Ten years." He didn't waste time remembering trivial things. That's just how he was. If it wasn't important enough to take up room in his brain, he usually deleted it.

"How come you remember it just like that?"

"I went to prison ten years ago, right after I gave that tackhead her walking papers. Then she turned me into the cops. Don't think I'll forget that too soon."

"Ten years, huh." Keith thought about how Iona looked to be around ten. *Could it be? The girl looked just like him.*

"Keith, why are you asking me about a female that you know I could go a lifetime without thinking about? The woman puts a bad taste in my mouth."

"I'll pick you up in the morning. We've got a lot to talk about."

6

Nina and Ebony were in the kitchen making the evening meal while Isaac and Donavan were at their little storefront church getting ready for Sunday service.

"Can you hand me the oven mitt?" Nina nodded toward the mitt on the kitchen counter.

Ebony grabbed the "Bless the cook" oven mitt off the counter and passed it to Nina. She stood back and watched Nina take the meatloaf out of the oven, put it on a serving plate, and slice several pieces.

Nina looked over at Ebony and smiled. "What are you thinking about?"

Ebony looked away, tears on her dark-chocolate face. "I'm worried about what my mom is going to think when she finds out what I've been doing."

"Based on the conversation I had with your mom, she seems like a caring and understanding person."

"I wish I had never given you my mother's telephone number."

Nina pulled Ebony into her arms and hugged her. "It's going to be okay. You've just got to have a little faith."

Ebony held Nina tight. "I don't want faith. I want to stay here with you."

Ending their embrace, Nina softly touched Ebony's cheek. How she wished that Ebony's mom was a wicked, unfit mother. That way she would have no problems fighting to keep her with them. Nina had even prayed that God would make a way for her and Isaac to be able to adopt the girl. But Ebony's mom wasn't wicked. She was simply a single parent doing the best she could, and the woman loved Ebony.

Nina would miss this woman-child, who'd found a place in her heart. She hated the thought of Ebony leaving, but she'd done the right thing by calling her mother. Even if Ebony's absence would cause her to mourn as if she were losing her very own child, Nina knew she had to do what was right for Ebony and her mother. She held back her tears, smiled and said, "You've got to go home, Ebony. It's where you belong."

They hugged again. Nina quickly wiped away a disobedient tear as it slid down her cheek before releasing Ebony. She cleared her throat and said, "Turn the oven off for me. We're done in here."

As Ebony turned off the oven she asked Nina, "Doesn't this all seem too normal to you?"

"Doesn't what seem too normal?"

Ebony pointed around the kitchen. "All of this—dinner, setting the table, your family coming home to eat and having normal conversations with you?"

Nina laughed. Some of the conversations she'd had with her husband were anything but normal. Especially the ones that related to the demonic forces oppressing the people within the inner city. They constantly talked and prayed about God's delivering power. She loved her husband and was in awe at times of the ministry-minded man she ended up with. But she would certainly not characterize their relationship as normal.

"Ebony, I'm glad you think we're normal . . . 'cause sometimes I wonder."

Ebony scrunched her nose. "Maybe you're not normal."

Nina playfully hit her with the oven mitt. "Gee, thanks, Ebony."

"What I mean is, your husband comes home every night, he doesn't beat on you, and I'd swear on a stack of Bibles that he wouldn't dream of cheating on you. That's not normal."

Nina laughed again. "Someday I'm going to sit you down and tell you our story."

Ebony took a seat. "Tell me."

"You're much too young. I can't tell you about all my drama."

Her eyes implored Nina. "Please tell me. I need to know that mistakes can be turned around."

Sitting next to her, Nina said, "All right. See, I wasn't married to Isaac when I had Donavan."

"No way. You had a child out of wedlock?"

"Yes, I did. See, back then, Isaac was very abusive, and he cheated on me. Well, I decided that I didn't want to be with a man like that, so I left him. I even considered aborting my baby. Thank God, someone took the time to tell me about Jesus."

"What did Isaac do when you left?"

"He found me." Then she drifted back in time to tell Ebony the story.

"I was on my knees, head bowed, lips moving, but no sound exited my mouth when Isaac opened my bedroom door. 'You're gonna have to pray a long time, if you're asking God to save you from my wrath,' Isaac told me. I stood and turned to face him. He looked at my stomach and said, 'Why didn't you tell me you didn't have the abortion?'

"I bent my head and touched my stomach, but remained silent.

" 'Nina, didn't you think I would find out about my baby?' " he asked.

"I remember looking up at him. One small tear escaped down my face. 'I thought you'd kill me before you found out the truth,' I told him.

"Isaac blushed and said, 'I'm sorry about that, babe.' He reached out to touch me, but I stepped back.

" 'I'll never put my hands on you again. You've got my word on that. My child will never see his mother battered and bruised,' Isaac promised. 'Get your stuff, let's go.'

"I put my hand on my belly and backed away from Isaac," Nina said as Ebony sat listening intently. "I can't go with you," I told him.

" 'What do you mean, you can't go with me? Nina, get your stuff.'

"I flopped down on the bed and looked at Isaac. He had been everything to me, but not anymore. Jesus had revealed Himself, and showed me that He was the only living God, and He alone was worthy of my worship. 'I cannot live in sin with you, Isaac.'

" 'We ain't living in sin! Stop trippin', girl, we live in Dayton,' Isaac said, as serious as ever."

Nina chuckled as she reminisced, but at the time it wasn't funny.

" 'You're carrying my baby. You belong with me,' Isaac said.

"I remember looking down at my hands and saying, 'We're not married.'

"Isaac opened the closet door and threw my clothes onto the bed. 'I don't know what these people have been filling your head with, but'—Isaac pointed at my belly—'that's mine. And that makes you and me family.'

"At that time, I didn't know where my strength had come from. I opened my mouth and said, 'I will not live with you.'

"Isaac kneeled down in front of me. He tilted my head toward him so he could look into my eyes. Then he said, 'You know I don't want nobody but you. It's you and me against the world. Come on, baby, come home with me, please.' "

Nina put her hands to her face as another tear fell to her cheek.

"I told him, 'I can't live in your world anymore. You have to let me go.' "

When Nina finished her story, Ebony said, "But he didn't let you go, or else you wouldn't be married today."

"No, he didn't let me go. But it took eleven years for him to convince me to take him back. I had to be sure that he was the man God had for me."

Ebony frowned. "But what if the man God has for me doesn't want to be bothered because of the things I've done?"

"Trust me, Ebony, when God gets through working on the man He has designed for you, your previous indiscretions won't matter to him."

Ebony sighed. "Too bad you won't know when that day comes."

"Why wouldn't I know? All you have to do is pick up the telephone and call me."

Ebony's eyes brightened. "You really want me to call you?"

"If you don't, I'll be forced to fly all the way to Pensacola, Florida just to see if your dialing finger is broken."

Ebony laughed. "Then I'll make sure to call you every week."

"You better," Nina said, laughing also. "Ebony, there's something I've wanted to know since you came to our home, but I've been waiting for the right time to ask." Nina paused, waiting for Ebony to give her permission to continue.

"You can ask me anything, Nina. I promise, I'll tell you the truth."

"How did you get from Pensacola, Florida to Dayton?"

Ebony lowered her head. "I left town with Jimmy Jones. The kids at school used to call him Jim Jones. They said he was poison, and they weren't far from the truth. I hit my first crack pipe with him. Then he got tired of me and ditched me in Cincinnati." She looked up at Nina. "That's where I met Charlie. He brought me to Dayton and made me turn tricks for my crack." Ebony covered her face with her hands.

They sat in silence for a moment.

"My mother is going to hate me."

Nina removed Ebony's hands from her face. "A mother could never hate her child. The two of you will get through this. And if it seems like she's having a hard time forgiving you, just remember what Jesus said."

"What did Jesus say that will help me deal with my mother?"

"Well, there was this woman who was caught in the act of adultery. A group of men brought her before Jesus accusing her of this horrible sin."

"Were they telling the truth? Had the woman really cheated on her husband?"

"Oh yes, everything they said was true."

Ebony's eyes dimmed. "So what did Jesus do about it?"

"The people that had gathered around picked rocks off the ground and demanded that the adulterous woman be stoned to death. But Jesus simply told them, 'He who is without sin, cast the first stone.' And not one person in that crowd was able to throw a stone at the woman. Jesus finally told the woman to go home and sin no more."

"Just like that, she was forgiven?" Ebony asked in amazement.

Nina snapped her finger. "Just like that."

Shortly after, Isaac and Donavan walked in the kitchen, and the four of them sat down to dinner.

Once the kids were in bed and Isaac and Nina had also gone to bed, Isaac informed his wife that Ebony's mom would be there the next day to get her.

"But I thought she wouldn't be able to make it here until next week?"

"She called," Isaac said. "Her sister is going to keep her other children so she can fly in and pick Ebony up tomorrow."

Nina turned away from her husband and pulled the covers tight against her.

Isaac leaned into his wife and moved her closer to him. He stroked her back and planted a kiss on her neck. "I promise, it will be okay."

Nina sniffled. "I know it's the right thing to do, but I'm not ready to let her go. I was just getting to know her and she's a wonderful kid."

"But she's not our kid."

Nina turned to face her husband, and tears fell onto her pillow. "I know she's not ours, but I want one just like her."

Keith and his crew had to pull a double to put the finishing touches on that building, so it was a little past eleven when he arrived home. Iona was on the couch asleep. The child looked precious and innocent, her eyes shut tight against all the evil of the world. This was Isaac's child. Keith was sure of it as he gazed down on her. What he wasn't sure of was why Cynda had never said anything. And he definitely wasn't sure what Isaac's reaction would be when he talked with him tomorrow.

Keith went into his throne room. Kneeling down, he bowed before the throne, determined to seek God in earnest. He needed the Holy Spirit to direct him. "Show me Your will in all this mess, Lord."

When he'd finished praying and God was still speaking into his heart about marrying Cynda, Keith rebelled. "I don't understand why You want me to do this. I want to be in love with the woman I marry. And besides, Lord, you know that I have been down this road before. I've seen what drugs and prostitution can do to a person. How it can destroy, how it can kill." He ran his hands through his hair and shook his head. "I don't know how I can love a woman like her."

As I have loved you.

Keith paced the floor. "What about Isaac, Lord? Cynda was his woman. I don't want my best friend's leftovers. She's got his child. How can I be with a woman who would deny a man the knowledge of his own child?" He shook his head. "I can't do it. Ask anything else of me, but not this."

Keith left his throne room and wandered around the house in search of Cynda. He wanted to get some answers concerning Iona. Cynda had put him in a bad position. What was he supposed to do when he picked Isaac up tomorrow afternoon? Give his best friend a cigar and tell him, "It's a girl"?

Keith couldn't get the answers he sought because Cynda was not in the guest bedroom, nor in the bathroom. She was nowhere in the house at all. He went back to the living room to wake Iona and ask her if she knew where her mother was, but she was sleeping so peacefully he didn't have the heart to disturb her.

He went back to his bedroom, took off his work clothes, and jumped in the shower. The hot water relaxed and soothed him. As he came out of the bathroom he listened for movement in the front of the house, but there was complete silence.

He put on his pj's, turned on the TBN channel, and stretched across the bed with the intentions of waiting on Cynda. His eyelids were heavy and his sleep-deprived body didn't much care where Cynda was at that moment, so he fell asleep.

He woke at six in the morning, just as Cynda opened and closed his front door. He jumped out of bed and angrily strutted into the living room to confront her.

Cynda put her finger to her lip as she pointed at Iona's sleeping form. Unzipping her jacket, she walked to the guest bedroom that was right next door to Keith's room.

Keith followed and closed the door. "Where have you been?"

Pursing her lips, eyebrows jutting upward, Cynda glared at him. He returned her stare, daring her not to answer him. Cynda finally shrugged and told him, "Out earning my money. I got to eat, don't I?"

Keith stood in the middle of the guest room, too stunned to move or speak.

She sat down on the edge of the dark-chocolate queen-size bed and began pulling off her stockings. Looking up, she noticed him staring at her legs. She patted the bed, lifted her chest to give him a good view of her breasts then licked her lips. she winked. "You wanna get something going?"

Keith looked to Heaven. *Do you see her, Lord? This can't be the woman You asked me to marry. Not me, Lord. I've been faithful to You."*

The gentle voice of the Lord told him, *My love covers all her sins.*

Keith took a deep breath and looked to Cynda. "No. What I wanted was to help you."

"You've helped us. Thanks for the place to crash."

Keith rolled his eyes. "What if I wanted to do more than
give you a place to crash?" *Where did that come from?* He
threw his hands up. "Just forget it." He opened the bedroom door to walk out.

Cynda yelled, "What's the matter? Look, I was going to
give you some for free. I mean, you are letting us crash here,
right?"

"I'm going to fix breakfast," he said, tight-lipped. *No way,
Lord. No way!*

Cynda rubbed her empty stomach. "Good. I'm starving."

"I bet you are," he mumbled under his breath.

While he was in the kitchen snatching food out of the refrigerator and throwing the skillet on the stove, he kept
mumbling to himself about not having to take this mess.
When he was flipping the eggs over in the skillet he sud-
denly remembered that Cynda had left her child home
alone to go out and make her "eating money."

He went back to her room to confront her. He didn't
even realize that the spatula was still in his hand, until he
was shaking it in Cynda's face and some albumin fell onto
the bedroom floor. "How could you leave your child alone
in the middle of the night like that?"

Cynda obviously had rummaged through the dresser in
his guestroom and located his old lounging clothes after she
got out of the shower. She had on one of Keith's T-shirts, a
pair of his jogging pants, and was putting on a pair of his
socks when he walked into the room. Even in his anger, he
still noticed how cute she looked in his lounging clothes.

"What's up your butt now?" she asked as she finished
putting on his socks.

"What's up my butt? Cynda, you left your child home
alone. At night."

She shrugged. "Iona can take care of herself."

"She's not *supposed* to take care of herself. That's why God gave her parents. And speaking of parents, who is Iona's father?"

Cynda sniffed the air. "Is something burning?"

"Oh, so you think you're going to ignore me?"

Keith went back to the kitchen, turned off the stove, took the bacon out of the skillet, and put the pieces on a plate. He then went back to his bedroom and made sure to keep his voice low as he said, "I already know who her daddy is. And how do you think he's going to feel, once he finds out you never told him that he has a daughter?"

With remote in hand, Cynda channel-surfed. "I don't know what you're talking about, Keith. How is a whore supposed to know who her baby's daddy is?"

"How old is Iona?"

"You need to get cable." She put the remote down.

"How old is she, Cynda?"

"She just turned ten. Why are you so interested? You want to be her sugar daddy, get her a present or something?"

The marks on her face told him that she was used to getting knocked upside her head. Maybe she'd grown to like stuff like that, but he refused to mess up his godly witness by putting his hands on a woman, no matter how much she was begging him to beat her down.

"Isaac stopped dealing with you ten years ago, and Iona looks just like him—Explain that."

Cynda got off the bed and strolled past Keith. She checked on Iona and then went into the kitchen and leaned against the stove, eating the bacon Keith had cooked.

Keith followed her. "Explain," he said with folded arms.

Cynda held up a piece of bacon and popped it into her mouth. "First of all, I didn't stop dealing with Isaac. He got rid of me, remember?"

"No, I wasn't around ten years ago when you and him broke up. I was paying my debt to society at that time."

Cynda snapped her fingers. "That's right. Well, you missed Isaac's finest hour. You should ask him about it some time."

Keith sat down at the table across from the stove. "Why do you hate Isaac so much, Cynda?"

"Ask him." Cynda began to open the kitchen cabinets and moved some of the canned goods around. "You got any coffee?"

Keith opened the cabinet above the sink and pulled out a can of decaf. He put a couple scoops of the coffee grinds in the coffee maker. "You're going to have to discuss this with Isaac sooner or later."

Cynda opened the cabinet that held the dishes and pulled down an acrylic mug.

"And since Isaac will be here this afternoon, I would say today is as good a time as any to tell him what's going on."

The mug in Cynda's hand fell to the floor.

Keith smirked as he witnessed the blood drain from Cynda's face. "I know you're not scared, not as bad as you act."

"Look, I don't want anything to do with Isaac, okay? Just call him and let him know that he can't come over here."

Keith leaned against the counter. "I can't do that, Cynda. I already told him he could stay here." He dropped his voice to a whisper. "So you're just going to have to fess up. I know that little girl in there belongs to Isaac. It's time for you to handle your business."

"Didn't you just tell me that you wanted to help me? Isaac don't need no help, so you need to be more concerned about what I want than what he wants right now."

"I can't do that, Cynda. I promised him he could stay here tonight."

Cynda rolled her eyes. "When you gon' stop being his boy and become a man anyway?"

7

"Have a seat, Isaac," Keith said. "We need to discuss some things before we go to my house."

Isaac put his suitcase on the floor and sat down. People were passing by them at breakneck speeds, either trying to get to their airplane or to a cab, so they could get to that all-important meeting. "What's up?" he asked.

Keith tapped his fingers on the table, trying to figure the best way to break the news. He wasn't worried that Isaac still had feelings for Cynda. Isaac hardly had any feelings for her when he was seeing her over ten years ago. But still, something seemed wrong with thinking about his best friend's ex.

Isaac hunched his broad shoulders. "You got something to say or not?"

"Yeah, I wanted to talk to you about something." Keith swallowed hard. "Remember when Cynda showed up at your wedding reception?"

Isaac's lip curled with disgust. "Yeah, I remember when she came in there and told me that she was the one who called the police on me. How could I forget that?"

"Well, you have to admit, it wasn't her fault that you were dealing drugs." Keith held up friendly hands before Isaac could react. "And, in a way, she saved your life. If you hadn't gone to prison, you probably never would have gotten saved in the first place."

"So you think I should thank that tackhead?" Isaac shook his head and then inhaled deeply. "Look, this is the second time in the space of a week that you've had that woman's name in your mouth. Why is she so heavy on your mind lately?"

"That's what I'm trying to tell you. See, I was in prayer a couple of weeks ago when God showed me who He wanted me to marry."

"You for real?" Isaac stood up and did the cabbage patch. "My boy is getting married."

"Sit back down, Isaac. There's more to it."

Isaac took his seat, but couldn't stop smiling. "I don't believe you, man. You ain't said nothing. Who is she?" He snapped his finger. "It's Janet, isn't it? I knew that woman had a thing for you." Isaac nudged Keith. "She'll make a great wife."

The mention of the woman Keith wanted but wasn't allowed to have brought a frown to his face. "Here's the thing, I think God wants me to marry Cynda."

"What?" The smile left Isaac's face with the quickness.

"I know, man. I can't believe it either. But this thing keeps coming back to me. I don't know whether to ignore God or go on and do His will."

"What you smokin'? Cynda is a whore. Now why would you want to marry a woman like that?"

Keith had no defense as he thought about Cynda walking into the house this morning, announcing that she had been out making her eating money. "I don't, but the thing is, I don't want to disobey God either."

"Man, she's a crackhead too. Why do you want to bring

drama like that into your life?" Isaac stood up again, but this time he wasn't doing the cabbage patch. He was huffing over Keith. "Why'd you have to tell me this before we go to your house? Is she there right now or something? Are y'all smoking crack together? Over there on the pipe, hearing voices, and thinking God is talking to you?"

"Shut up, Isaac. I'm not on crack. But, yes, Cynda is at the house."

"You sleeping with her?"

"No, it's not what you think."

"Why do you want Cynda . . . just tell me that? There are so many other women in this world that you could have. Why can't you stay off of the women that belonged to me?"

Keith just looked at his friend.

"You thought I didn't know that you had a thing for Nina? I knew it, but I also knew you would never stab me in the back." Isaac lifted his hands to the heavens and shook his head. "At least I can understand your wanting to be with Nina—she's good and kind—but this whore?"

Keith got out of his seat. "That's enough, Isaac. I'm just mulling things over. It's not as if I'm jumping at the chance to marry her. But whether I do it or not, you don't have to disrespect her like this."

"Cynda has to earn my respect, and she's never earned anything but a two-dollar tip from a john."

Isaac regularly rescued drug addicts, drug dealers, and prostitutes from their horrid lives, introducing them to a better life. A life with Jesus Christ. And so Keith knew that he didn't have a problem with his attempting to rescue a prostitute, especially since God was directing him. Keith wondered, *How would he react when I tell him the rest of the story?*

Isaac shook his head and then put his hand on Keith's shoulder. "It wasn't your fault, man."

"What wasn't my fault?"

"You did everything you could for your mother. It wasn't your fault that she died. You can't keep punishing yourself for not being there for her. And, believe me, marrying Cynda is too high a price to pay for something that happened twenty years ago."

Keith sharply brushed Isaac's hand off his shoulder. "That's not what this is about."

"Who are you kidding? I was there. I saw what your mother's death did to you. It wasn't your fault that she became a prostitute. Her heroin addiction put her on those streets, not you."

"I heard God, Isaac."

"Don't do it, Keith. Cynda's just going to bring you down."

"Let me worry about that."

Isaac threw his hands up. "More power to you. I'm out." He turned in the direction of the cabs that lined the street.

"Where are you going?"

"I'll catch a cab to Spoony's then I'll get a hotel. I'm not trying to put you out."

Keith grabbed Isaac's suitcase. "Man, let me take you where you're going. And then if you don't want to stay at the house, I'll drop you at a hotel." Keith couldn't just sit there and let Isaac catch a cab. Besides, there was one other thing he needed to tell his friend.

"Get up, Iona. Come on, honey, we've got to go." Cynda stood over her daughter, who was still lying on the couch she'd fallen to sleep on the night before.

Iona stretched and yawned.

Cynda nudged her shoulder. "Get up, girl."

Turning over, Iona rubbed her eyes then stretched again. "What's wrong, Mama?"

"Nothing's wrong." She handed Iona her shoes. "Here, put your shoes on. We can't stay here."

Iona took the shoes from Cynda and started putting them on. "But I thought you said Uncle Keith wanted us to stay with him." She crinkled her pert nose. "I don't want to go back to Uncle Spoony's. I like it here."

Cynda folded the queen bed back inside Keith's bulky, green-grey sofa and put the mammoth seat cushions in place. "Things change, baby girl. That's one thing you have to understand about life. Now come on, we need to be out of here before Keith brings Isaac home."

"Isaac, my daddy?" Iona questioned.

Cynda stopped in her tracks and turned to face her child. "What did you say?"

"I know his name, Mommy. Uncle Spoony told me all about him. So if my daddy's coming here, why can't I stay and meet him?"

"Because he don't want you. Remember how I told you that your daddy was real mean to Mommy?"

Iona nodded.

"Well, how mean do you think he'd be to you if he knew where you were?" Cynda handed Iona her coat, then took the key Keith gave her out of her purse and put it on the coffee table. "Let's just say, he's not someone either of us wants to see right now." She opened the front door and left, dragging Iona behind her.

"Where are we going, Mommy?"

"Getting out of the way of two maniacs." Cynda pulled out her cell phone and dialed Jasmine's number. "Hey, girl, do you have room for me and Iona?"

"So it's true," Jasmine said on the other end of the phone.

"What's true? What are you talking about?"

"Spoony just left. He said you stole something from him. My guess is you stole Iona."

"I can't steal my own child, Jasmine."

Spoony was truly crazy. She'd spotted him earlier that morning while she was out trying to earn enough money to feed and clothe her child. She hightailed it off that corner and made it back to Keith's house, where she thought she'd be safe. Enter maniac number two, Isaac.

"Don't tell me, girl. Tell that fool you hooked up with. He's down the street at Cooper's house waiting on you to show your face over here."

"Thanks, girl. I'll check with you later."

Just as soon as Cynda hung up with Jasmine, her phone rang. It was Linda.

"What do you want?" Cynda asked.

"Where is Iona? Why did you keep her out all night?"

"She is *my* daughter, Linda."

"I know that, but you've never kept her out all night before."

"I'm just trying to keep my daughter safe from pedophiles like your husband."

"What are you talking about?"

Cynda flagged a cab down and she and Iona hopped in. "Ask your man."

"Look, Cynda, you've got this wrong. Spoony has never touched Iona."

"No, he hasn't touched her. He just wants to let other freaked-out weirdos do it for him."

After a brief silence, Linda asked, "So what are you going to do?"

"Take us to the bus station, please," Cynda told the cab drive. Then to Linda she said, "We're getting as far away from Spoony as possible, that's what we're going to do."

"Look, if you're set on doing this, come to the house and I'll give you some money. I don't want Iona out there starving to death."

"Meet us at the bus station."

"You know I can't leave the house before Spoony gets back."

"Where is he?"

"Out looking for you."

"How do I know you won't call and tell him that I'm on my way over there?"

"I wouldn't do that."

Cynda contemplated Linda's offer but then thought better. "Keep your money, Linda. We don't need you." Cynda hung up. She then opened her purse and counted all the money she had, about four hundred dollars. Not hardly enough for her and Iona to escape from Spoony and Isaac. And what if she got the urge to get high? She didn't want Iona to go hungry. And her clothes were still at Spoony's.

Reconsidering Linda's offer, she thought about how she could really use the money after all. Not to mention she could get the money, pick up some of Iona's clothes, and get out the way before Spoony came back home. She gave the cabbie Spoony's address and sat back.

When the cabbie pulled up in front of Satan's house, Cynda got out and paid the driver.

Iona stayed in the back seat, a frightened look on her face. "I don't want to go in there, Mama."

Cynda saw the fear on her daughter's face and turned back to the cab driver and asked, "Can you wait on me and let my daughter sit in the cab while I go inside?"

He shook his head. "I wouldn't wait on my mother in this neighborhood. You're going to have to call another cab."

Iona repeated, "I don't want to go in there."

"Get your kid, lady. I've got to go."

"All right, all right," she said to the cabbie. "Get out of the car, girl. I don't have all day."

Iona got out of the cab, and she and Cynda walked to the house and knocked on the door.

Linda opened the door. "I thought you weren't coming?"

"Can't let you know all my moves," Cynda told her. "You got the money?"

"Wait a minute."

Linda went into her bedroom. When she came back out she handed Iona two thousand dollars. "This is all I've got. I'd give you more if I had it."

Cynda took the money out of Iona's hand and counted it. "Girl, you're working way too cheap. After all the mess you've taken off that Negro, you should be a millionaire by now."

"Where will you go? Spoony and I will be worried sick."

"Oh yeah, he's worried all right."

Cynda went to the kitchen, grabbed a trash bag, and then told Iona, "Go throw your clothes in this bag."

"Think about what you're doing, Cynda. If you take her, Spoony will kill you."

Cynda turned and faced Linda with fire in her eyes. "You've got that right. That Negro will have to kill me before he turns my daughter into a whore."

Linda backed away from Cynda. "Spoony would never do something like that to Iona. We love her."

"Wake up, Linda. Spoony has already told Iona what he plans to do to her. And we both know that you would just stand by and watch him do it."

"No, no, you're wrong."

"If thinking that I am lying on Spoony helps you sleep at night, then so be it. Go on, get yourself a good night's sleep, but I'm taking my daughter out of here today."

Iona ran back into the living room. "Mama, don't yell at Aunt Linda."

Cynda grabbed her daughter's arm and took her back to her bedroom. "Girl, we got to get out of here and you worried about me yelling at that woman?"

"But Aunt Linda is nice to me," Iona said, holding the half-filled trash bag.

"That woman don't care nothing about you, just like Spoony don't care about you, you hear me, Iona?"

"Yes, Mama."

"Now let's finish getting your things so we can go."

They shoved some more of Iona's things in the trash bag and then headed back toward the front door. Cynda couldn't resist. She turned to Linda. "Tell Spoony to send me a bill for the money he lost by not putting my daughter on the street."

"Why don't you tell me yourself?" Spoony closed the front door behind him and walked into the living room.

Cynda jumped, and then turned to face him. "We're leaving, Spoony. You can't stop us."

Iona started crying.

"Hush, baby," Cynda told her. "We'll be out of here in a few minutes."

Spoony walked toward them. "What's the matter, Iona? You don't like it here no more?"

Iona continued to cry as she moved closer to Cynda.

"So how much do you think I should bill you for my loss of income?" Spoony asked Cynda, venom in his eyes.

"Tell her it's not true, Spoony. Tell her you would never do something like that to Iona."

He turned his glare on Linda. "Did I ask you to open your mouth?"

Linda cowered. "No."

"These two belong to me. I'll do what I want with them." He turned back to Cynda and put his finger in her face. "How much should I bill you?"

"I-I-I-"

Spoony put his hand under his ear. "What? Speak up, Cynda. I can't make out what you're saying."

Cynda stepped back. "W-we're leaving, Spoony."

Spoony grabbed Cynda by her throat and backed her against the wall.

Linda pulled Iona out of the way.

"No, no. Don't hurt my mommy!" Iona yelled as Linda pulled her by the arm to the back bedroom.

Spoony smacked Cynda. "You think you're just going to walk out of here with my property? You got another thought coming."

"You can't have her. I won't let you do this." Cynda pushed at him, but his body was too rock-solid to be moved. She looked around for something to hit him with and saw a glass lamp. She tried to reach out for it, but Spoony began punching her in the face and pushing her downward. He kicked her several times, and she rolled around on the floor, trying to cover herself.

"Stop, Spoony. Just let us go. Let me and my daughter go, please."

He bent down and grabbed a handful of her long, black hair. Yanking her off the ground, he stood her in front of him and punched her in the face again. "I'll let you go when you're in a pine box and not before."

The punch sent Cynda reeling backward, and she fell against the wall. Something in her snapped. Spoony wanted her dead. He wanted her in a pine box so her daughter could look down on her and hate her for not protecting her, just as she'd hated her mother. History would not repeat itself today! She leaped on Spoony. Stuck her claws into him and tried to peel the flesh off his bones.

"Have you lost your mind?" He pushed her to the ground and touched the blood spots on his face. "I'm gon' kill you for that."

Cynda pulled herself up against the wall as Spoony advanced on her. Once again she eyed the lamp that sat on the table next to her. But Spoony was choking her before she could grab it. Thoughts of her mother's dead body flittered through her mind. The mother she lost because of a man like Spoony. She'd sworn that she wouldn't be like her mother, but here she was, dying just like her. "S-stop." She tried to pull his arms from around her neck, but her strength was waning. She could barely hear her own voice as she pleaded with him.

Spoony continued choking her. "I told you. Didn't I tell you I was going to kill you?"

Just like Mama. She lived and died just like Mama. Her vision was blurring. But somehow she managed to touch the lamp. She brought her hands down to the table and reached for it. Tears stung her eyes as she swung the lamp and then floated into darkness.

8

"Look, Isaac, there's something else I need to tell you about Cynda," Keith said as they turned onto Spoony's street.

"Didn't I tell you I didn't want to hear another word about that woman?" Isaac turned away from Keith to study the commotion going on around Spoony's house.

Keith couldn't hold it in any longer and blurted out, "Cynda has a daughter."

"Why would the police and ambulance be surrounding Spoony's house?" Isaac turned back to Keith. "I thought you said you weren't sleeping with her?"

"I'm not, man. Her daughter is ten years old."

"Yeah, well, good for her. Why are you telling me?"

The door to Spoony's house opened, and the paramedics carried out a body bag.

Isaac and Keith got out of the car. Soon after, the police brought Cynda out of the house in handcuffs.

Keith ran to her. "What happened? What's going on?"

The burly officer pushed him out of the way. "This is police business. You need to move."

Cynda's eyes were glazed as she stumbled beside the offi-cer.

"Tell me what happened," Keith yelled as Cynda was placed in the back seat of the police car. The police slammed the door after putting her in the back seat.

Through swollen lips she answered matter-of-factly, "I couldn't let him prostitute my baby."

"I'll get you out of this, Cynda," he yelled as the police drove off. "You've just got to trust me." Keith felt ill. He blamed himself for everything. What if he'd done what God wanted and asked Cynda to marry him? Would this be hap-pening? Would Cynda be on her way to prison? *I'll fix it, Lord.*

Isaac watched as Linda walked outside with a little girl clutching her arm. He then walked over to Linda. He had to find out if he had arrived too late to tell his old friend about a God that loved him no matter what. But the closer he got to Linda, the better view of the little girl he got. Then Keith's words hit him. *Cynda has a little girl. She's ten.*

Isaac looked from Linda to the little girl. He turned to Keith as his friend walked over to them. "What's going on here?" Isaac looked from Keith, to the child, then back to Keith again.

"That's what I've been trying to tell you." Keith pulled Isaac away from Iona and Linda. He then whispered, "I think Iona is your daughter. She looks just like you."

Isaac glared at his friend as he stepped back. "How long have you known this?"

Keith held up his hands. "I swear, man, I just met Iona yesterday. I asked Cynda about who the father was, but she wouldn't admit it."

Isaac walked back over to Linda, whose gaze was fixed on the paramedics as they lifted the body into their truck. "Is that Spoony?" he asked.

Without looking at him, Linda nodded.

"Linda, I know this is a bad time, but I need to talk to you."

She looked at Isaac with dull, unfeeling eyes. "Now is as good a time as any. Don't suppose things will get any better or worse for me."

Isaac followed Linda as she walked up the steps and back into her house. She acted as if she didn't notice the turned over chairs and coffee table or the busted glass that lay in pieces on the floor. She asked Keith to sit with Iona in the living room while she took Isaac to the dining room.

When they sat down, Linda simply said, "Iona is your daughter." She picked up her pack of cigarettes off the table, put one in her mouth, and lit it. "I love that little girl. I wanted to keep her." She puffed on her cigarette. "But when I saw you standing outside I figured that God must have sent you here to get her."

As they sat in silence, Isaac tried to put this nightmare together. Spoony, his old friend, was dead, and Cynda had killed him. She had also given birth to his baby but never told him. Now he would have to go home and tell his wife that he'd fathered a child that wasn't hers. Nina was the best thing that had ever happened to him. But how much could she take from him?

Linda stood up. "Well, I think it's about time you met your daughter."

Isaac numbly followed Linda as she walked into the living room.

"Iona, honey, come here. I want to introduce you to somebody."

Iona walked over and said, "I already know who he is."

"You do?" Linda asked. "How do you know?"

"Uncle Spoony showed me a picture of him." Her eyes got sad as she looked at Isaac. "He said you didn't want me."

Isaac bent down and looked into his little girl's eyes and wished he could tell her that Spoony was wrong. He wished that he was excited at the thought of being her father. But Lord, he wished Nina had birthed this child for him. "We'll work through this, okay?"

Iona nodded, and Isaac grabbed her hand and walked out of Spoony's house with his daughter.

"Ebony, your mom is here," Donavan hollered from the porch.

Nina and Ebony were in her office. Nina was going over a scene she was writing for her next book with Ebony. Nina turned away from her computer screen and looked at Ebony. "Are you ready for this?"

Ebony leaned against the wall in Nina's office. "I don't know. I'm scared."

Nina stood and put her hand on Ebony's shoulder. "Have a little faith."

Tears flowed down Ebony's face as she hugged Nina. "I love you, Nina. I'm so glad I met you."

Nina started crying also. How she wished that Ebony was her child, but she had to face facts and play the hand she'd been dealt. Wiping her eyes, Nina said, "I love you too, honey. But no matter how much I love you, I guarantee, your mom loves you more. Come on, let's go talk to her."

Slowly, they moved down the stairs to greet Ebony's mom. Ebony stopped midway down the stairs as her mother's profile came into view. She bit her lip.

Nina nudged her forward. "Nobody is without sin, so nobody can throw stones at you. Remember that."

Ebony smiled and walked a bit faster. Her pudgy mother was standing in the entryway watching her walk down the stairs. When Ebony was on the last step her mother ran to her and enveloped her in sweet love. "Oh, baby. We've missed you so much." She twirled Ebony around then stepped back and looked at her child. "Are you all right? Nothing's happened to you, has it?"

Somberly Ebony told her, "A lot's happened to me, Mama."

"It doesn't matter, baby. You'll be all right, even if we have to get you some therapy. I just need you home. That's all I want." She turned and faced Nina. She stuck out her hand. "I'm Gloria Jones. I guess you've figured out that I'm Ebony's mother. Thank you so much for calling me."

Nina shook Gloria's hand. "Yes. And you have a wonderful daughter. We enjoyed her company this past week."

Gloria beamed and looked back toward her daughter. "Ebony is wonderful, isn't she? I've been going out of my mind ever since she disappeared."

Nina invited Gloria to have a seat. "I think Ebony wants you to know a few things before you take her home."

There was a granite-white sofa and loveseat in the living room. The cherry maple entertainment center with a 48-inch plasma TV was against the wall facing the sofa. Ebony sat on the loveseat and put the multi-colored throw pillow in her lap, while her mother sat on the edge of the sofa. Ebony was so nervous that her hands were shaking. She put them in her lap and lowered her head as she said, "I've done some things since I left home, Mama."

"Things? What kind of things?"

Ebony lowered her voice as she sunk back into her seat. "I've been selling my body."

"What?" Gloria jumped up and walked the length of the living room. She turned then came back to stand in front of Nina and Ebony. "How could you have done something like this, Ebony? How?"

Ebony turned to Nina with tears in her eyes. "I told you."

Nina was leaning against the wall between the living

room and the entryway, trying to give mother and daughter some space, but when she saw the look of desperation in Ebony's eyes, she knew she had to intervene. She rushed over to Gloria and put her hand on the woman's shoulder. "Please listen to her, Ms. Jones."

She brushed Nina's hand off. "How can I listen to this? Ebony wasn't raised like this. We are a Christian family with morals."

Donavan had been sitting on the stairs in the entryway. He stormed into the room, stood in front of Ebony's mother and said, "If your family is so Christian, then why don't you practice some of that love the Bible talks about?"

"Donavan!"

"No, Mama, she's wrong," Donavan said as he turned back to Gloria. "I've been in trouble myself, and because my parents are Christians, they forgave me and stuck by me."

Gloria slumped back in her seat. "But things like this aren't supposed to happen to Christians."

Head still bowed low, Ebony said, "I'm sorry I disappointed you, Mama. But you're not perfect either. Before you started going to that church, you had three children by three different men."

Gloria's mouth fell slack. "How dare you bring that up in front of these people!"

"I'm not trying to embarrass you, Mama, but if God forgave you, don't you think He can do the same for me?"

Tears cascading down her cheeks, Gloria went to her daughter and held her. "I'm sorry, baby. I'm so sorry. We'll make this right, I promise."

They held each other and cried. Held on to one another tighter, and then cried some more.

Nina and Donavan walked into the kitchen, made a couple of sandwiches, and headed back toward the living room. When they returned and Donavan saw that Ebony and her mother were still crying and that his mother's eyes were beginning to water, he told his mother that he had some homework to finish.

Nina smiled at her son and let him escape. The last place he wanted to be was in a room full of crying women. Like father, like son.

Nina allowed Ebony and her mother time to bond as she sat across from them silently praying that God would mend this broken family. She knew firsthand that God could do just that. She, Isaac, and Donavan had been living separate lives for many years. She and Isaac both loved God and tried to do His will, but they just couldn't connect. And their disconnection caused Donavan to stray. Almost caused the end of their family.

"When you two get home," Nina said, "don't forget this moment. Don't forget to love each other. It'll help you get past the pain."

Ebony pulled away from her mother's embrace and walked over to Nina. She bent down in front of her and hugged her. "Thank you."

Tears filled Nina's eyes. "I'll miss you more than you'll ever know. You are precious to me."

Ebony gathered her things and left with her mother.

"What am I suppose to do with Cynda's child?" Isaac was treading back and forth in the living room of Keith's small home while Iona slept in the spare bedroom. He had much on his mind. Most of all, Nina. She'd been told a little over a year ago that she would never be able to have another child. How could he now bring her a child that he had with another woman?

When he'd first met Cynda about twelve years ago, he thought she was gorgeous. At the time he was already dating Nina for about a year, but their relationship was on the outs. Nina wasn't happy with his lifestyle, didn't want to be a part of his world. Isaac thought if he spent time with Cynda, she would take his mind off of Nina. But it didn't happen. The more time he spent with Cynda, the more he disliked her. She was shallow and self-centered. Thought the world owed her something just because she was beautiful. When he cut her loose, her vindictive behavior sent ripples of tidal waves through his life. But he had no idea that it would eventually turn into a tsunami.

Nina loved him. He knew that without reservation. But he had put her through so much mess during their rocky years together, and even more during their years apart. Would this child prove to be the final straw?

Isaac turned to Keith. "You still want to marry Cynda?"

"I never used the word *want*," Keith told him.

"Point taken. But do you still believe that God wants you to marry her?"

Keith put his head in his hands. "I don't know. I just don't know."

"Look, why don't we see if we can get her out of jail before anything?"

"I can get her a lawyer," Keith said. "I can do that much for her."

"All right, and I'll stay here with Iona until we know something concrete."

Keith smirked. "Scared to face the little woman, huh?"

"That way I can be here to see if Iona's no-good mama can get out of jail. Then I'll at least have an answer for Nina as to whether or not we will be keeping Iona, or if Cynda will be able to do it."

They agreed on their course of action and then went to bed. But Isaac couldn't sleep. Or rather, he didn't want to sleep. He knew what was coming and fought hard to not let it overtake him again.

People always wondered how God was able to get big bad Isaac Walker's attention. God wasn't subtle or lovingly kind with the way he dealt with hardheaded Isaac. No, Isaac was so bad God had to drag him to the altar via a first-class trip to Hell.

Isaac would never forget the smell of decay, death, and dying he endured on his guided tour. Pain still consumed him every time he reminded himself that his brother, the original Donavan, now resided in Hell forever.

Donavan was only fourteen when he was murdered during a back-alley crap game. He had never committed his life to the Lord, so when his life on earth ended, a torturous life in Hell began and Isaac had been forced to watch it happen. He wished he could forget the agony on Donavan's face that he'd witnessed as the demons tortured his frail body. But things like that were impossible to forget when he was forced to relive them over and over again in his sleep.

Try as he might, Isaac couldn't keep his eyes from closing. And no sooner than they did, he drifted back into the place where hundreds of menacing spirits stood, growling and snarling. The demons were of varied shapes and sizes. Some were as big as a grizzly bear with heads like bats and ten-inch fangs. Some were small and monkey-like, with big hairy arms. Still others had large heads, large ears, and long, jagged tails. The most dreadful of all were the smaller piranha-like imps, which infested their victims in swarms and gnawed at their flesh.

As it always happened, when he was forced to experience this episode, two of the big grizzly demons stepped from the pack carrying Donavan like a Ken doll. When one of the demons put his spear in Donavan's flesh, Isaac heard his little brother scream and beg for mercy.

Isaac ran to the demons screaming, "Noooo!" as if he would be able to change destiny this time around, never mind the fact that he hadn't changed the outcome the sixty-five other times he'd relived this episode in the past ten years.

The demon lifted his spear again, positioning it for Donavan's chest cavity. Isaac grabbed the spear and tried to yank it out of the demon's hand, but its grip was much stronger than anything Isaac had ever known. The demon, venomous fluids oozing from his mouth as he hissed, swatted Isaac to the ground. His beady eyes centered on Isaac. With his lip curled and fangs fully exposed, he lunged.

Isaac scurried out of the way. Scrunched in a corner, he was forced to witness every painful moment of Donavan's torture. Two demons grabbed Donavan's arms and stretched him out crucifixion-style

Isaac called out to his brother as another demon lifted his spear, "Donavan, run!"

"Aaarrhhh!" Donavan yelled as the spear pierced his left shoulder.

The demon pulled the spear from Donavan and lifted it to impale him again.

Isaac yelled, "Nooo!" Isaac was no punk, and he wasn't about to hide in a corner and take this mess. He got up and ran full speed toward the offending demon. He jumped on its back and tried to pull the spear from his hand.

The demon hissed and cackled as he shook Isaac off his back. He picked Isaac up like he was a Raggedy Andy doll and threw him across the room.

Isaac hit the wall. *Whoosh*. His breath exited his body as he slid down the wall and landed on a heap of limbs. Dazed, he shook his head.

The nine-foot-tall demon turned jaundiced eyes in Isaac's direction and pointed at him. "Stay there," he ordered.

Isaac climbed down from the pile of limbs and ran back to the demon.

Jaundiced eyes was waiting for him. He put his spear down.

Isaac advanced.

The demon spat green slime on the ground. He picked

Isaac up by the collar and pimp-smacked him and threw him against another wall.

Isaac didn't get up.

The demons then brought another person into the room. It was Iona.

Isaac closed his eyes tight to this new pain.

Both of the grizzly demons took one of Iona's arms and pulled her until she stood crucifixion-style. A third demon walked toward her with spear in hand.

Iona looked to Isaac with fear in her eyes. "Daddy, daddy, help me," she cried out.

The spear-toting demon turned to Isaac. "If you don't want her, we sure do."

"Nooo!" he screamed as he jolted upright in bed. Panting, he wiped the sweat from his face and declared to the forces of darkness, "You can't have her. My family belongs to the Lord."

9

Keith couldn't sleep either. He stayed up half the night praying and petitioning God for a way to save Cynda without sacrificing himself. In the end, he relented. He would marry Cynda and love her and she would break his heart, just as the prophet Hosea's heart had been broken by Gomer, the prostitute God required him to marry.

Isaac was right about one thing. Keith did feel responsible for his mother's death. He'd done everything he could to get Dorthea Williams off drugs, but she couldn't let it go. He'd finally given up, walked away. The night he'd told her he wanted nothing else to do with her was the night she turned her last trick.

He wouldn't give up on Cynda. He promised God that he would go the distance to ensure a better life for Cynda and Iona. He mortgaged his house and hired the best lawyer he knew. If she was going to beat the charges against her, Jim Reid was the man for the job.

Jim and his wife Marline attended the same church as Keith. He'd always enjoyed fellowshipping with Jim, and now he was putting his future wife's life in this man's capable hands.

Reid worked his magic and was able to get Cynda released on house arrest until her trial. One catch—Since Iona was in the house when the incident took place, Cynda was not allowed to remain the custodial parent.

"Is the child's father able to take custody?" the judge asked during the custody hearing.

"We haven't heard from him in ten years," Cynda answered.

"Well, if the father cannot be located, we will have to put the child in foster care."

Isaac, who was sitting in the back of the courtroom with Keith, stood up, nostrils flaring. "I'm Iona's father," he said. "I'll take her."

Cynda began to scream vulgarities at him. "You can't just give him my child!"

The judge had to bang the gavel to get her to shut up. "That's enough, Miss Stephens."

Cynda continued on with her obscene rant.

Impatiently, the judge asked, "Is he the father?"

Cynda turned fiery eyes on Isaac. "He thinks he is, but I'm a prostitute, Judge. Anybody could be Iona's daddy." With a glint in her eye, Cynda added. "She might even be yours, Your Honor."

He banged the gavel once again and then pointed at Cynda. "I can tell you right now, Ms. Stephens, this is not the *Maury* show. This court does not have time to sift through possible fathers for your daughter. You should be grateful this man is willing to step up to the plate."

"Your Honor, Cynda doesn't care anything about her own child. She would rather let you send my daughter to a foster home than tell you the truth."

The judge jotted a few notes down on his notepad and then turned toward back to Isaac. "I'm ordering a DNA test. If the child is yours, I will make sure that you receive full custody until Ms. Stephens can prove to this court that she is a responsible citizen."

"Thank you, Your Honor," Isaac said. "I'm going to need to receive temporary custody papers so I can enroll her in school while we are waiting on the DNA results."

The judge jotted more information on his notepad. "Bring the child back this afternoon for the test, and my clerk will have the documents you need waiting."

With that, Cynda had to be removed, kicking and screaming from the courtroom.

Isaac and Keith left the courtroom shortly after the team of security guards carted Cynda back to jail.

"She acts like I am thrilled to be the father of her child. Who would want a child by that nasty wh—"

"Look, Isaac," Keith said, cutting him off, "if you don't want to take Iona home with you, just leave her with me."

"I don't need you to take over my responsibilities. I got mine." Isaac stalked away from Keith and mumbled something about Cynda being a no-good guttersnipe.

Keith caught up with Isaac. "I didn't mean to upset you. It just seems like you don't want to take Iona."

"Iona has nothing to do with this. It's not her fault that her mother is a—"

Keith held up his hand. "Then take her home. Introduce her to your wife."

"It's not that simple, Keith. I can't just walk her in the front door and say, 'Surprise, honey. I've got a daughter. What's new with you?' "

Keith rubbed his jaw. "I guess you've got a point there. But you're married to Nina, Isaac. She will understand." Keith smiled at his friend. "Matter of fact, the Nina I know would welcome Iona with open arms."

"Well, the Nina I know is still grieving over the fact that she can't have any more children." Isaac closed his eyes and shook his head. "I got to go pick Iona up from school. I'll talk with you in a couple of days." His shoulders slumped from the weight of his troubles, Isaac walked away from his friend. He lifted his face to God. "I need your help with this one."

Keith's heart went out to him. He hoped that he and Nina could work this out. But right now he had his own problems. He left the courthouse and went to his office to talk with Janet.

As usual, faithful Janet was seated behind her desk typing away. She looked up and smiled at Keith. "About time you decided to come to work." She lifted a Burger King bag off her desk and handed it to him. "I figured you were running around taking care of so much stuff that you wouldn't have time to get lunch. I picked you up two chicken sandwiches, no pickles, lots of mayo."

Again, Lord, why not Janet? The smile on his face was awkward as he said, "Thank you, Janet."

"What's wrong?"

"Can I talk to you for a minute?"

"Sure. What's up?"

He hesitated. "Come into my office for a minute, okay."

She followed him, closed the door, and sat down in one of the office chairs in front of his desk. She had on a beige pants suit that tastefully accented the curves on her body. She looked good in that suit. In fact, she looked good in all of her clothes.

Instead of sitting behind his desk, Keith plopped down in the chair next to Janet, and they stared at each other for a moment.

Keith scratched his throat and then broke the silence. He looked Janet in the eye. "You know how much I depend on you, right?"

Janet nodded.

"And you know that I think you are a wonderfully spiritual person, and well . . . how much I enjoy your company, right?"

Slowly, she answered, "I think so."

"So, anyway, I have been praying and seeking God for the woman I'm supposed to marry." He saw the smile on her face and turned away from it. "God showed me who that woman is, and I just wanted to tell you about it before I talk to her."

Her hands went to her hips. "Excuse me."

"Well, to tell you the truth, I had hoped God would tell me to marry you."

She held up a hand. "Are you telling me that God told you to marry someone else?"

Elbow on the armrest of the chair, forehead in his hand, Keith said, "Yes, that's what I'm telling you."

"Why?"

He saw the tears forming in her eyes and could do nothing to stop them from falling. But he could at least tell Janet the truth of the matter. "She's headed to prison, and it's partially my fault. If I had obeyed God when he first told me to marry Cynda, she probably wouldn't be in this predicament. But I wanted a woman like you. Someone thoughtful and kind."

She stood. "I don't understand you, Keith. You say you want a woman like me, but instead of getting to know me better, you're just going to marry some woman who might be headed to prison?"

"It sounds crazy, I know."

She walked out of his office. He got up and followed. "What are you going to do?" he asked.

Janet sat down behind her desk. "I'm going to get back to work."

He looked at her as if she was crazy. "Just like that?"

Shuffling some papers, she asked, "What do you want me to do, Keith? We never really got anything going. I know we both thought something would happen, but hey, I am not about to fight against God."

"So you're going to continue working here?"

With a wicked smile, she told him, "Yeah, I'm going to act like some of the women in the church that want to be the pastor's wife so bad that they secretly hope his current wife passes away in her sleep. Except, I don't need your future wife to pass away. Just maybe get a long prison sentence. Then you'll come to your senses."

Although Janet had some seriousness to her tone, after uttering the words, both she and Keith began to laugh. Keith then covered her hand with his and said, "I'm sorry."

Keith went back to the jail so he could have a moment alone with Cynda, who was jumpy and anxious. Both held a telephone to their ear so they could hear the other through the thick glass partition.

As soon as Cynda sat down, she asked, "So when can you get me out of here?"

"Well, first I need to know if you have family here in Chicago," Keith said.

"What do you need to know that for?"

"For them to put you on house arrest, you need to have some place to go."

Cynda shifted in her seat. "I ain't got no family. Only person I ever had besides Iona was my grandmother, and she died twelve years ago."

Keith wanted to just take Cynda into his arms and hold her. She put on this tough-girl façade, but he saw through her.

"Why can't I just go to your house?"

Here was his chance to convince Cynda to marry him. Keith thought that if she had to pick between jail and life with him, surely, she would pick him.

"The only way you can stay at my house is if we are married."

Her head jerked. "What?"

"I've been praying about this, and I believe that God wants me to marry you."

With a smirk she asked, "What did you do to God?"

"This isn't about me. It's about what God wants to do for *you*."

Cynda laughed at him. "You're willing to marry a soon-to-be-convicted murderer. Man, you are ate up, for real."

"You can't live in my house if we're not married."

Cynda was silent for a moment, but then she quickly turned an accusing finger at Keith. "Why'd you let me spend the night a couple days ago if you are so moral and upright that you can't have a woman live with you unless you are married to her?"

"That was for one night. I wasn't going to let you and your daughter spend the night on the streets. But this is different. You will be in my house every day and night for months before all this mess is resolved."

Cynda sneered. "Too much temptation for you, daddy?"

Way too much. "If you want to marry me, I'll take you home."

"I don't want to marry you or anybody else, got it?"

He stood. "Call me if you change your mind."

Cynda rolled her eyes, and watched Keith walk out of the visitation area, leaving her in this place to fend for herself. No matter, nobody looked out for her, and she'd taken care of herself for as long as she could remember.

Cynda was beautiful and she knew it. God should have been more careful with His beautiful people. But maybe it was like her grandmother had told her when fat o' Suzy Stelson busted her lip and sent her running home.

Then, Cynda's grandmother opened the door and demanded to know what had happened to her.

"Fat o' Suzy hit me," Cynda cried.

"Well, what made her hit you?" her grandmother inquired.

"She told me that I was a whore just like my mama, and I told her she was just mad because Jerome didn't like ugly and neither does God."

Grammy pulled Cynda into an embrace. "Chile, God don't care nothing 'bout pretty or ugly. What God don't like is *wrong*."

And hadn't her life been wrong since the day she was conceived? Her daddy was some married Hispanic man. That was wrong. Her mother wanted to be with her pimp, even though he abused her until the day he killed her. Something was definitely wrong with that. She'd never experienced love in all her twenty-nine years. Just a bunch of users. God just didn't like her. And *that* was wrong.

When Cynda returned to her community cell, a big, muscular biker chick said, "Hey, Cynda, we heard you offed Spoony. Is that a fact?"

Lying on her musty cot, Cynda glanced up and snarled, "Get out of my face."

"Oh, so you think you're bad now? Kill one played-out pimp and all of a sudden you don't have to speak to us common folk no more."

Cynda ignored her.

"Oh, so you don't have to answer Big Rosa? Is that what you think?"

Cynda kept her head turned and her mouth shut. She just wanted to be left alone. Was that too much to ask?

An instigating inmate yelled to Big Rosa, "I know you're not going to let that piece of crap disrespect you like this."

Rosa turned on the instigator. "I don't need you to tell me what to do." She turned back to Cynda. "You gonna answer me or what?"

This time when Cynda didn't respond, Rosa grabbed her by her shirt and pulled her off the cot.

Cynda spat on her.

As Rosa pounded her big fists into Cynda's face, she didn't even try to fight back. Didn't care if Rosa killed her. As she dropped to the ground, she felt multiple feet kicking and stomping her. Someone kicked her in the head, and her brain rattled as she floated into unconsciousness for the second time that week.

Before darkness overtook her, she thought of the disappearing man she met when she was nine and had gotten lost.

The man had told her that the Good Shepherd loved her, and that if she got lost, he'd leave all that he had to come find her. The one that got away. Her last thought was of the Good Shepherd. Where was He?

When Cynda's attorney told Keith that she'd been rushed to the hospital, he went out of his mind with worry. Isaac and Iona had left an hour before he got the news. He could have called Isaac's cell phone, but Isaac wouldn't have much sympathy for Cynda right now, so he suffered alone.

Driving to the hospital, Keith kept praying that God would spare her life. This was the woman that God had ordained for him. "God, please let her live."

Keith went to Cook County Courthouse right after he'd received word of Cynda's brutal beating. He tried to get a marriage license, but the clerk of courts told him that he had to bring Cynda with him. So he went to the hospital to convince Cynda that he was a better deal than getting beat in prison.

When Keith stepped into Cynda's room, he was unprepared for what he saw. He'd gotten used to the scars and bruises. Cynda seemed to live for the opportunity to be someone's punching bag. But he'd never seen her face as swollen or as black and blue as it was now. Her right arm was in a sling. He was more determined than ever to marry her and give her a better life.

He leaned down and whispered into her ear. "Cynda, it's

me, Keith. I don't want them to lock you back up. I want to take you home with me, okay?"

Slowly, she nodded.

He put her hand in his, held his breath and prayed that the Lord had softened her heart toward him. "Will you marry me, Cynda?"

"Whatever, man. I don't care," she mumbled in a barely audible voice.

Keith had been single for a long time, but he'd always imagined that the day he asked his future bride to marry him, she would be so full of joy that tears would fill her eyes as she jumped out of her seat to hug and kiss him. None of that happened, of course, and Keith felt cheated. He vowed right then and there that Cynda would never feel cheated. He would do everything he could to ensure that her life with him would be a happy one.

It took three days before Cynda was able to leave the hospital. When her court appointed counselor came to the hospital to go over the house arrest details, Keith told him that he needed to take Cynda to Cook County Courthouse to get a marriage license, and the counselor agreed to go with them.

Because Keith knew that Cynda was still in a lot of pain he rented a wheelchair to get her from the hospital to the courthouse and then to the house he would share with her.

Once they filled out the paperwork and received their license, the clerk of courts told them that the license would become valid twenty-four hours after receiving it and invalid after sixty days.

Cynda's home detection device was strapped to her ankle the moment she walked in Keith's house.

Keith put her to bed in his bedroom once Cynda's counselor and the technician left and told her, "My pastor will come to the house tomorrow to marry us. Is that all right with you?"

"I don't care. Just no jail, no beatings," Cynda told him, half-delirious from the pain medication.

Pastor Norton arrived at Keith's house at three o'clock the next afternoon. He went into the bedroom to meet Cynda and was immediately taken aback by her swollen and bruised face. Pastor Norton turned back to Keith. "Do you want to wait until she recovers? Maybe give her a little more time to think this through?"

In his heart Keith felt that this opportunity would not come again. "Let's do it, Pastor. We're ready."

Pastor Norton opened his Bible and then closed it. "Are you sure about this?"

Keith looked down at Cynda's bruised body and saw the scars life had inflicted on her. He wanted to be the one to help her heal. He wanted to be around when God took away the pain. "I'm sure."

Pastor Norton rushed through the vows, but even so, it didn't escape his attention that when he asked Cynda if she would take Keith Hosea Williams to be her husband, Cynda replied, "Man, I don't care."

Keith saw the shocked expressions on his pastor's face but ignored it. He prayed that God would give him the ability to love Cynda until she loved him back. As he slipped the diamond ring he'd purchased at Tiffany's the day before on his wife's finger, he decided that he was going to show her what true love was all about. He'd make a believer out of this woman if it was the last thing he did on earth.

10

Nina was rushing around the house getting ready for a doctors appointment that she was sure would bring good news when the telephone rang. Caller ID told her that her best friend, Elizabeth Underwood, was on the line. Nina had first met Elizabeth when she was pregnant with Donavan and contemplating life as a single mother. Their friendship had weathered the tests and trials that life brought their way, even surviving Elizabeth's moving to Atlanta, Georgia and her career change from housewife to gospel diva.

Nina picked up the phone and asked, "What's up, girl?"

"I don't know. You tell me what's so important in Ohio that you can't pick up the phone and call me."

Nina laughed. "Sorry about that. I've been dealing with a situation here. I'll tell you all about it later. I'm on my way out so I'll give you a call this evening, okay?"

"All right, girl. Just call me later. You know I'm not going to be home much in about a month. Kenneth is working out all the final details for the tour as we speak."

Kenneth, Elizabeth's husband and manager, was working diligently to ensure that his wife's tour would be successful.

Snapping her finger, Nina said, "That's right. It's time to promote your new CD. Don't worry, I'll call you later." Nina hung up, proud of herself for not telling Elizabeth that she was going to the doctor. Elizabeth would have wanted to know what her appointment was for, and Nina didn't want to tell anyone until she was sure.

Nina had been so preoccupied with Ebony's needs that she hadn't noticed when she missed her period. But now that Ebony was gone, one glance at her calendar told her that she was six days late. And she was hardly ever late. She called Dr. Hopson, and he gave her an appointment. Only problem was, she had to get to his office within an hour and couldn't find the left side of her tennis shoes. She looked under the bed and in the hall closet. She finally gave up and put on a pair of low-cut black boots, grabbed her Fendi purse, and ran to her car.

All the way to the doctor's office, Nina kept thanking God for His faithfulness. "But Lord, You're not just faithful. You are good to Your children. I thank You, my Father, that no weapon formed against me can prosper, and no doctor has the final say over my body."

Nina did a two-step praise dance all the way into the building. She patiently waited to be escorted to the back of the doctor's office into an examination room. As she sat in the room with a hideous blue-and-white striped hospital gown on waiting for Dr. Hopson to bring her the good news, she wondered why she hadn't just gone to the drug store and bought one of the home pregnancy tests and gotten it over with.

But truth be told, Nina knew why she hadn't taken the test in the privacy of her own home. She wanted her doctor and everyone else to know that her God could restore her womb.

There was a knock on the door. Then Dr. Hopson opened it and walked into the room.

Nina watched him closely. There was no let's-break-out-the-cigars kind of smile on his face, no light in his eyes. *That's okay*, Nina thought. Dr. Hopson didn't have to be happy for her. Isaac will be happy. Nina's greatest joy would be to give her husband another child, one that they would raise together from day one. This child wouldn't have weekend visitation with the father. Daddy would already be in the house. Nina couldn't wait to tell her man what God had done for them.

"How are you feeling, Nina?" Dr. Hopson asked.

She adjusted her gown. "I feel really good, Dr. Hopson. What took you so long?"

"I had to re-check the results."

Nina laughed. "What's wrong? You still don't believe that my God is a miracle worker?"

Dr. Hopson pushed his wire-rimmed glasses back toward the bridge of his nose. "I don't dispute whether or not your God is a miracle worker. But you also can't dispute my findings. He sighed and put his hand on her shoulder. "You're not pregnant, Nina."

"What do you mean, I'm not pregnant? I'm late, so I must be pregnant."

Dr. Hopson shook his head.

"Stop shaking your head." She removed his hand from her shoulder. "I know my body. How do you explain the fact that I'm late, when I'm never late?"

"I hate to tell you this, Nina, but you might be going into menopause."

No, no, no! Lightning doesn't strike in the same place twice. God would not do this to her. The shock registered on her face as she told him, "But I'm only thirty-eight."

He looked at the papers in his hands. "Sometimes it happens early."

"That's not true," Nina screamed. "It can't be true. God is good to me. This isn't happening."

"So, what do you like to do when you're not in school?" Isaac asked Iona as he drove the SUV he'd rented from Hertz down I-70.

Iona glared at her father and then turned to stare out the window.

One hand on the wheel, the other rubbing his chin, Isaac contemplated this situation. He hated to admit it, but his biggest worry right now was that Nina would walk right out the door the moment he walked in with this child. A child who looked more like him than his son. Donavan was a carbon copy of Isaac's brother, minus Nina's hazel eyes. And since Isaac's brother was killed before his fifteenth birthday, Isaac was happy to remember his brother through his son. Seeing his son and knowing where his brother now resided also helped to keep Isaac focused on bringing as many souls to the Lord as possible.

But Iona had Isaac's skin color, his dimples, and when she turned and gave him a what-are-you-looking-at stare, he recognized those dark, cold eyes she rolled at him.

He couldn't stand the child's mother, but he didn't see much of Cynda in Iona, so it was becoming easier for him to separate the child from the hooker that birthed her. Would Nina be able to do the same?

He turned off the highway and took his daughter to Steak and Shake. They were only two hours away from home, but Isaac couldn't go there just yet. He'd talked to Nina several times a day since arriving in Chicago. He told her about Spoony's death and about his need to stay in Chicago for a few more days. Isaac knew that Nina assumed he was staying to help Linda with funeral arrangements.

Isaac didn't have the heart to tell her about Cynda or Iona. For one thing, Cynda had tormented Nina for years back in the day when he was dating both of them. And even after he and Nina broke up, Cynda would still seek out every opportunity to tell Nina about her escapades with Isaac.

After he and Iona placed their orders, Isaac decided to call Nina. "Hey, lady, are you missing your husband yet?" Isaac said into his cell phone.

"More than you know, baby," Nina said somberly.

Isaac could hear the sadness in her voice. It now made him want to rush home. But he thought about the camel then looked at the straw that sat across from him. "I stopped in Indianapolis. I might stay here overnight."

"No, Isaac. I need you home with me. I'm really feeling a little down after letting Ebony go, and . . . I need to talk with you about something."

"Look, Nina, I might as well tell you now. There were some problems in Chicago. I've got a little girl with me." He hesitated. "I'll be bringing her home with me."

"No, Isaac. I can't take another little girl that doesn't belong to me. It's too hard to give them back."

He closed his eyes. "This one can't be helped, baby." He shifted in his seat so Iona couldn't read his lips as he whispered, "Her mother has been arrested."

"Oh, Isaac, no."

The waitress put Iona's burger and fries and his chicken sandwich on the table.

Isaac caught Iona's look of disapproval and told Nina, "The food is here, baby. I'm going to call you later tonight, okay."

"I'd rather you come home tonight."

"I know. I'll get there as soon as I can." Before hanging up, he added, "I love you, Nina. You do know that, don't you?"

"I've been wondering why you kept stalking me until I finally agreed to marry you. All this time I just thought you were a little off, but now I find out it's been love all along."

He could hear the laughter in her voice and wanted to join in, but his life was no laughing matter at present. "I'll see you when I get home." He closed his flip phone and said grace over his and Iona's food.

Brows furrowed, Iona asked, "Why did you do that?"

"Do what?"

"Pray over the food."

This kid looked like him and had his former bad traits. There was a time when he thought praying was stupid also. "Iona, do you believe in God?"

She took a bite of her hamburger, chewed a little, and then answered, "Naw, my mom says all that God stuff is just a myth."

"What if your mother is wrong?"

Chewing some of her fries she shrugged.

"Look, Iona, you're going to be staying with me until this stuff with your mother gets straightened out. Me, my wife, and son all believe in God. I would just appreciate it if you would open your mind to the possibility that God does exist, okay?"

"You have a son?" Iona rolled her eyes. "I bet you didn't wait until he was ten to introduce yourself to him, huh?"

The seed of unforgiveness toward Cynda grew deeper roots in his heart. How was he supposed to give back ten years of missed hugs, ten years of butterfly kisses, and ten years of holding daddy's hand and receiving daddy's love? He was no miracle worker. He never professed turning water into wine. But thank God he knew the man who did. And right now he was calling on Him for help. *Lord, Jesus, I need You to show me what to do. I need to know how to make this right.*

"Let's get something straight, Iona. I didn't know that I had a daughter. If I—"

"Yes, you did. My mama said you didn't want nothing to do with us." Iona's cold, dark eyes accused Isaac of lying.

"She said you were too busy chasing after some woman who didn't even want you to care about what happened to me."

She was right on one count. He didn't want anything to do with Cynda's deceitful, snake-in-the-grass self. "Your mother didn't tell you the truth, Iona."

"My mother always tells me the truth. You're the reason she had to work with all those bad men. You're too cheap to pay child support."

He wanted to tell her that her mother was on crack and that was the reason she "worked" with all those bad men. But no matter how bad he was hating on Cynda right now, he refused to defame her to this child.

They ate the rest of the meal in silence.

By the time Isaac received the check he decided that he needed to get back on the road and face the music at home. Nina was more equipped for handling pre-teen girls than he was.

Nina and Donavan were in the dining room going over his homework when Isaac pulled into the driveway. Donavan jumped up.

"Not so fast, mister," Nina said sternly. "Finish this math paper before you go anywhere."

"But Dad just pulled up."

Nina smiled. "He lives here, Donavan. You'll be able to see him when your homework is finished."

Donavan sat back down and got back to work on his paper.

Nina reminded herself to walk, not run, as she rushed to the front door to greet her man. As his key clicked in the lock, she ran her hand through her short-layered hair. She wished she'd made time to wash and style her hair today instead of just letting it lay flat on her head. She wished she had put on some makeup too. But it had been a blah kind of day for her, and she chose to let her appearance reflect her mood.

Her heart beat a bit faster as the door slid open. She couldn't help it. This man set her soul on fire. It was those deep dimples of his. Every time Isaac smiled, Nina wanted to scream, "What you want? Just tell me your dreams so I can make them come true." Her adoptive mother used to tell her that she loved her husband so much that she would drink his dirty bathwater. Nina didn't know if she was ready to drink dirty bathwater, but she'd do just about anything else for this strong black man walking through her door.

She grabbed him and covered his mouth with hers. He was a whole foot taller than her, but she still felt right in his arms. She needed to forget what her doctor had said. She needed to wrap herself in Isaac's arms and believe that all things were possible. He lifted her onto their handcrafted cocktail table without caring if they cracked the glass top. The kiss deepened, and Nina became mesmerized. How could this man walk back into her world after being gone only three days and cause her to yearn so deeply for him?

"Baby, you make me *want* to come home," Isaac told his wife.

Smiling, she pulled her man closer. His statement thrilled her because she understood the meaning. Many married men came home as a sense of duty, because they had to. But *wanting* to come home was a whole 'nother-other. She whispered in his ear, "Let's go to our room and make a baby."

His eyes clouded as he pulled away from her embrace.

"What's the matter? The man that wars with demons doesn't trust that God is able to perform a miracle for us?" She needed him to believe for her, to tell her that every doctor in this world could just shut up.

"It's not that, baby."

"Well, what is it? Because I choose to trust God before I

trust what some doctor has to say. I thought you were in agreement with me on this?" *Please be in agreement. You don't know the day I've had.*

His head hung low as the dark-chocolate little girl stepped in front of him.

Nina's face flushed red. "Oh my God, I totally forgot that you were bringing someone home." Nina bent down in front of the little girl and put out her hand. "Hello, I'm Nina."

Iona ignored Nina's hand. She gave her the once-over then said, "My mother looks ten times better than you."

Nina's mouth hung open. She stood and looked at Isaac who had jumped in front of the little girl, his finger shaking in her face.

"Now look here, Iona, you are not going to disrespect my wife. This is our home, and you will appreciate that fact."

Iona shrugged. "Whatever."

Nostrils flaring, Isaac said, "What did you say to me?"

Nina grabbed his arm and turned him toward her. She felt as though the girl's mother was in jail and that she needed compassion rather than a good thrashing right now. "Let it go, baby." She ran her hand through her hair. "She's right. I do look a mess."

Iona said to Nina, "I don't need you taking up for me."

As the two of them stood side by side, Nina looked from one to the other. Their complexions were the same, the shape of their eyes and the bone structure, the same. Iona smirked at Nina, who put her hand to her mouth and backed away. Those dimples on the little girl were exactly like her husband's. As a matter of fact, this little girl looked exactly like her husband.

Isaac walked toward her. "Baby, now I know this seems a little weird."

Nina looked from the child to her husband, from her husband and back to the child. "Who is her mother."

Isaac lowered his head.

"My mother's name is Cynda Stephens and she is triple times prettier than you," Iona spat.

Nina's hand went to her mouth again. As she backed away from Isaac, tears formed in her eyes. Now Nina understood why Cynda had made such a scene at her and Isaac's wedding last year. All this time, that woman had Isaac's child. As cruel as Nina knew Cynda to be, she imagined the woman sitting in a jail cell somewhere laughing at the thought of Nina having to raise a child that belonged to her.

Isaac reached out for his wife. "Let me explain, baby."

Donavan walked into the room. "What's going on?"

Nina brushed by Donavan and ran towards her bedroom.

"What's wrong with mom, Dad?"

"It's complicated, son. Can you show Iona where the spare bedroom is while I go see about your mother?"

"Does this mean I don't have to finish my homework?"

"That's fine, son. Whatever you want," Isaac answered, hardly paying attention.

By the time Isaac reached their bedroom, the door was locked. "Nina, baby, let me in."

She didn't respond.

He leaned against the door. "I can hear you crying. Open the door so I can hold you . . . please, Nina. I just want to hold you."

11

Five days after the attack in the county lockup, Cynda's body was still sore. Her face and arms were also still swollen and black and blue.

As Keith gently pulled the covers over Cynda, he asked, "Can I get you anything?"

"Get out of my face," she replied, shoving him away from her.

Keith frowned as he backed out of the room. Cynda had been unruly for two days now, accusing him of tricking her into marriage. Maybe he did take advantage of her at a vulnerable time, but she went to the courthouse and signed those papers with him. She knew exactly what she was doing. She'd been handed a get-out-of-jail-free-while-awaiting-trial card, and she took it.

He pulled a vase out of the kitchen cabinet, filled it with water, then put the white roses he'd purchased from the hospital gift shop in the vase. The faucet continued to drip even after he'd turned it off. Keith made a mental note to call the plumber to have that little nuisance fixed.

He took a can of tomato soup down from the cabinet, put

it in a bowl, and microwaved it. Putting the roses, the soup, a glass of 7 Up, and some pain pills on a dinner tray, he walked back into his bedroom. Smiling at his disagreeable patient, he set the tray on the nightstand next to the bed. He took the roses off the tray and placed them on the dresser across from the bed so that Cynda could see them.

Picking up the bowl of tomato soup, Keith sat down in front of her and held up a spoon. "I figured that you must still be in a lot of pain, so the sooner I can get some food in you, the sooner I'll be able to give you something for your pain."

Cynda rolled her eyes and shot an accusing glance his way. "Don't you have a job? Shouldn't you be there?"

Putting a spoonful of soup in her mouth, Keith answered, "I'm working from home this week. I want to be here to care for you."

As Keith tried to give her another spoonful of soup, Cynda turned her head. "So when they fire you, I guess you think I'm going to take care of us?"

Keith knew all about Cynda's skills. He'd go on welfare before allowing her to take care of them. "You need to eat." He held out the spoon again, and Cynda relented. "You've already lost weight."

"Don't worry about me getting fired. I own the company, remember?"

"A regular Daddy Warbucks, huh?" she asked through clenched teeth.

"You okay?"

She nodded, and he shoved another spoonful of soup in her mouth.

"Nothing like that. This is my first year in business. Things are still real tight, but we'll manage, don't worry."

"Yeah, that's what Spoony said before I started tricking for him."

Keith sat with the spoon in his hand. He knew that life

had kicked Cynda around so much that she didn't know how to receive him. He sat the bowl on the nightstand. "I'll be in my office just across the hall if you need me. The pills are on the nightstand, but I really think you should eat a little more before taking them." He got up and walked out of his bedroom.

Keith had been sleeping in the guest bedroom and his office, whichever he felt like sleeping in. He didn't want to get too comfortable in either. As soon as Cynda was well enough and not in so much pain, he intended to move back into his bedroom, or better yet, *their* bedroom.

He wasn't in his office an hour when Cynda called out to him. She needed his help getting out of bed so she could relieve herself. He then put her back in bed, warmed up her soup, and fed it to her.

She took the pills Keith offered and then asked, "Where are the pills the doctor prescribed for me?"

"A person coming off drugs shouldn't have such a high dosage of pain medication."

Smirking, she asked, "Oh, so when did they put M.D. behind your last name?"

"I'll be in my office if you need me." He turned and walked out of the room.

"I need my pain medication," she screamed. "Don't get it twisted. I'll never need you."

Later that evening Keith gave Cynda a sponge bath. Her face tightened with every touch. She winced, and then jumped when he tried to apply soap to her rib area.

"Sorry," he told her then quickly finished up.

"You're not sorry. If you cared at all, you would give me my real pain medication. Can't you tell how much I'm hurting?"

He let her air dry while he dumped the water out of the hospital pan he'd used to sponge-bathe her. As he walked back into the room he said, "I'm just trying to keep you from having to withdraw from pain medication along with all the other stuff you are going to be having withdrawal symptoms from."

She picked up the dinner tray off her nightstand and hurled it at Keith's head. "You're a fool," she screamed. "You think it's better that I be in agonizing pain and have withdrawal symptoms?"

Picking up the tray he told her, "I'm just trying to help."

She tried to lift her bruised body off the bed. "Give me my clothes. I'm getting out of here."

"You are on house arrest, Cynda."

"I don't care. If the police pick me up, at least I'll get some real pain medication from the prison nurse. They won't just let me suffer."

He eased her back down on the bed and pulled the covers over her naked body. "Calm down, Cynda." He opened the bottom drawer next to his bed and pulled out the addicting doses of pain medication and handed the bottle to Cynda. What else could he do? She was right. If the police took her back to the hospital, they would give her this stuff. He handed her a glass of water and then asked, "Do you want me to put a gown on you?"

"Naw, I sleep like this all the time. You do remember what my profession is, right?"

"I'll have to put something on you in the morning, but hopefully, you won't be so raw by then."

"Thanks for the bath, daddy. I'm not up for sex this week. But at least you were able to feel me up."

The comment gut-punched him. Sent him to his throne room, crying out to God.

"Lord, I really need Your help. I did what You asked, but now I need something from You." Falling on his knees, tears stinging his eyes, he pleaded, "I can't be in a loveless marriage. Teach me how to love this woman, and teach her how to love me back."

He leaned his back against the wall as he sat on the floor and moaned. Tears creased the corners of his eyes as he realized that he had let Cynda down by giving in and handing her those pain pills, just as he had let his mother down when he was nineteen.

"I can't take this any more, Mama. You have got to get off drugs," Keith told his mother.

Dorthea Williams was stretched out on her dirty couch. It had once been orange, but now it was brown with tints of orange. She was leaning over, vomiting on the carpeted floor. Between vomit and wipes of the mouth, she told Keith. "I-I'm gon' give this stuff up, son. You believe me, don't you?" She heaved, turned back to the floor, spilled out the rest of her guts, then told him, "This stuff don't mean me no good."

Keith stood at the door, his hand on the doorknob. He wanted to go to her, put her in the shower, and clean up that mess, but he was tired of being her fix-it man.

"You're not getting another dime from me. Do you understand what I'm saying, Mama?"

She didn't respond.

"And I won't keep my stuff here any more. You've stolen your last crack high from me."

Dorthea pulled herself into a sitting position and wiped her mouth again. "Boy, why are you being so high and mighty? You're the dope man, remember? If you and your friends didn't supply the stuff, I couldn't use."

His face was set. "And you won't blame me for your addictions ever again. At least, not to my face. I'm not coming back here again. I refuse to see you until you get clean." He opened the door and walked out of his mother's life. He didn't realize that he'd just given her a death sentence. That the next time he saw her, she would be in a body bag.

* * *

Cynda wanted to die. She wanted the sharp pains that were ripping through her body to just take her out. Life had already had a joke at her expense. Didn't she turn out just like the kids said she would? Her mother's pain had been extinguished at twenty-seven. Why was she still here? Couldn't God be merciful enough to just allow someone to put a bullet in her head?

Spoony had almost done the job, but Cynda distinctly remembered a glowing form over her body, blowing life back into her and begging her to live and not die. Who would do that for her? Certainly not Linda. She hated Cynda's guts. And Spoony the devil was dead, so he didn't do it. Maybe Iona tried to resuscitate her, but where did she learn such a thing?

She wanted her Grammy to make it all better. Or better yet, maybe her Grammy could take her to the place where there was no more crying and no more dying. The place she'd gone off to. But to get there, Cynda would probably have to make amends with God. She'd rather stay alive, or go to the Devil, thank you very much.

No matter which way you looked at it, God was just cruel. She could be dead, all her troubles over, but instead she was on house arrest and married to Keith the do-gooder.

She didn't ask him to marry her. Hadn't asked for anything from him. So what right did he have to look so sad when she screamed at him? If he didn't like what she said, why didn't he do something about it?

When he'd brought dinner to her last night and she threw it on the floor, he'd said, "I know I'm not the best cook in the world, but my food isn't that bad."

"I don't want anything from you!" she screamed.

"I'm just trying to help."

"No, you're not. You want something. All of you want something. Everybody has a motive."

As he bent down to pick the food off the floor, she saw his lips move.

"And stop praying for me. I don't want anything from your God either, do you hear me?"

He walked out of her room without saying a word, but she knew he was in that office of his, praying. Like she wanted anything from a God cruel enough to allow her to be born to a whore like Flora Stephens.

She rolled over in bed and whispered, "At least I protected my child, Mama. Why couldn't you do the same for me?"

A single angry tear rolled down Cynda's face as she lay in bed, too weak to lash out. Too weak to get high and relieve some tension. Too weak to do anything but hate. She hated life for the pain it brought her, and Keith for the way he took everything in stride. Her taunting didn't cause him to yell or hit. He just backed up and prayed, so she decided to ignore him. Once she was able to move around again, she'd show him that he had no restraint. Not with her.

12

By the time Isaac and his children woke up, Nina was on an airplane, halfway to Atlanta. She'd packed her clothes and wrote Donavan a note right after she slammed her bedroom door in Isaac's face. She didn't want her son to think she'd abandoned him, so she told him that the only reason she wasn't taking him with her was because he had school that Friday morning. She assured him that she would be back home soon. She just needed to see Elizabeth.

Nina was sure that her best friend would be able to lift her out of this cloud of darkness she'd fallen into. Elizabeth had been there, had weathered her own storms. Nina needed her faith strengthened, needed to know that God was still on her side.

As the plane descended, Nina started crying again. How many tears could one woman have? She thought she'd cried up a storm the night before and couldn't imagine that she had more to shed. Just like that old Natalie Cole song, "Good Morning, Heartache." She bundled up her wet tissues and put them in the trash as the stewardess stopped next to her seat.

"Are you all right?" an elderly woman seated next to her asked.

No, I'm in early menopause, and my husband had a child by another woman. "I'll be okay," Nina told her. She dabbed at her eyes with another tissue.

Nina took a cab from the airport to Elizabeth's house. When the cab pulled in the driveway, she got out and knocked on her friend's door. As she heard someone running down the spiral stairs toward the door Nina wished she had called first, but she knew that Elizabeth wouldn't be starting her promotional tour for her new CD for another next month.

The door swung open, and Elizabeth grabbed Nina's arm, pulling her inside. "Girl, get in here. Isaac called. He told me that you left a note for Donavan stating that you were on your way here, but when I didn't hear from you, I got worried."

Nina allowed herself to be pulled into Elizabeth's mammoth foyer. Every time Nina visited her friend, all she could think was, *Go on, girl. Do your thang.* There was no jealousy between these two friends. Both knew they had chosen their God-given path in life and were satisfied with the fruits of their labor.

Elizabeth was a dark-skinned beauty with long, shoulder-length hair, while Nina was several shades lighter with short-layered hair. The contrast between the two best friends, the introvert and the extrovert, didn't end there. Elizabeth was always more flamboyant, more of a risk-taker than Nina. When shopping, Elizabeth always picked bold, colorful outfits, while Nina preferred the serenity of earth tones. As one of today's premier gospel singers, Elizabeth was constantly on tour and in the public eye, while Nina preferred to sit behind her computer, writing best-selling Christian fiction.

"Why don't you have your cell phone turned on?" Elizabeth asked Nina. "I've been trying to call you."

Tears welled in Nina eyes once more. "I didn't want to talk to Isaac, so I turned it off."

"Ah, hon, stop crying." Elizabeth hugged Nina. "Isaac has called here about ten times already. He was sure you were on your way here."

"Did he tell you what he did?"

Nodding, Elizabeth suggested that they sit in the living room.

Nina followed her friend into the living room and sunk into the soft cushions of the orange and beige sofa and cried some more.

Elizabeth rubbed Nina's back and waited for her tears to subside. As she began to quiet down, Elizabeth wiped away tears from her own eyes. "I have to call Isaac and let him know that you made it here safely."

Nina grabbed Elizabeth's arm. "No! If you call him, he'll come down here, and I don't want to see him right now."

"Nina, do you know the man you're married to?" Elizabeth laughed. "If I call him, he might come, but if I don't call, he'll be on the next plane out of Dayton. Let me check in with him so we can work this out on your terms."

Nina let Elizabeth's arm go. "Okay, call him." As her friend walked out of the room, Nina added, "But tell him I don't want to see him right now. Tell him that I need a few days for myself."

Elizabeth came back into the living room. "Okay, I told him, but I can't guarantee how long he will stay away."

"I don't want to look at him right now."

Elizabeth plopped back on the couch and put Nina's hand in hers. "It was ten years ago, hon. Are you really going to hold this against him?"

A lone tear slid down Nina's face, and she wiped it away. "I thought I was pregnant."

"You didn't tell me that. When? I mean, how far along?"

Nina lifted her hand to silence Elizabeth's questions. "I wasn't. My doctor said I'm in early menopause."

Elizabeth shook her head, lifted her eyes to God, and then turned back to Nina. "I refuse to believe that. I won't believe it."

Nina hugged her friend. "Thank you for saying that. But right now you have more faith than I do. I'm having a hard time getting back up from this blow from my doctor. And then that man of mine brings home a child he had with some other woman."

Sighing deeply, Elizabeth squeezed Nina's hand again. "I'm sorry that your doctor said that to you, but I know you didn't let a mere man destroy your faith. You've been telling me for a year now that no doctor could dictate whether or not you can have another child. Remember that, Nina? You told me that your fate was in God's hands."

Elbows on her knees, hands under her chin, shoulders slumped, Nina said, "I really believed that, Elizabeth. But it's one thing for a doctor to say I might not be able to have any more kids because of a gunshot wound."

It still terrified Nina when she thought of just how close she came to losing her son that night crazy Mickey Jones hunted her son down and shot both her and Donavan. But God had His angels looking out for them that night.

"But when a doctor tells you that you've entered menopause, that's kind of it. A dead situation, you know what I mean?"

Elizabeth smirked. "Yeah, I know all about dead situations. Don't forget that my husband was in the World Trade Center when it collapsed, and everybody, including yours truly, thought he was dead. But God didn't see it that way. So, if I don't know anything else, I know that you've got to hold on to your faith. Don't turn your back on God like I did, Nina."

The thought of Elizabeth trying to commit suicide all

those years ago when she thought her husband was dead sent chills down Nina's spine. That was a time she didn't want to go back to. Looking around the expansive room, Nina asked, "Where is Kenneth?"

"Girl, you know that man is off on another crusade." Elizabeth laughed. "But I'm not mad at him. If nothing else, this family is going to get into Heaven because we fed, clothed, and visited everybody that ever needed anything."

Nina laughed with her. "Don't I know it? I've got the same crusader in my house. He's even worse than me with it."

Elizabeth softly rubbed Nina's shoulder. "You've got a good man, Nina."

"I need to lay down and rest for a bit."

Elizabeth took Nina upstairs to the guestroom and told her to come down when she was ready to eat. But once Elizabeth closed the bedroom door behind her, Nina lay on the firm mattress and didn't want to get up again. She slept all day, only waking when Erin, Elizabeth's oldest daughter, knocked on the door.

"Telephone, Auntie Nina," Erin said from the other side of the door.

"Tell Isaac that I'll talk to him later," Nina yelled.

"It's Donavan. He wants to talk to you."

Nina pulled herself out of bed and opened the door. "Thanks, hon," she said to Erin as she took the phone from her. "Hey, Donavan. How was school?"

"It was fine. Ma, why'd you go to Atlanta? Is Aunt Elizabeth sick again?"

"No, baby, nothing like that. I just needed to get away for a little while, that's all."

"When are you coming back home?"

She felt the tears getting ready to spring forth again. *Good afternoon, heartache.* "Soon, honey. I'll be home soon."

"Okay. Daddy wants to talk to you."

"Wait, Donavan, I've got to go. Just tell your dad—"

Isaac's strong voice came across the line. "You tell me, Nina."

When she didn't respond to him, Isaac trotted on, "Look, baby, I know I was wrong, but this happened a long time ago. You can't hold this against me now. Besides, I didn't even know anything about Iona all this time."

"Don't tell me what I can't do, Isaac. I'm sick and tired of dealing with your mess."

"You just left, baby. How could you leave me like that?"

Nina ran her hands through her hair. "Maybe we never should have been. Maybe we made a mistake by getting married."

"Don't say that, baby. I messed up. You can blame this all on me. But that doesn't change the fact that I need you." He sighed. "Baby, if there was no us, I'd probably be dead right now."

The tears filling Nina's eyes dropped onto her cheeks. How could one man have so much power over her heart? She was tired of giving him this much power. "I've got to go, Isaac. I'll come home when I'm ready." She hung up and then curled up on the bed again. Isaac didn't need her. He had gotten himself another child without her help, so why couldn't he just get along with the rest of his life without her?

On Sunday morning as Elizabeth, Erin, and Danae, Elizabeth's younger daughter, started getting ready for church, Nina decided to do something she hadn't done in over a decade—Skip church, and sleep in.

Elizabeth knocked on the guest bedroom door. "Hey, sleepyhead. The pancakes are done. We're leaving in fifteen minutes, so hustle."

Nina couldn't turn down her favorite breakfast food. She got out of bed, put on her baby blue silk robe, and descended the stairs. She was at the kitchen table squeezing syrup on her pancakes when Elizabeth walked into the kitchen.

Elizabeth glanced at her watch. "Where's your clothes?"

"Is Kenneth still out of town?"

"Yeah, he won't be back until later tonight. Where's your clothes?"

"I'm not going to church today. You tired me out with all that shopping yesterday." Nina stuffed some of the yummy pancakes into her mouth.

Elizabeth looked worried. "Are you sure about this, Nina?"

Nina put her fork down and gave Elizabeth a solemn look. "I'm sure, hon. I just need a day off, okay?"

Elizabeth put her hand on Nina's shoulder and squeezed. "I'll see you when we get back home."

Nina ate three fluffy pancakes before Elizabeth and her children headed out for church. When she was sated, she put her plate in the sink and climbed the stairs, heading back to her room. But her full stomach did nothing for the emptiness of her soul. She had trusted God, and He had let her down. How was she supposed to bounce back from that?

Feeling restless in her room, Nina put on her tan-and-white sweat suit and went for a walk. There was no breeze in Atlanta today, only hot, humid air. Coming from Ohio, where the sun definitely didn't shine all year round, Nina wondered how anyone could put up with the constant assault of heat and humidity. But then she thought about it. Hadn't she been putting up with a constant assault of her own? First, a maniac shot her and Donavan. Then when she woke up in the hospital she was told that where the bullet was lodged made it near impossible for her to ever conceive again. But her pain wasn't over. She was forced to watch her only child fight for his life.

Not only did she have to face the fact that she would probably not be able to provide her husband with another child, but now her doctor informed her that she might be in the early stages of menopause. Now her husband had the audacity to bring home a child he'd had with another woman.

Sweat dripped from Nina's forehead as anger caused her to pick up the pace. Her arms swung back and forth in rhythm with her short legs. She looked to Heaven, wanting desperately to tell God how she was feeling, but she was just too angry. No, talking wasn't what she wanted. Her fist balled as she marched. She wanted to fight. Satan didn't want to mess with her today. She would take care of God's light work, freeing up some of His time so He could solve some of her problems.

Her clothes were sticking to her by the time she returned to Elizabeth's house. She jumped in the shower, changed her clothes, flopped on her bed, and tried to channel surf, but her eyes kept turning toward the Bible on her nightstand. She could almost hear the Lord saying, *I missed you today*.

Her eyes misted over. She got out of her bed and fell on her knees. She had been angry with God and had hoped that missing church would remove all thoughts of God from her mind. But she couldn't get away from her life-giver. Couldn't turn her back on all she knew to be true.

"I missed You too, Father. I've had an awful morning," she bellowed through the current of her tears. "But I don't know where to go from here. I'm hurt, Lord, can't You understand that?"

The tears were flowing down her cheeks as she continued to pour out her sorrow. Her Heavenly Father understood her better than anyone, so while pancakes, walks, and channel surfing couldn't soothe the trouble in her soul, this talk with God was making her want to believe again.

Wiping away the tears that cascaded down her face, Nina prayed, "But how can You turn my situation around?"

God's answer came in a gentle whisper. *Beloved, where is your faith?*

Head bent low, Nina admitted that her faith had weakened as she waited for God to turn her situation around. But didn't Sarah, Abraham's wife, wait on God for decades? So who was she to give up after only one year?

Someone was leaning on Elizabeth's doorbell. Nina had a pretty good idea who it was.

She got off her knees vowing to trust God. Downstairs, she opened the front door.

Isaac was leaning against the door jam, that deep chocolate skin and those drive-me-wild dimples were beckoning her. "Time's up," he said.

13

Keith wondered if Cynda had taken too much pain medication. She'd become silent and withdrawn. Hadn't opened her mouth to curse him in three days. Was she delirious? The swelling was going down, her lip was no longer fat, so he knew it didn't cause her pain to talk. Maybe she was just tired of being ornery.

Keith put a bowl of ham and bean soup on the table next to her bed. "Are you hungry?"

She scooted up in bed. "Yeah, I could eat something," she moaned.

He sat a couple of novels on the table next to her soup.

She picked them up. " 'Sunday Brunch,' 'More Than Grace,' 'Divas of Damascus.' What's this?"

"Just some novels I thought you might enjoy while recuperating. I figured that since the sling was off your arm now, you'd want something to do." He then replaced her high dosage pain medication with the store-bought bottle he'd given her the first day he brought her home. "You won't need this high dosage any more since your pain isn't as severe."

Cynda lifted her leg. "I need this thing off." She shook the detection device around her ankle. "Then I can get out of here and get back to my life."

"You need to eat."

She grabbed the bowl and ate some of the soup. Then she asked Keith, "Can you call Isaac's house? I need to ask Iona something."

Keith smiled. "This is the first time you've asked to speak to Iona since you've been here. She'll be happy to talk to you."

"Are you criticizing me about how much I talk to my daughter?"

Keith held up a hand. "Look, I'm not trying to start an argument with you. I just think Iona will be happy to talk to you."

"Well, she could have talked to me every day if that judge didn't give my child to that man."

Keith left the room to get the telephone. He walked back into the room and handed Cynda the telephone and told her that Iona was on the line.

She took the phone and stared at Keith. "Can I have some privacy?"

Keith went to his office to check his e-mails and return about fifteen calls. Of course, he would have to use his cell phone, since Cynda was on the house phone.

On Friday, Cynda's attorney stopped by. She was feeling good enough to sit in the living room with Jim and Keith. "So what's up, man?" she asked. "How are you going to get me out of this?"

Jim took a pen and pad out of his briefcase, and then sat down across from Cynda. "That's up to you. What can you tell me to get you out of this?"

"I don't know, man. You're the one with the law degree. Shouldn't you already have an angle worked out on this case?" She turned to Keith. "How much you payin' this slacker?"

Jim cleared his throat. "Mrs. Williams, I'm here to help you. But I wasn't a fly on the wall when Mr. Richard Davidson was murdered. You need to fill me in. That's the only way I'll be able to help you."

With a puzzled look on her face, Cynda asked, "Whose Richard Davidson?"

Jim looked up from his pad. "The deceased. The man you lived with for several years."

Cynda sat back in her seat and shrugged. "Oh, just call him Spoony."

"Okay. So far we know that you lived with a man whose first name you didn't know. Did you ever meet his parents?"

She smirked. "I didn't even know Spoony had parents. They sure didn't call him." She rolled her eyes. "Why are you asking me all these irrelevant questions?" Cynda glanced at Keith again and raised an eyebrow.

Tapping his pen to his pad, Jim began, "Well, Mrs. Williams—"

"Stop calling me that. My name is Cynda. Cynda Stephens."

Jim pointed his pen in the direction of Keith. "You did marry Mr. Williams, did you not?"

Cynda bent over and touched the home detection device around her ankle. "I had to get out of jail, didn't I?"

It was Jim's turn to steal a raised eyebrow glance at Keith. "Well then, Mrs. Williams, the reason I asked you about your relationship with the deceased is so we can prove to the court that you had a long-term committed relationship that turned violent."

She sat up and leaned over so that she was almost nose-to-nose with her attorney. "The last six, seven years I've been hooking for him. Is that long-term committed enough for you?"

Jim slammed his pen and paper on the table and stood. "Look, Keith, I don't understand why you want to help this woman when she has no respect for you or herself. I can't waste any more of my time on this case."

"What's up his butt?" Cynda rolled her eyes. "I'm the one facing life in prison."

Keith looked at his friend. "She's my wife, Jim. Wouldn't you do everything you could to help Marline?"

Jim shook his balding head then sat back down. He turned to Cynda. "Can you please tell me what happened the day Mr. Davidson died?"

"He was trying to kill me. I just happened to get the job done on him first."

Jim was writing in his pad. "Did Mr. Davidson have a history of hitting on you?"

"He was mean. He loved beating on me. And I would just sit there and take it."

"Why didn't you just take it that time?"

"The fight wasn't about me this time. He wanted my daughter."

Jim looked up from his notepad. "What do you mean when you say he wanted your daughter?"

She twisted her lip and ran her hands through her long, black hair. "I mean he wanted to put my baby on the street." She lowered her head and averted her eyes. "Look, I know I'll probably never win any mother-of-the-year awards, but I'm not a monster, and I couldn't let him have my baby." She scooted back in her seat, brought her knees up to her chest, and rocked back and forth. "Not like my mama let them take me."

Keith and Jim exchanged glances.

"He told my daughter that I wasn't bringing in enough money and that she would have to take up my slack." Her lip curled as she whispered, "Never."

Keith watched his wife struggle with demons from her

past. *Help me to love her pain away, Lord.* He stood. "I think that's enough for today, Jim."

Jim turned away from Cynda, shook himself, and then stood. "Yes, I think we can dig a bit deeper next week. The preliminary will be next month. We'll need to talk to the little girl."

"No!"

"Your daughter has a lot to do with this case."

"I've done enough to Iona. Just leave her alone."

"Do you think that's necessary, Jim? I have to agree with Cynda. Iona has been through a great deal already."

Jim picked up his briefcase and headed toward the door, and Keith followed him. He whispered to Keith, "If what she says is true, I probably would have killed that lowlife myself. We'll need that little girl's testimony. She's her best hope."

"I'll see what I can do."

Cynda was still on the couch rocking when Keith walked back into the living room. He stood behind her and touched her shoulder. "You ready for bed?" he asked.

She stood without answering and walked toward their bedroom.

Keith followed her and went into the adjoining bath. Cynda's story had made him feel dirty, and although he knew that kind of dirt didn't come off with mere soap and water, he stripped and jumped in the shower anyway.

The hot water assaulted his body as he stood under the jutting stream, praying for his wife. He wanted God to do something special for her, to make her clean.

When he'd finished praying and was soaping up, Cynda opened the shower curtain and stood in front of him. The heat that boiled in Keith right now had nothing to do with the temperature of the water. His wife stood before him naked. Her body was still slightly bruised, but she was toned, kind of athletically built. How she had time to exercise to get such a lovely figure, God only knew. Maybe, it was from dodging blows.

Her gaze scanned his body. "You want some company?" She ran her hands through the hairs on his chest. "I'm not in pain any more. We can make it happen tonight."

He moved her hand. "No, Cynda."

She stepped into the shower to confront him. "What's your problem? Are we married or not?"

He stepped back. She was too close. "It doesn't mean anything to you. It's just your profession, remember?"

Advancing on him, she played with the hair on his chest again. "Look, man, I'm offering you some free sex. What more do you want?"

Moving her hand away from his chest, he said, "Please get out of this tub so I can finish showering."

She looked down at him then triumphantly back into his face. "You want me. So what's the problem?"

"You're right, Cynda. I want you, and we will be together like that one day. But when you join with me, it's going to be more than just a job."

She rolled her eyes and stepped out of the tub. "It's just sex, Keith. You don't need to make more out of it than it is." She closed the shower curtain, leaving Keith alone.

When his tormentor was gone, Keith turned the water to cold and lingered until he could walk into his bedroom without wanting plain and simple sex. Cynda had taken his towel, so he walked into the bedroom in his birthday suit. She'd seen all of him and a whole lot of other men anyway. He was quite sure his body wouldn't make her blush.

She sat up in bed as Keith entered the room. She opened her mouth, as if in shock. "Husband, do you think you should walk around your wife like that? I might assume you want to sleep with me."

He grabbed the towel off the end of the bed. "I do intend to sleep with my wife." He pulled a pair of navy blue cotton pajamas out of the drawer and put them on. Pulling up the cover and getting in bed with her, Keith said, "And that's all I intend to do—*sleep*."

Cynda turned on him. "You don't normally sleep in here." She pointed toward the door. "Go back to your office and sleep."

"This is our bedroom, Cynda, and I'm sleeping in here with you from now on. The only reason I haven't been sleeping in here was because you were in pain and I didn't want to bump you during the night and cause you more pain."

"Well, I still might be in pain, so get out of here."

"That's not what you told me in the bathroom."

She rolled her eyes.

"You know, you roll those eyes an awful lot."

"That's because you irritate me an awful lot."

Keith got out of bed, pulled out a flannel nightgown from the dresser, and brought it back to Cynda. "Here, I picked this up for you yesterday."

She again rolled her eyes. "Is this a joke?"

"No joke. I need you to wear a nightgown, so I can get to sleep without thinking about jumping your bones."

"If you don't want to have sex with me, why do you want to sleep with me? Aren't you afraid that I will contaminate you and cause all your good choirboy tendencies to fade away?"

He held up the gown. "Can you please do this for me?"

She got out the bed, snatched the gown from him, and wiggled her hourglass form into it. Before jumping back into bed, she posed. "Happy now?"

Actually, he wasn't happy. She looked just as good in that gown as she did nude. And it had been a long time since he'd been with a woman.

Sliding in next to her, he grabbed his Bible off the night-stand. He prayed, while Cynda tossed and turned. He read from his Bible until his eyes drooped.

Pulling the covers over his body, he pulled his wife close to him, and she scooted to the edge of the bed.

14

Nina was back home, but in three days, nothing was resolved. She was laying in her king-size, dark cherry oak bed, facing the wall, tears streaming down her face.

Isaac pulled her close to him, feeling the warmth of her back as she rested against his chest. He couldn't stand the thought of living without her. He'd spent too many years without her already. "We'll get through this, baby. Don't give up on me."

"That child hates me," she said sniffing. "No matter what I do, she won't even talk to me."

The child's name was *Iona*. Nina hadn't once used it since Isaac had brought her home. How was Iona supposed to show affection to Nina, when she was treating her like an inconvenience? Isaac knew Nina didn't mean to do it. His wife didn't have a mean-spirited bone in her body. But the truth of the matter was, he saw what she was doing, and Iona saw it also.

"Maybe if you spent some time with her, the two of you would learn how to communicate with one another."

Nina turned to face him. "I can't spend time with someone who hates me. Your daughter doesn't want to be bothered with me." Wiping the tears from her cheeks, she said, "But you think I should suck up to her, don't you? You think I should try to make her like me."

Isaac kept his voice level. He didn't want to get upset and go off, but they'd been having the same conversation for the past three nights with nothing being resolved.

"Nina, Iona is ten. You are the adult." He wanted to add that she was also a Christian, but he left that out and hoped that God would convict her Himself. He continued, "So quite naturally I would expect that you would make more concessions than Iona."

She said nothing.

"Nina, I need your help. The night before I brought Iona home I had one of those nightmares, you know, the one where I'm in Hell." His voice trembled. "But this time Iona was in Hell too. Those demons told me that if I didn't want her, they did." He rubbed her shoulder. "Honey, don't you see what this means. If we don't love and care for Iona, she could end up in a place we don't want her to go."

Nina flipped back the covers and got out of bed.

Isaac sat up. "Where are you going?"

She opened their bedroom door. "I need to be alone," she said without looking back. "I just need to pray right now."

Even with prayer, Nina couldn't get her heart to change.

The next morning, Donavan and Iona were sitting at the table playing a game of hangman while she fixed bacon and eggs. The two of them were getting along so well, Nina wanted to lean over the table and shout into her son's face, "Traitor." Couldn't he see that this was tearing her apart? Where was his loyalty? But then she also asked herself, "Where is all this Christian love I'm supposed to have?"

She didn't even say good morning to Iona, covering it in a roundabout way by saying a generic good morning to all. She'd even heard the Lord gently saying to her, *If you don't*

*forgive others their trespasses against you, how can I forgive the
things you've done?*

There was a time when that gentle rebuke from the Lord
would've changed her heart and mind. She always felt that
God had gifted her with a forgiving heart, which made her
feel special. She just didn't know that something could hurt
so bad that she wouldn't want to forgive.

The telephone rang, and Nina turned off the stove and
picked up the wall phone. "Hello," she said.

"Where's my daughter?" Cynda asked angrily, as if Nina
had done something to her, other than feed, clothe, and
house her child.

Nina took a deep breath. "She's right here getting ready
to eat breakfast."

"Well, why am I still listening to you talk? Put *my* daughter on the phone right now."

Tears seeped through as Nina tightly closed her eyes. She
wanted to tell this woman off so bad, but she refused to act
the fool in front of her son. She handed the phone to Iona
and then told Donavan, "Breakfast is on the stove. Go ahead
and make your own plates."

She went into her office, closed the door, took a few deep
breaths, and waited for Iona to hang up with her wonderful
mother.

Nina then called her best friend Elizabeth, who she'd been
on the phone with every day since she came back home. "I
can't take this. I really can't," Nina told her through sobs.

"Stop crying, hon. You know I cry whenever you do, and
I'm tired of crying."

"I can't help it. Every time I look at that child I remember how her mother used to taunt me. I hear her telling me
that she and Isaac are going to Chicago for the weekend.
And I just keep thinking that she probably got pregnant that
weekend."

"I remember you telling me about that. Girl, you should

have tripped her and let her fall headfirst into one of them big dryers you had at that Laundromat you used to work in."

Nina laughed through her tears. "Do you think I'm an awful person because of the way I feel about this child?"

"Now you know I don't have no stones to throw at you. If Kenneth had brought some long-lost child in here from one of his previous indiscretions, I don't know which side of crazy I would have gone to first. And Isaac is over there wanting you to get over it and feed his flock. The only thing I don't understand is why the police haven't been called over there yet. Girl, you are better than me."

"Stop making me laugh. I want to have a pity party."

"Then come on back to Atlanta, and I'll treat you to the pitifulest time of your life."

Nina smiled at the thought. "That sounds good."

"Nina, can I ask you something?" Elizabeth asked in a more serious tone.

"What?"

"Have you told Isaac about your doctor visit yet?"

"I haven't had time to tell him yet."

"Maybe you should make time, huh, hon? That way he can help you pray about this thing."

"I think I'd rather come back to your house."

"Well, come on. But make sure you tell him where you're going before you leave. That man was absolutely frantic the last time."

Nina frowned. "I probably can't come right now anyway. Isaac is planning a tent revival, and I can't leave the kids on him while he's working on that."

"Like I said, you're better than me, because I would have left everything and let his congregation see him pulling his wavy hair out."

"He hasn't been too bad. He's taken the kids with him a couple times this week. That way I was able to work on my book and not be distracted by them. He even made dinner last night."

Elizabeth sighed. "Well then, Nina, if he's not so bad, why don't you give him a chance? I know you can get through this if you try."

"Oh, so this was your little reverse psychology, huh? You figured if you talked about my husband I would come to his defense, is that it?"

"Now, calm down, Nina. I'm only trying to help."

"Well, from now on, Ms. Elizabeth Underwood, just be a friend and listen, okay?"

She hung up and put her head in her hands. She knew exactly what was wrong with her but didn't want to admit it. Iona reminded her of the little girl she desperately wanted to have. The little girl she would never have.

The phone rang, and Nina snatched it up, prepared to let Elizabeth have it again.

"Nina, it's me, Ebony."

Nina smiled. "Hey, honey. How's everything going?"

"Fine. I know you're usually writing during this time of day, but I had to call and share my good news."

Nina had heard from Ebony a couple times since she'd left with her mom. Thank God she was able to communicate with her. "Don't keep me in suspense. Spill it."

"I got an A on my math test, you know, the one I didn't think I was smart enough to pass."

"See . . . I knew you could do it. You just keep studying, girl. The sky is the limit for you."

"Okay, well, I've got to let you go. I'm going to the movies this afternoon with my mom."

How Nina wished that she was Ebony's mom and that she was spending girl time with her. "All right. Call me soon, okay?"

After that conversation, Nina locked herself in her office for the rest of the day under the guise of working on her book. In reality, she hadn't typed a single sentence. She was playing solitaire, wishing she was alone on a deserted island. Then, nobody would have unrealistic expectations of her. She would get along nicely with the swaying trees and God's cool breeze.

Isaac knocked on her office door, dashing all her palm-tree dreams.

She opened the door and let him in. "What's up?" she asked, as if he needed a reason to enter her domain.

He sat in the chair in front of her desk. "The kids said they haven't seen you since breakfast."

She pointed at her computer. "I've got to get this story finished. My editor has been hounding me for it."

He looked at his watch. "Are you planning to fix dinner?"

"I really don't feel up to it tonight. Can you just order a pizza or something? Maybe you could take the kids out for pizza. I bet they'd like that." *Just go. Take them on a month-long trip around the world. Have fun with your children.*

Isaac pulled himself out of the chair and walked around the desk to face her. "Nina, Iona said that she screamed for you earlier when Donavan punched her in the arm. Why didn't you go help her?"

Yeah, Nina did hear her screaming, but it was the first time Iona had bothered to say her name all week. And, anyway, Donavan wasn't going to hurt her. *The little snitch.* "So we have an informant in the house now? Do I have to watch everything I do and say around here?"

"Nina, I don't know what's happened to you, but you're not acting like the same woman I married."

She stood up. "*You* happened to me, Isaac Walker."

Isaac looked at the door. "Lower your voice."

"Oh, do you think they don't know that I've been disgraced and wronged by you yet again?" She moved to the window, putting distance between them. "Just when I thought you'd changed, that I actually mattered to you, you go and bring some other woman's child in here and expect me to raise her?" She laughed, but the sound was bitter.

"What do you want me to do, Nina? She's my child. I couldn't just leave her to Children Services."

"But she's not *my* child, Isaac. Do you know how much that hurts? Do you even care?"

He reached his arms out to comfort her, but she stopped him, raising her hands. "Don't. Don't try to make it better."

"Tell me what to do."

She turned her back on him. She was getting good at turning away from him. "I don't know if I can raise that woman's child."

"She can become just as much your child as she is Cynda's, if you give her a chance."

Nina opened her office door and went into her bedroom, locking the door behind her before Isaac could even turn the knob.

On Monday, Isaac received a call from Iona's school. She was being suspended for two days. A teacher had tried to instruct her on how children should respect adults and not roll their eyes or flip them off when they didn't agree with something said and Iona spat in her face. Like mother like daughter.

Although Isaac had stopped dealing with Cynda ten years ago, he'd seen her twice since. A year ago at his wedding, and a year before that when he'd spotted her in an alley trying to get some crack. He'd tried to help her then, offering to get her some help for her drug problem, and she spat in his face.

Mondays were his day off, so he was in a brown and tan Nike jogging suit and his size twelve Jordan's. Comfortable clothes, beat-down clothes.

Mrs. Walsh, the school secretary, was rubbing her temples when Isaac walked in. She sighed. "Mr. Walker, thank God you could come so quickly."

Iona was sitting in the chair in the corner, elbow on her leg, hand in a fist under her chin.

"Where's her teacher? I'd like for Iona to apologize to her," Isaac said to Mrs. Walsh.

"Ms. Days went home. This incident really shook her up."

Isaac turned to Iona. "Well, young lady, what do you have to say for yourself?"

"Like you care."

In a rage, Isaac stepped to his daughter. "What did you say to me?"

"She's been like that all morning, Mr. Walker. You can't talk to her."

Iona glared at Mrs. Walsh. "Didn't nobody ask you nothing."

Isaac yanked Iona out of the seat. His gaze bore into her as he leaned close to her ear. "If you open your mouth again, this woman is going to call Children Services on me . . . 'cause I'm going to beat you half to death right here in this office."

Iona swallowed hard. Eyes bulging, she said, "But they'll take you to jail if you hit me."

"I've been to jail. And before I let a child disrespect me, I'd rather catch another case." He tightened his grip on her arm. "Do you understand me, Iona?"

"Yes, sir," she stuttered.

He turned her toward Mrs. Walsh and released her arm. "Apologize."

Iona turned back to him. "But—"

He gave her the look, the one that said, "Don't mess with me."

Iona turned back around. "Sorry for what I said, Mrs. Walsh."

They walked out of the office in silence.

It was raining when they opened the school door, so they ran to the car. Once inside, Isaac looked at his daughter and shook his head. "What am I going to do with you, Iona?"

"Just throw me away. My mom has thrown me away, so why don't you go ahead and do the same?"

"Your mother didn't throw you away." He really hated taking up for Cynda. "The courts took you away from her."

"She was glad. She hates me."

"Nobody hates you, Iona."

Tears were in her eyes as she screamed, "Everybody hates me! You hate me because you think I'm ruining your happy little home. And my mom hates me because she thinks I kept her alive or something."

His eyebrows furrowed in confusion. "What are you talking about?"

"Mom thinks I somehow breathed life back into her while she was unconscious on Spoony's floor."

"What would be the problem with that?"

The tears flowed down her face as she said, "She said she would have rather died." She wiped at the tears, but they kept coming. "You don't want me, and she doesn't want me. Maybe I should just die."

Isaac pulled his daughter into his arms. True, life wasn't kind to her, but it didn't exactly tiptoe around him either. He would just keep praying for God to take away her pain.

"I don't want you to think that I don't want you. You're my flesh and blood, and I love you."

She lifted her head, eyes wide open, and a little smile etched on her face. "You love me? For real?"

Isaac wiped the tears from her face. "Yes, I really do." Then he added, "But you're still getting punished." He started the car, and they headed for home.

15

Keith and his crew were on a job site on the north end of town. Pete, Chris, and Sam were using the jackhammer to knock down the concrete wall, while Keith searched through his truck for the blueprints and work order. He finally gave up and called Janet.

"What's up?" Janet asked.

"Did I leave the work order in the office?"

"Hold on, let me check."

When she came back, she told him, "It's not here. I thought you took them home last night?"

He snapped his finger. "You're right. Now we're going to get further behind. I can't believe I left those plans at home."

"Why don't I drop by your house and pick it up? I can swing by the job site, and you won't have to fall behind."

"Thanks, Janet. I really appreciate it. I don't know where my head is lately."

"I know," Janet said, and then hung up.

An hour later, Janet, her face ghostlike and horror-stricken, pulled up at the job site with the blueprints and his work orders. She handed them to Keith and turned to get back in her car without as much as a single word.

"What's wrong, Janet?" Keith assumed that Cynda did something to her when she went to the house to pick up the blueprints.

She clasped her hands together and opened her mouth, but no sound came out. She stepped back, scratched her head, and turned away from him.

As she opened her car door, Keith again asked, "What's wrong?"

"Go home, Keith. Go check on your wife." She slammed her palms against the steering wheel, and as tears slid down her face she asked him, "What was God thinking? You deserve so much more."

She closed the door, and Keith watched her drive away and wondered what Cynda could have done to upset her like that. He wanted to rush home, but didn't want to feel like a fool if nothing was wrong.

He pulled out his cell phone and called the house. The line was busy. It stayed busy.

What was he supposed to do? Leave his crew to do all the work while he spied on his wife? He couldn't do it. His personal life wasn't going to affect his business anymore than it already did. After dialing the house for the sixth time and still getting a busy signal, Keith allowed the crew to knock off about two hours early.

As he pulled into his driveway next to a midnight-black Lexus that had never been in his driveway before, he kicked himself for not coming home sooner. He got out of the truck and sprinted toward his ranch-style house, stepping on the tulips and chrysanthemums that the ladies from his church had planted last spring.

The front door opened, and a man dressed in workman's overalls stepped onto his porch. "Same time next week, sugar?" the man asked.

Cynda leaned against the doorpost. She had on a short, black silk gown that Keith didn't remember buying her. She winked. "Yeah, baby, same time."

Keith barreled his way onto the porch and put his hands around the man's throat. The 5-11 stranger was no match at all for Keith's 6-2, and 220-pound body.

"Don't you ever come to my house again, do you hear me?"

Cynda stepped onto the porch and grabbed Keith's arm. "Are you crazy?" she yelled. "What are you doing?"

Keith let the man go and stepped back. "Stay away from my wife."

The man sputtered something about calling the police.

Cynda pulled Keith into the house. "Just leave, Joe. Get out of here."

Keith pulled his arm from Cynda's grasp and jumped in Joe's face again. "Are you deaf?"

Joe stepped off the porch and headed for his car. Before opening the door, he yelled back, "She invited me over here, man. I didn't even know she was married. Geez! Where I come from, men don't marry hookers."

Deflated, Keith went into the house and shut the door. "What was he doing here?" Keith demanded to know.

Cynda stood in the living room, her hand on her hip. She lifted her leg, displaying the monitor around her ankle. "I can't exactly go to him now, can I?"

He advanced on her with his fist clenched. "Did he bring this gown for you?"

"No, my first customer brought the gown."

"Your first *what*? How many men have you had in my house?"

She didn't move. "Enough."

He was foaming at the mouth, madder than a lion chasing after the animal stupid enough to mess with his cub. "What did you say?"

"So I guess you're going to beat on me." She shrugged. "Go ahead. It's not like I haven't been down this road before."

"Why, Cynda? You are my wife."

"Boy . . . please, don't color it up. We're roommates."

Keith's mother once told him, "Son, don't ever put your hands on a woman, but if she acts like a man, treat her like one."

This one was certainly begging for it, in his face, daring him to hit her. Only men acted like that, right? If he hit her in the eye, she'd probably treat him with a little more respect. He wanted to beat some sense into her, but he couldn't put his hands on a woman, no matter how wrong she was. He looked at her for a moment. Her eyes were glassy and wide open, like toothpicks were holding them apart.

"What's wrong with you?"

She started fidgeting, walking in circles. "Why something gotta be wrong with me?"

"You on something?"

"Why I got to be on something? Why can't I just like sex?"

He grabbed her arms and looked deep into her eyes. "You're on crack?"

She pulled away from him. "I just had a little hit. What's the big deal?"

"The big deal is, I opened my house to you; took care of you when you couldn't do anything for yourself, and you thank me by prostituting and doping up in my house?"

"You don't own me. I can pay my own way." She took a fifty out of her bra and tried to hand it to him. "Here, put this on the rent."

"If you think I could take money that you earned by, by"—He turned away and walked toward his office.

She put her hands on her hip and posed as she sneered, "How does it feel, dear husband, to know that someone else wants what you don't?"

And there was the reason she'd done this to him. She wanted to punish him for not having sex with her.

He stormed into his office and slammed the door. Kneeling before the throne he prayed, "Father, I know You love me and desire good things for me, but I just don't know if I heard you clearly about this marriage. She can't be the one for me, Lord. The woman has nothing but contempt for me."

He waited, hoping to hear God say, "Son, you're married to a coldhearted devil. Get out while the getting is good," but there was no reply.

Keith continued calling out to God. "She doesn't want me, Lord." *My bride whores after others, and I love her still.* "But I'm not like You, Lord. I don't know if I can stay with someone who treats me this way."

Keith bowed his head lower as he continued to pray. His own words had condemned him. If he was to be Christ-like, then he would have to love in spite of the treatment he received. Whether or not he received love back was not the issue. Jesus loved while He was being crucified. He got off his knees and exited his office, carrying his cross.

His wayward wife was sitting on the couch in the living room with the remote in her hand and the phone to her ear. "The next time Donavan hits you, I want you to pick up the biggest stick you can find and wear him out with it," Cynda said.

With Iona on the other end of the phone, Cynda was putting more poison in her mind, rather than encouraging her to make the best of her situation.

"Just because you're under their roof don't mean you have to put up with their mess. You let me know if anything else goes down, okay?" She hung up and looked in Keith's direction and continued to flip channels.

"You really shouldn't encourage Iona to disrespect Nina and Isaac."

Fire flashed through Cynda's eyes. "So I'm supposed to let them treat my child like an unwanted orphan and just keep my mouth shut? Is that the way you want me to handle it?" She mumbled under her breath, "The way you handle everything."

Keith could barely look at her. Didn't want to be in the same room, same city, or same earth with her. But he was honor-bound to treat her right anyhow. "I'm going to go pick up some food," he said. "Do you want Chinese or pizza for dinner? I would have asked before I came home, but the line stayed busy."

"Chinese works for me." She pulled the same fifty out of her bra and tried to hand it to him again.

He ignored her outstretched hand. "So, this is the way you dress to sit around the house?"

"You don't like it?" She looked down at the skimpy gown then back at Keith, who rolled his eyes and walked out the door.

Driving to the Chinese restaurant he kept reminding himself, Love is kind, love does not think evil. Love does not mix rat poison into a box of shrimp fried rice.

When he got back home Cynda had changed into a pair of jeans and a T-shirt he had bought her. He set the food on the table and opened the boxes. Cynda grabbed the plates out of the cabinet. When they sat down, Keith held her hand and said grace over their food.

"Why do you find that necessary?" Cynda asked.

Keith put some sweet and sour chicken on top of his rice. "What?"

"Praying. Like somebody cares enough to listen."

"My God listens when I pray."

She put some pepper steak and an egg roll on her plate. "Yeah, that's why you're stuck with me."

"God has a plan for me."

"God's plan must be for you to suffer."

Chomping down on his food, Keith looked at her through pain-filled eyes. "With suffering comes growth. The more I grow, the more I will be like Him."

She shook her head. "I don't understand you."

"You don't have to understand me. Just love me."

"I'm not into all this love stuff." She walked to the refrigerator and took out a diet coke. "You want one?" she asked, holding it up.

"Yeah, I'll take one."

She sat back down and handed him the soda, and they ate in silence for a while.

"Look Keith, I don't think this is going to work out. When I get through with this court case, I'm going to move out, okay. We can get a divorce or an annulment or something."

He wanted to remind her that she might go to prison before this was all over, but apparently she looked at her court case as nothing more than a traffic ticket that she could just go into court for, bat her eyes, and the judge would let her walk out with a small fine.

"You're my wife, Cynda. I'm not only here to make sure you walk out of court without going to prison. I'm here till we part in death."

"Keith, let's be real. You don't even want to have sex with me. How long do you think you can stay married to a woman you're too good to touch?"

He saw the pain in her eyes. He put his hand over hers. "I never said I didn't want to touch you. My God, Cynda, just being in the same room with you makes me want to claim my rights as your husband."

"Then, why don't you?" she asked, as if she was truly interested in what he had to say.

"Because it doesn't mean anything to you. You give away

sex like it's the toast you add with eggs for breakfast. When we make love, I want it to be a joining of two people that love and care for each other."

"You expect too much from me."

"No. I think you expect too little of yourself." He scraped the container for the last of the chicken. "Like this whole drug thing . . . you've got a ten-year-old daughter you claim to love, but you're a dopehead."

She stuck out her tongue at him. "Sticks and stones."

"I'm not trying to fill you with guilt. I just want you to see how much you are putting at risk by doping up."

"I don't do it every day. I just need a pick-me-up every now and then."

"I'll tell you what, Cynda." He took his plate to the sink and rinsed it out. "Don't do your drugs or invite old customers to our home. If you want to do something to help pay your way, try fixing dinner and keeping the house clean."

Cynda got up and started clearing off the table. "I can do that. Cleaning a house isn't a big deal." She put the leftover containers in the refrigerator and ran some dishwater.

Keith got in the shower and let the hot water sting his flesh. As he soaped up, he asked, "Lord, what am I going to do with this woman?"

Love her.

"How, when she's so, so unlovable?"

When no answer came, he shut off the water and got out of the tub. He dried himself and then put on his pajamas. Before walking out of the bathroom he noticed the black gown Cynda was wearing earlier in the trashcan, and ripped apart.

He turned on the light in his bedroom, got in bed, grabbed his Bible, and began looking up scriptures on love: Beloved, let us love one another: for love is of God; and everyone that loves is born of God, and knoweth God.

Another scripture said: Herein is love, not that we loved God, but that He loved us, and sent His Son to be the propitiation for our sins. Beloved, if God so loved us, we ought also to love one another.

About an hour into his study, Cynda appeared in the doorway. She leaned against the door and waited for him to look up. "I'm sorry," she said when he finally looked her way.

He put down his Bible. "What are you sorry about?"

Wringing her hands, eyes downcast, she said, "For not being grateful for all you've done for me. I'll try not to disrespect your home any more."

She took her flannel nightgown out of the drawer and went into the bathroom. When she emerged, she had on the gown he'd bought her. She walked over to the bed. "Do you want me to sleep on the couch?"

Keith lifted the covers and invited her to join him . . . for love bears all things, hopes for good things, but endures all that comes.

16

"Get out of my room," Iona spat.

Nina's mouth dropped, as well as the basket she was carrying. Dirty clothes spilled out, mixing with the clothes Iona already had on the floor.

"Did you hear me? Y'all put me on punishment. Said I have to stay in my room. Well, that's just fine with me. I don't want to see any of you anyway, so get out of here."

"Look, little girl, I don't know how you were allowed to talk to your mother, but we have rules of conduct around here," Nina said.

Iona rolled her eyes.

"First off, no room in this house is off-limits to me or your father. Secondly, if I feed you, don't disrespect me. It's just that simple."

Iona rolled her eyes again. "Whatever."

Maury was blaring through the room. "You are not the father."

Nina turned off the television, wondering where Maury was when she needed him.

"Hey, don't touch my stuff," Iona said to her.

"You're ten, Iona. You don't have any stuff. I've got news for you—You are not allowed to watch *my* television for the rest of the day."

"I'm gon' tell Isaac."

"Go right ahead." Nina picked up the dirty clothes that had fallen out of her basket.

Iona sucked her teeth. "I hate you."

"You want your telephone privileges taken away next?"

Arms crossed, Iona glared at Nina.

"And that reminds me, I don't want you dialing long-distance until after seven in the evening. And use either Isaac's or my cell phone to make the call."

Iona's eyes were lifted to the ceiling as Nina looked around the room.

"Pick the rest of these clothes up and bring them downstairs so I can wash them," Nina said and stormed off.

Later that evening, walking past Iona's room, Nina wished she had taken her phone privileges away when she overheard Iona on the phone with her mother.

"Come get me, Mama. I'm tired of being in this house."

She must be tired of having three meals a day and a mother who doesn't run the street.

"I hate her. She makes me sick. She thinks she can tell me what to do. She's not my mother."

Nina put her hand on Iona's doorknob. *Time to show this knucklehead some love with a leather belt*, but then she stopped herself. The way she was feeling, she'd probably kill the girl.

Forget it. She was tired. Finished. Out of here. Nina went into her room and pulled her suitcase out of the closet.

Isaac walked into their bedroom. "What are you doing with that?"

Nina pulled some clothes out of the closet. "I'm going to spend a little time with Elizabeth and her family. I think the trip will do me some good."

"So you're just going to leave me again?"

She kept packing.

"What about till death do us part, Nina? Did you listen to the words the preacher spoke to us just last year?"

Throwing a pair of pj's in the suitcase, she turned to face him. "What about *love, honor,* and *cherish?* Did you understand what those words meant?"

He pulled her into his arms. She didn't stop him, and even put her arms around him and squeezed a little. "I love you, Nina. Don't do this."

"I love you too, but I got to get away for a little while."

He lifted her head and looked into her eyes. "We can work this out, baby. Stay."

"That little girl is driving me up a wall."

"I need you, Nina."

"How can you say that? You can't like the way I am right now."

"I'll take you any way I can get you, babe."

She squeezed his hand and then sat down on the edge of the bed, her head hung low. "You don't think I see how I'm treating your daughter, but I see it, Isaac, and it sickens me." She looked at her husband as tears filled her eyes. "I should be able to treat her better than this. I have more compassion for Ebony than I do for Iona."

"Look at me, Nina. I'm pastoring a church, and I can't forgive Cynda. I know it's not right, but that's where I'm at right now." He sat down next to her and wiped her tears. "We all need help to overcome things. That's why God sits on His throne and we don't."

"But I've never had a problem with being kind. But the way I treat Iona . . ."

Isaac put his hand in hers and allowed her to continue.

"When that little girl called her mother, she just sat there and talked about me as if I wasn't in this house. As if I wasn't feeding her."

"What if that was Donavan on the phone talking about you to his friends? What would you have done then?"

"I would have snatched his ungrateful behind off that phone and then I would have felt bad and sat down and talked with him to find out why he was so upset with me."

"So why didn't you do the same thing with Iona?"

"She's not my child."

"Yes, she is."

Nina let go of Isaac's hand and stood. "Don't say that to me. She is yours and Cynda's child. She has no part of me in her."

"She's your child also, because you're my wife. Can you see that, Nina?"

Just a few weeks ago, Nina thought that the only thing she wouldn't do for this man was drink his dirty bathwater. Now she would gladly drink that water, if only his prodigal seed would disappear. Was God showing her that Isaac's seed *was* his dirty bathwater? Maybe that's what her foster mother was referring to all those years ago when she told Nina that she loved her husband so much that she was willing to take the dirtiness that life thrust upon them and help him clean it up. *Oh God, teach me to love that way.*

"Look, Nina, we both know what the main issue is. It's the same one that's been between us since we got married."

"What are you talking about?"

"I don't care if you have another child or not, Nina. I love you the way you are. You are the woman God gave me."

She opened her mouth to deny it, but before any words came forth, she decided to speak from her heart. "Isaac, I need to tell you something." She squeezed his hand, seeking the strength to continue. "The day you brought Iona home, I had just come back from the doctor."

He pulled his hand from her grasp. "What did the doctor say? Is something wrong with you?"

She patted the bed. "Sit back down, Isaac." He obeyed

her command, and she continued. "I had missed my period, so I thought I was pregnant." She willed herself not to cry, not again. "But he told me that I was more than likely going into early menopause."

Isaac waved that away. "You were on your period last week, Nina. How can you be going through menopause?"

"It was three weeks late."

"But it came."

"I've never been late before, Isaac, not three weeks. Anyway, I don't want to dwell on this. I've decided to trust God and let it go. The only reason I told you is because I want you to understand why it hurts so much every time I look at Iona."

"It doesn't have to hurt, baby."

But it does hurt. Oh God, please take this pain away. "How can I change the way my heart feels, Isaac?"

"Make Iona the most blessed child in the world. Give her two mothers to love." When she didn't respond, Isaac picked up her suitcase and dumped the contents on the floor. He turned back to her and said, "Stay."

She opened her mouth to respond, but he was upon her, covering her mouth with his. He moved her toward the bed, and she allowed it to happen.

As he stripped her clothes from her body she knew that she would love this man for a lifetime. Couldn't let him go. She would enjoy her husband. Just enjoy this moment, kiss and make love to him, and then go out there and drink his dirty bathwater.

17

During the weekend Keith had set his mind to fast and pray for Cynda's deliverance from drugs. Cynda walked into their bedroom and found Keith on his knees calling out to God on her behalf. She then went over to the dresser and rummaged through the drawers, knocking things around, anything to distract him from praying for her.

On Sunday morning when he got up and got ready for church, Cynda asked, "Are you going to put my name in the prayer box?"

Fixing his tie, he answered, "I think I just might do that. Corporate prayer is always a good thing."

She got out of bed and moved his hands from his tie and knotted it for him. "Don't do me any favors, Mr. Williams. You told me you don't want me doing drugs in your house, and that's all you had to say."

"Are you serious? Or just too crazy to know you need God's help?"

"Keith, you were right. If I want to get my daughter back, I have to do it without drugs."

"But you don't have to do it without God."

"I don't need your God to kick my habit. And I'm going to prove it to you."

"Everyone needs God, Cynda."

Walking away from him, she said, "Well, I'll just show you, mister doubting Thomas."

He grabbed her arm and pulled her toward him. "You know something about the Bible? Where did that come from?"

"I'm not completely ignorant, Keith. My grandmother was a God-fearing, Bible-toting Christian till the day she died . . . for all the good it did her." She walked with him toward the front door.

"Why do you think it didn't do your grandmother any good to serve the Lord?"

She opened the front door, and Keith stepped onto the porch.

"My grandmother's only child was killed by her pimp while she stood by, praising the Lord." She closed the door and left him standing on the porch, stunned.

At church Keith was yet again amazed as Pastor Norton stood behind his Plexiglas podium and preached from the seventh chapter of Luke. Pastor Norton explained that when a prostitute stood at the feet of Jesus, then washed his feet with her tears and dried them with her hair, and then anointed them with ointment from her alabaster box, the Pharisees became offended and accused Jesus of not being aware of the sins the woman had committed.

"Then Jesus said to them, 'There was a certain creditor who had two debtors: the one owed five hundred pence, and the other fifty. And when they had nothing to pay, the creditor forgave them both. Tell me, which of them will love him most?' "

Pastor Norton studied the congregation for a moment. "One of the Pharisees answered and said, 'I suppose the one he forgave the most.' Then Jesus said to him, 'You have rightly judged. Therefore I say to you, her sins, which are many, are forgiven; for she loved much.' "

Pastor Norton closed his Bible and turned back to the congregation. "What I'm trying to get across to you all is this—Don't judge people by who they are today because the same person you condemn to hell, God may be trying to raise to glory, if only He can get you to pray for them."

Janet was seated next to Keith. She touched his shoulder with her newly manicured hands. Her hair was in one of those "up 'dos" with pin curls dancing around the front and back of her head. Keith liked the way it drew attention to her sparkling brown eyes. He liked brown eyes. His wife had fake hazel eyes, but Janet's were real.

"I'm praying for you," she told him.

Keith sunk back into the well-cushioned pew and turned his gaze away from her eyes. She wasn't the woman God had for him. Pastor Norton was preaching about the woman God gave him, and he would do everything in his power to love and treat her right.

"Would you pray for my wife also? She needs to know the love of God."

Janet turned her attention back to Pastor Norton.

As Keith continued to listen to the message, his faith grew. He had taken it upon himself to pray for Cynda's deliverance from drugs. But did he think that the rest of her sins were too much for God to do anything with? *Lord, forgive my unbelief. Please deliver my wife from all her past sins. Wash her whiter than snow.*

When the benediction was given, Jim came over to Keith. "Man, I need to apologize. Sometimes, I forget that God is still in control."

Keith patted him on the shoulder. "I know. I was just thinking the same thing."

"How's Cynda doing?"

"Will you two excuse me." Janet left them to join a group of women having a conversation at the sanctuary door.

"Not too good. But after today's message, if I don't know anything else, I know that God is still on the throne, my brother."

"I'll be over tomorrow evening so we can finish putting this case together. We will know this week whether the grand jury has decided to indict her or not."

"What do you think her chances are? Be up front with me."

Jim put his hand on Keith's shoulder. "They'll indict. She's looking at about ten years if she's found guilty."

Keith went home with heaviness on his heart. His wife was a handful, but he didn't want to see her in prison. He didn't tell Cynda about his conversation with Jim. Her spirits were high. She was floating around the house, talking about some TV commercial that told her how she could make millions of dollars working from home. He smiled and listened to everything she had to say. No way was he going to take her hope away.

On Monday when he arrived home after work, Cynda had fixed steak and potatoes for dinner. "I would have fixed some salad with it, but all you had was tomatoes and green peppers in the fridge," she told him.

"If you give me a list, I'll go to the grocery this evening."

Keith was washing the dishes after dinner when the doorbell rang.

Cynda opened the door and let Jim in, and Cynda and Keith sat down with him.

Jim got right down to business. "I know you already gave your statement to the police, but I need to go over it with you again."

Cynda nodded. Keith put her hand inside his as she told Jim, "I spent the night here with Iona. I needed a place to lay low while we figured out what to do."

Jim had his notepad out again and jotted down something as he talked. "Why did you need to lay low?"

"I told you that already. Iona told me that Spoony wanted to put her on the street."

"Okay. So why'd you leave Keith's house?"

She gave Keith a sideways glance. "That morning, Keith told me he knew who Iona's father was. He tried to get me to admit it, but I denied everything. Then he told me that her father was coming to town that day. I couldn't allow him to see Iona. I didn't want him to take something else from me." She lowered her head. "But he took her anyway."

She stopped talking, and for a moment, no one said anything; allowing her to adjust to her pain.

"Why did you go to Mr. Davidson's house when you left Keith's?"

"I wasn't trying to go over there. But he was staking out my girl Jasmine's place, and Linda promised me some money. So I figured, since he wasn't home, I could go get the money and some of Iona's clothes. Then I wouldn't have to buy any more when we got to where we were going."

"And where were you going?"

Cynda shrugged. "I'm really not much of a planner. I was going to figure that out once we left Spoony's."

"So, before you could get out of the house, Mr. Davidson showed up?"

"Yeah. He got mad because I was taking the only thing he had left to hold over me. See, he knew Isaac was Iona's father, and he knew I never wanted Isaac to know about her. So he kept me on the street, supplying his drug money. He started knocking me around as usual, but I didn't care. I told him we're getting out of there. That's when Linda took Iona to the back."

"So it was only you and Mr. Davidson in the front room?"

"Yeah. He knocked me around the room. At first I thought he was just going to beat on me. I was used to that. But then he started choking me, and all of a sudden I was that little nine-year-old girl again, looking down on my mother's coffin and hating her for letting some man kill her. I couldn't let that happen to Iona. I mean, at least I had my grandmother. Who did Iona have?"

Keith squeezed her hand. "It's okay. Go on. What happened next?"

"That's just it. I can barely remember anything after that. I started blacking out. But I think I picked up the lamp. After that"—Cynda shook her head—"nothing."

Jim wrote down Cynda's last comments then told her and Keith, "A shattered lamp was found next to the body. I'm going to pick up the autopsy report tomorrow, so I'll know more about what the coroner thinks killed him."

Cynda glared at him. "You haven't gotten the autopsy report yet?"

Jim lowered his head. "No."

"Look, Mr. Reid, you and I handle business in a similar fashion. We both collect our money up front." Cynda paused, and then backhanded him with, "But I do my job once the money has changed hands."

Jim put down his pad. "You're right, and it'll never happen again. But I'm going to be straight with you. I really need your permission to speak with your daughter."

"Why do you want to bring Iona into this?"

"Your daughter brings another aspect to the case. No jury is going to forget how this little girl felt while watching her mother get attacked."

Cynda turned to Keith. "I don't know. What do you think?"

Keith thought of the ten years she had coming to her if the jury didn't see eye to eye with her, knowing firsthand that she didn't have the most lovable disposition. "Maybe we should at least let Jim speak with her. Then we can decide whether or not we'd put her on the stand, okay?"

She told Jim, "Okay, but just talk to her. Don't badger or try to pull stuff out of her that's not there."

Jim's eyebrow jutted upward, and his mouth went slack. "I would never do that."

They finished with Keith offering to travel to Dayton with Jim to introduce him to Isaac and Iona. The truth of the matter was that Keith knew that Jim wouldn't get past the crack of an open door at Isaac's house. No way would his friend volunteer his daughter for the sake of Cynda. He had to make Isaac see reason. So he planned to leave his wife alone and hope for the best.

When Jim left, Cynda picked up the phone and called Iona. Isaac answered the phone and refused to let her speak to Iona.

"I have a right to speak to my daughter, Isaac."

"You gave up that right when you smoked your dope and prostituted yourself in front of her," Isaac told her. "Oh, and just so you know, I received my papers from the family court today. The DNA test is 99.8% positive that I am Iona's father, so you know that I'll be filing for full custody."

"Put Iona on the phone!" Cynda screamed.

Keith took the phone out of Cynda's hands. "Man, why are you acting like this?"

"How do you think I feel, Keith? That woman kept my child away from me for ten years. I can't get a single day of those years back, and I'm supposed to bend over backward for her?"

"No one's asking you to bend over backward," Keith said. "Just put Iona on the phone."

"My daughter is doing her homework, and I'm not interrupting that so she can talk a bunch of nonsense with Cynda." Isaac slammed down the phone.

Cynda rolled her eyes. "That man is insufferable. I don't know how you tolerated him all these years."

"He's all right. Just give him time to adjust to the situation. He'll come around."

She pulled one of the pillows off the couch and threw it at Keith. "You always take his side. When are you going to stop being his boy and become a man?"

Keith picked up the pillow off the floor. "I don't know what you want me to do, Cynda. You created this situation when you refused to tell the man that he had a daughter, so you and Isaac are going to have to work through this together."

Keith didn't want to argue. He sat down next to his wife and invited her to watch a movie with him. Having no one to argue with, Cynda agreed. They picked *The Gospel*, with Boris Kodjoe and Clifton Powell.

When it was over, Cynda said, "See, that's why I don't like going to church. More mess is in the church than on the street."

"But you stayed in the street, even with all the mess you had to deal with, didn't you?"

"Yeah, but God wasn't on the streets watching me do my dirt."

Keith shook his head. "You're wrong, Cynda. God is everywhere. The Bible says that God sees both the good and evil we do. I think you missed the point of the movie. What they were trying to show was that although we're not perfect and we slip up from time to time, we can turn back to God and He will forgive us."

"If you say so." Cynda yawned and walked toward their bedroom.

Keith lingered in the family room, bowed his head, and asked the Lord to help Cynda see it His way. He joined his wife in bed and picked up his Bible.

"Why do you read that thing every single night?"

He smiled. "It gives me strength. Helps me to see things the way God sees them."

She turned toward the wall and drifted off to sleep, but before Keith could finish studying, Cynda started tossing and turning, flailing her arms.

"No! Get off me. Get off me!" she screamed in her sleep.

He shook her. When her eyes focused on him and she stopped swinging, he asked, "What was that about?"

Cynda closed her eyes tight and didn't respond.

Keith put the Bible back on the nightstand. "You want to talk about it?"

She shrugged. "Ain't nothing to talk about."

"Who did you want to get off you?"

"Look, I don't know nothing about nobody getting off me. What I do know about is this crick in my neck and how bad my back is aching because of this rotten mattress."

"The mattress on the bed is old. It was passed down to me when I first got out of prison. I just never thought about replacing it."

"Well, you need to think about it. Got my back aching and carrying on."

"Where are you in pain?"

She pointed to a spot just above her buttocks.

"Lay on your stomach," Keith told her. She did as he asked, and he began working his magic on her back, rubbing and kneading where it hurt.

Cynda moaned, "Ah! Yeah, right there."

He continued massaging her back until desire for her overtook him. He pulled her hair back and lowered his lips and kissed from the nape of her neck to her earlobe. "How 'bout that, baby? How does that feel?"

"Feels like you know what I like."

He turned her over and kissed her soft cheeks. Then he leaned in and covered her mouth with his. He took her face in his hands and forgot about what might have been with someone else. Anyone else. There was only one woman for him, and she was beneath him, soft and warm.

"You're so beautiful," he told her, tracing kisses from her eyebrows to the tip of her chin. He closed his eyes and allowed himself to feel. "I love you, Cynda Williams."

Her eyes shot daggers through his heart. "You ain't got to say all that, Keith. I'm gon' give you some. Just stop lying, okay."

His body went stiff. He got caught in the moment, forgetting that she wasn't yet his. But those words brought it back to him loud and clear. There were certain parts of her he couldn't touch.

Keith slowly pulled away. He got off of her and situated himself on his side of the bed.

"What's wrong?" Cynda shoved him. "What's the matter with you? Why'd you stop?"

"I'm your husband, Cynda. It's okay if I love you."

She rolled her eyes and turned toward the wall.

18

"You're worried, aren't you? Think that once you leave I'll have some wild party in your house and your neighbors will call the police, and before you know it the police will come to Dayton and arrest you for running a brothel?"

Thoughts like that did cross Keith's mind, but he was determined to live his life. He wasn't going to keep close tabs on her, rummaging through the trash to see what she'd thrown away. He wasn't going to install a nanny cam. He was just going to step out of the way and let God work on her.

"Are you worried that you might do something like that while I'm gone?" Keith had his duffel bag open and was headed to the drawer to pack for his overnight trip.

Cynda blocked him. "Let me do that. It's how I earn my keep around here, remember?"

He smiled at her and sat down on the bed to watch her pack his duffel.

"Anyway, I already told you that I won't use your house to entertain clients again. And I've been drug-free for two weeks. I'm good." She put his socks, toothpaste, and a toothbrush in the bag.

Cynda was still trying to prove to him that she could kick the stuff without God. He hoped she could kick it, but he knew that if she did, it would be because of God's mercy.

"Can I ask you a question?"

"Shoot."

"Why'd you throw that black nightgown away?"

Silence filled the room. Keith wasn't sure if she was going to answer him.

"It was the way you looked at me when I had it on. Iona had given me the same look when she told me she didn't want to do the type of work I do. It made me feel dirty, so I threw it away." She averted her eyes. "Guess that makes you feel superior, knowing that you could make me feel bad about my line of work."

"It's not your line of work anymore, baby."

He kissed her, and she held onto him. "I'll give Iona your love. Oh, I almost forgot. A new mattress will be delivered tomorrow, so make sure the house is clean."

"Aye, aye, sir," she said, her hand to her forehead military style.

Nina and Iona sat in one of Nina's favorite Mexican restaurants eating fried ice cream and talking about the movie they'd just seen. Nina thought it had way too much adult stuff in it to be rated PG, but Iona didn't have a problem with all that. She told Nina she'd seen more stuff than that just sitting on Spoony's porch.

This outing was Nina's attempt to finally become a part of Iona's life. They'd gone shopping before the movie.

"I didn't think you were going to take me with you today." Iona scooped some of her ice cream.

Matching Iona scoop for scoop, Nina said, "Why? I told

you yesterday that we were going to have a girl's day, shopping and a movie, remember?"

Iona twisted her lips and lowered her head. "I know. But my mom always promised that we would go places, and then she would have some excuse why we couldn't go."

Nina put her hand on top of Iona's. "You can trust me, Iona. If I make a promise to you, I will keep it. I learned the hard way with Donavan that your children can be taken from you in the blink of an eye, so we've got to make the most of every moment we have."

"You don't have to make the most of any moments with me. I'm not your child."

Sadness filled Nina's eyes, but she shook it off. "I know that, but if you let me, I'd like for us to become friends. And then one day maybe you will even think of me as a second mother."

"Linda was like another mother to me. She was nice."

"I want to apologize to you, Iona. I wasn't nice to you like I should have been when you first arrived."

"It's all right. I know you don't like me because of my mother."

Iona was way too grown for the ten years she'd been on this earth. But maybe that came from all she'd been through.

Their waiter stopped to check on them. Nina assured him they were fine then leaned closer to Iona and said, "Your mother has nothing to do with this."

"She already told me what went down between you, her, and Isaac, so I know you hate her."

Tears that Nina couldn't hold back filled the corners of her eyes and drifted down her cheeks. "I'll admit that I have a problem with your mother."

"See, I told you," Iona said triumphantly. "That's why you hate me."

Nina held up her hand. "I don't hate you, Iona. But, from

this time forward, I promise you this, I'm going to do everything in my power to make you feel like a wanted member of our family." Nina held out her hand for Iona to shake it. "Can we start over?"

"Will I still be able to call my mom?"

Nina nodded then put her hand down. "Yes, of course you can call her. We have to wait until a certain time when the rates are cheaper, like I asked you to do before, but that's the only stipulation I have on phone calls to your mom."

Iona rubbed her chin and pondered. "I guess that will be okay."

They sat in silence, finishing up their fried ice cream, and then Iona asked, "Nina, can you tell me something?"

"Sure, honey. What do you need to know?"

"It's about my mom." She hesitated for a moment. "Do you think she will go to prison?" She held up her hands. "And don't give me the little-kid answer, tell me the truth."

Nina scraped her plate then put the last of her ice cream in her mouth. "The truth is, she might go to prison. Killing someone is a serious offense."

"But what if she had help?"

Nina put down her spoon. "Iona, do you know something that you haven't told us?"

She hunched her shoulders and looked away. "I was just asking."

"Baby, if you know something that will help your mother," Nina said, putting her hand on top of Iona's, "you need to speak up."

19

Isaac was in his office at the church, working out the final details for the tent revival when Keith walked in. Isaac stood, and they clasped hands.

"Hey, man, what brings you to Dayton? Why didn't you let me know you were coming?"

Keith smiled. "I figured a sneak attack would be better for this one."

Isaac looked over Keith's shoulder and noticed the man standing in the doorway, briefcase in hand. "What's up?"

Keith motioned for Jim to come forward. "Isaac, this is Cynda's attorney, Jim Reid. He needs to speak with Iona about what happened that day."

"Are you crazy?"

Keith held up his hands. "Look, you know I wouldn't ask if it wasn't important."

Isaac sat back down behind his desk. "Keith, you can bump your head over Cynda until the white meat shows, but I'm not about to expose Iona to more of that woman's drama."

Keith and Jim sat down in front of Isaac's desk.

"She's Cynda's only hope, man."

Isaac reviewed some papers on his desk as if Keith hadn't said a word.

"She's Iona's mother, for God's sake. Do you want your daughter to know that her mother went to prison because you refused to help her?"

Flinging the papers across his desk, Isaac asked, "Would that be the same woman who kept the knowledge of my child from me for ten years? Would that be the same woman responsible for the fact that I don't even know the child that's in my house? Is that the woman you're asking me to help?"

Keith leaned closer to Isaac. The desk was still between them, but their gazes locked on each other. "Isaac, as long as we've been friends, I've known that you have a problem forgiving people. It's why you still keep your father at arm's length."

"My father has nothing to do with this."

Isaac's father had beaten his mother to death when he was only thirteen. Isaac also blamed his father for his brother's death. The way Isaac saw it, if he hadn't been in "juvie" for attacking his father, his brother wouldn't have been in that alley shooting craps. He just wouldn't have allowed it.

"And it's why you are refusing to help Cynda," Keith continued. "Now, I'm not saying that you don't have a legitimate beef with both of them, but when are you going to realize that you did more to God than anyone has ever done to you, and yet He still forgave you?"

Isaac leaned back in his chair and rubbed his chin. He looked to Heaven. *Lord, why is this world full of so many people who need to be forgiven?*

My son, they are just like you were. In need of a Savior.

Isaac turned back to Keith. "I'll let you see Iona, but I won't let you upset her. Is that clear?"

"Cynda has already expressed that to Jim."

"And we all know how much Cynda cares about the well-being of her child, don't we?" Isaac said sarcastically. He looked at his watch. "Nina and Iona should be home by now. Come on, you two are invited for dinner."

"That's not necessary, man," Keith said. "We can grab something before we check into the hotel."

"Now you know Nina would have my head if I didn't invite you over for dinner."

"She always was the more sensible one." Keith grinned.

They all headed out of the church, and Keith and Jim followed Isaac home.

When they arrived at the house, Nina ran toward Keith and embraced him. "It's so good to see you," she told him.

Isaac cleared his throat loud enough for the next-door neighbors to hear him, and Nina and Keith turned to face him.

"Yes?" Nina said lovingly, her arm still around Keith's neck.

"All that running should have been for me, not this knucklehead. I don't see you getting all excited like that when I walk in the door," Isaac said, striking a mack daddy pose.

Nina waved him off. "I see you every day"—She nodded in Keith's direction—"but this is the man who helped to bring my son out of a coma."

Nina still didn't understand how Keith had done it. After Donavan got shot, he was in a coma for days. Nina and Isaac watched and prayed, but nothing happened. Then one day Keith walked into Donavan's room and started talking, and Donavan's eyes opened, as he called out for Keith.

Keith smiled. "Yeah."

Isaac pulled Nina away from Keith. "I keep telling you that Donavan was getting ready to wake up anyway. Ain't nothing magical about Keith's voice," Isaac teased.

"Whatever." Nina extended her hand in Jim's direction. "Hello, I'm Nina Walker."

"I'm Jim Reid, Cynda's attorney."

She looked back at Isaac then at the attorney. "Well, how did you know?"

"Know what?" Jim said.

Her eyebrows furrowed. "How did you know about Iona?"

Keith frowned. "Nina, we're not following."

"When Iona and I were at lunch today, she said something that led me to believe that she might know more about Spoony's murder than she told." She looked at Keith. "I was going to call you after dinner tonight."

Jim's brown eyes lit up. "We really need to talk to her."

"Well, y'all come on in here and get some dinner before you do anything else. I just fixed a big pan of lasagna. We'll have tons of leftovers if you two don't help us eat it."

As they all broke bread together, Keith talked with Donavan about school, grades, and football practice. Donavan made sure to include Iona in the conversation. Nina tried to involve Jim by asking questions about his work and the church he and Keith attended. Isaac stayed quiet through most of the meal, watching Iona, trying to determine if she was nervous and feeling uncomfortable.

When dinner was over, Nina and Iona stayed behind to wash the dishes.

"Why do I have to wash the dishes? Y'all just got me here to be the maid."

Putting the cups in the sink, Nina asked, "Was Donavan our maid when he washed the dishes last night?"

Iona rolled her eyes and stepped to the sink.

"Don't say nothing when your eyes get stuck"—Nina mimicked her eye-roll—"like that."

Iona rolled her eyes again, and Nina tickled her.

"Stop," Iona said between giggles. "Leave me alone."

Still tickling her, Nina said, "Every time you roll your eyes, I'm going to tickle you."

"Stop," Iona begged, "I'm going to pee on myself."

"Are you going to stop rolling your eyes?"

Jumping around, Iona replied, "Yes, I'll stop."

"Good. Now let's get these dishes done."

Isaac told Jim and Keith, "I want to be in the room when you talk with Iona."

Keith held up his hands. "That's fine. I'll just hang out with Donavan until you are finished."

When Keith turned to go find Donavan, Jim told Isaac, "I think you might want to know a few things before we bring Iona in here."

"Like what?"

"Well, first, it's going to be important that you don't get upset at some of the things Iona might have to say. She needs to feel comfortable exploring the events of her past."

Isaac hollered into the kitchen and told Nina to bring Iona into her office when they were done with the dishes. He took Jim into the office and shut the door behind them.

"I will sit behind this desk and quietly observe while you talk with her," Isaac said. "I'm not in here to interfere, I just want to make sure you don't go overboard."

Jim touched Isaac's shoulder and stopped him from walking to the recliner behind the desk. "Sit right here please, Mr. Walker." Jim pointed to the chair in front of him.

Isaac sat down asked, "What's up?"

"The reason I asked that you not get upset while Iona is speaking is because I believe she will divulge some things that a parent might become very angry over. Remember, Mr. Davidson is dead. He can't hurt your little girl any more."

Isaac was seeing red. His hands clenched around the armrest. "What things do you think Iona will tell you?"

Jim cleared his throat. "I think Mr. Davidson was about to turn your daughter into a prostitute."

"What?" Isaac barreled out of his chair. How could Spoony do such a thing to his daughter? Had their old friendship meant so little to him? He vigorously rubbed his forehead as he walked in circles around Jim. "You mean to tell me that this man was so low that he would prostitute a ten-year-old child?"

"I don't know how far he would have gone. All I know is that he supposedly threatened your daughter with it. That's why Cynda was at the house that day. She was trying to get Iona's clothes so they could get away from Mr. Davidson."

A knock came on the office door, and Jim reminded Isaac, "I need you to be calm."

Calm? Isaac thought. How could he be calm when he just found out that someone he once trusted wanted to prostitute his only daughter?

The door opened and Iona stood there with her white and sage green ribbons in her hair, a pleated skirt, and knee-high socks on. What type of sick freak would want to destroy her innocence?

"Have a seat right here, Iona." Jim pointed at the chair that Isaac just got out of.

Iona sat down and put her hands in her lap.

Jim started slowly with, "Iona, I want you to know that I'm not here to make you talk about things you don't feel comfortable discussing. But I do have some questions for you, and I think your answers might be helpful."

"Is this about my mother?" she asked.

Jim nodded. "Yes, it is."

"She told me that you were coming to see me."

I sure wish she'd told me. Wish she'd told me a lot of things. Isaac pulled up a seat next to his daughter.

"She told me to tell you what I know only if I feel like it."

"Do you feel like talking to me today, Iona?"

"Yeah, I want to help my mama. I don't want her to go to jail."

"Okay." Jim opened his briefcase and took out his note-pad. "Can you tell me why your mother wanted to get you out of Mr. Davidson's house?"

"Who's Mr. Davidson?"

"Spoony," Isaac told her.

"Oh."

Jim tried again. "Do you remember why she wanted to get your clothes and leave his house?"

Iona turned to Isaac, but kept her eyes downcast. "It's bad, Daddy. I don't know if I should say it."

This was the first time she'd called him *Daddy*, and a spring of emotion bubbled in Isaac as he grabbed his daughter and held on to her. He wanted to protect her from the world her mother had created, but to do that he had to know the demons she was dealing with. Pulling back and releasing her, Isaac said, "I'm here, pumpkin. I won't let anything happen to you. But what I want you to do right now is tell Mr. Reid why your mother wanted to leave Spoony's house." He wanted her to do this, not to help Cynda, but to help her-self. If she said it out loud, she could release herself from it.

Iona looked down and fidgeted with her hands. "Spoony told me that my mama wasn't bringing in enough money, so I was going to have to"—She buried her head in Isaac's shoulder—"I can't say it, Daddy."

"That's all right," Isaac told her. "You don't have to say another word about it."

"I'm sorry, Mr. Walker, but she's going to have to tell me what Mr. Davidson said to her."

Isaac glared at Jim. "She didn't cause Cynda's problems, and you're not going to sacrifice my daughter to save that, that . . ." He clamped his mouth shut.

Jim looked down at his pad. "Okay, let's skip that one. But can I ask her some other questions?"

"No," Isaac roared. "You cannot ask her another thing. She's done!"

Iona peeled herself off Isaac's chest and sat back up. She told Jim, "I want to help my mother."

"You don't have to do this, Iona."

"I want to, Daddy."

Isaac relented. "Go ahead."

"Can you tell me what happened when Mr. Davidson came home?"

Twisting her hands again, Iona said, "He told my mother that she wasn't going to take me out of his house. Then he grabbed her by her throat and slapped her." Iona held on to the cushion in her chair. "I begged him not to hurt my mama, but he didn't listen. He just kept hitting her."

"What happened then?" Jim asked, taking notes.

"Linda took me into the back room so I wouldn't see what else he did to my mother."

Jim was writing so fast on his notepad that he didn't bother to look up when he asked, "Did you hear anything?"

"I heard my mom screaming. She begged Spoony to just let us go, but he said he was going to kill her, so I asked Linda to help my mother."

Jim looked up. "What did you say?"

"I said, I asked Linda to go help my mother. Linda can't stand to see me cry, so she went back into the living room."

Jim's eyes lit up again. "Now this is real important, Iona. How did Linda help your mother?"

Iona leaned back in her seat and rubbed her chin, and Isaac smiled, thinking, *Like father, like daughter.*

"I don't know how she helped her. I wasn't in the room."

"Okay. Right after you asked Linda to help her, what did you hear going on in the front room?"

"Well, Linda took the plastic flowers out of the vase that was in my room. Then I heard a crash, but I didn't hear my mother screaming any more. Then Linda went in there." Iona rubbed her chin again. "I think I heard Linda say, 'No, you.' " She hunched her shoulders and continued, "Then I heard another crash. Only, it wasn't really a crash, more like a boom."

"What kind of vase did Linda take out of the room?"

"Linda made a ceramic vase for me. She's an artist." Iona smiled. "She decorated my vase with all kinds of colors, but it's broke now."

Isaac couldn't help himself. "Why do you think it's broke, Iona?"

She turned to her father. "Because she didn't have it when she came back to the room. I asked her where it was, but she told me to be quiet. She said we had to get out of the house."

"When you left the house, did you see anything else?"

"No. Linda covered my eyes when we got to the living room, and when we got outside she called the police. I heard her tell them that there were two dead bodies in the house. I started crying because I didn't want my mama to be dead."

"How did you find out that your mother wasn't dead?" Jim asked, still vigorously scribbling notes.

"When the police got there, Linda opened the door, and we heard mama screaming, 'I killed him, I killed him.' Then she started laughing. The police put handcuffs on her, and then I saw her spit on Uncle Spoony."

Jim looked up.

"She didn't mean to do it. I think she was just mad," Iona said, twisting her lip."

Isaac turned to Jim. "Would you step out so I can talk with her for a minute?"

"Yeah, sure. No problem."

When Jim left them alone, Isaac turned to his daughter and put his arm around her. "You've been through a lot more than any ten-year-old should have to endure."

She snuggled closer to him. "Sometimes I dream about Uncle Spoony. I think he's coming back to kill me."

"Do you feel comfortable talking to me or Nina about some of your thoughts and feelings?"

She shook her head.

"If I took you to see someone, like a counselor, would you talk to her?"

She shrugged.

"Would you try?"

Her answer came softly. "I'll try."

Upstairs, Keith was trying his best to whup Donavan at a game of Need for Speed, but since the last computer game he'd ever played was Pac-Man, he wasn't coming out on top. He shook his head as Donavan racked up more points.

"You aren't going to take Iona, are you?" Donavan said out of the blue.

Keith put the control down and looked at his godson. "No. Why would you ask me that?"

"No reason."

Keith grabbed Donavan's arm and turned him around. "Talk to me."

Donavan put his hands in his pockets. "I was just hoping Iona would stay with us. Mom needs the company. You know, I'm getting older, and she's not going to have me around much longer."

Keith lifted Donavan's strong chin. "Look me in the eye, young man." When Donavan looked up Keith said to him, "How many times do you have to be told that your mom doesn't blame you for what happened?"

Donavan turned away.

"Are you listening to me?"

Donavan's eyes clouded with sorrow. "I'm the reason she can't have any more kids." His voice broke. "If I hadn't gotten involved with those guys, she wouldn't have gotten shot."

"Donavan, you were shot too. Remember that? Your mother doesn't blame you. Hear me on this one."

Isaac knocked on Donavan's door then opened it. He looked at Keith. "We need to talk."

20

Isaac, Jim, and Keith stood on the porch outside of Isaac's house. Isaac told Keith, "We think Linda may have also been involved in Spoony's death."

Jim added, "She told the police that the only time she came out of the back room was when she and Iona ran out of the house, but Iona just told us that Linda went into the living room with a vase in her hand before she and Iona left the room."

Keith's eyes widened.

Jim continued, "And the autopsy report indicates that there was a foreign particle in Spoony's skull, besides glass from the lamp Cynda admits to throwing."

"And you think the foreign particle was the ceramic vase?" Keith asked.

"It's quite possible, but we won't know for sure until we talk with Linda," Jim said.

Keith pulled the keys out of his pocket. "Well, let's go talk to her." He started to walk off the porch.

"Not so fast," Isaac said. "Linda isn't going to let us in

her house if we show up there at two in the morning. Which is how long it will take us to get there. The two of you can bunk here. We'll go see her in the morning."

Keith couldn't keep the disbelief out of his tone. "You're going to go to Linda's with us? To help Cynda?"

Isaac let out a long sigh. "I'm not interested in helping Cynda. But I don't want Iona having to visit her mother in prison if she didn't actually do the crime. And I don't want you wasting your life waiting ten years for her to get out of prison to figure out she wasn't worth it."

When they arrived at Linda's house the next day, Isaac told Jim and Keith, "Let me do the talking." He had history with Linda. They'd always gotten along well, so Isaac thought she would respond to him.

"Let's get this done," Keith said.

Once they were in the house, Linda fixed each of them a cup of coffee. Her eyes weren't as clouded over with sadness as on the numerous occasions Isaac had visited this house.

"How you doing, Linda?" Isaac asked. He cared about this woman, and wanted her to know he was in her corner.

She just kinda stared off into space. "You remember those letters you sent to Spoony years ago? The ones 'bout how you turned your life around, and fell in love with Jesus?"

"Yeah, I remember." When Isaac was in prison he'd sent similar letters to all the peeps he'd run the streets with. He still didn't know how much good came from those.

"Spoony laughed at what you wrote. Said you'd gone soft, lost your nerve with all of them roughnecks facing you down in prison." She smirked. "I didn't agree with him though." She looked at Isaac. "I didn't agree with Spoony about a lot of things. Anyway, I kept your letters. And the other night I was listening to one of them TV preachers. He said Jesus Christ was the atonement for our sins. I was lying in bed about to take some sleeping pills and die because I was so filled with guilt, but when he said that, I remembered your letters."

Isaac thought, *Did my letters really save her life, Lord? Had I really been directed by You to write those letters all those years ago?*

"Your letters talked about how God forgave you for all the stuff you'd done." She smiled, and her eyes shone bright. "And I knew that you'd done an awful lot of stuff. So I asked God if He would forgive me too, and you know what?"

"What?" Isaac asked.

She smiled again. "He did."

"What did you need anointment for?"

She patted Isaac's hand. "You already know. That's why you brought them with you, isn't it?"

Jim leaned forward in his seat. "Linda, can you tell us what happened the day your husband died?"

Her mouth twisted, and without much ado she admitted, "I killed him."

Isaac, Keith, and Jim looked at each other but said nothing.

"That man took everything from me. He whored around, beat me up when I complained. He beat me so bad when I was pregnant that I lost that baby and never conceived again. The only thing he ever gave me was Iona. I couldn't let him take her too."

Keith asked, "Cynda says that Spoony wanted to prostitute Iona, is that true?"

Her eyes got that faraway look in them again before she answered, "When I asked him about it, he told me to shut up before he started beating on me again. So I took Iona into her room and I grabbed the ceramic vase I'd made for her and went back into the living room. At first I wasn't sure if I could do it. But Cynda was unconscious when I went back into the room. I think she tried to hit him with my glass lamp but she must have missed, 'cause his mean ol' self was standing over her kicking her even while she was unconscious." Linda eyed the three men. "I thought she was dead. Spoony had his back to me while he kicked her. I heard him say, 'Now I'm going to go get Iona ready for her new job.' I knew he planned to rape her and I couldn't let that happen, not to Iona. So I screamed at him, 'No, you won't,' and smashed him in the head with that vase and watched the evil seep out of him as he dropped to the floor."

21

Isaac and Jim followed Keith to his house. Keith and Jim were excited to tell Cynda the good news.

Isaac told Keith, "I want to see Cynda. I need to know why she never told me I had a daughter."

When Keith opened his front door and saw chairs turned over and lamps broken on the floor, he frantically looked around the living room expecting to see Cynda's body stretched out on the floor. When he didn't see her, he started screaming, "Cynda! Where are you? Cynda!"

Their bedroom door opened, and Cynda's bruised body came running toward him. She clung to him like a cat clawing a tree and trying to get rid of the dog on its tail. Kissing his neck, face, and lips, she told Keith, "Please don't leave me again. I was so scared."

Keith pulled her off of him and wiped the blood from his lips. He handed her a handkerchief to hold up to her lip, which was dripping blood. Her eye was swollen, and her clothes were torn. He looked around the living room. "What happened here?"

"He beat me, Keith. I thought he was going to kill me."

Cynda tried to cling to him again, but he held her at arm's length.

The eye that wasn't swollen was wide open and glassy. She couldn't stand still in front of him.

"Who did you have in my house?" Keith demanded to know.

Shaking her head, she said, "I didn't call anybody to come over here. I told you I wouldn't do that again."

Isaac said, "Look, Keith, man, the girl is a junkie. She obviously let some crackhead tear up your house. How much more has to happen to you before you realize that loving her is the wrong thing to do?"

Keith held up his hand. "I can see, Isaac, but she's still my wife. Let me handle this, please."

"Fine." Isaac threw his hands up. "I'm out, man." He turned to Jim. "You want me to take you home? My boy has his hands full."

"If I'm not taking you too far out of the way, I'd appreciate it."

"Don't worry about it." Isaac then turned back to Keith. "You should have married Janet. Hopefully, it's not too late." Then he shut the door.

Keith turned back to Cynda. "Who did you have in my house?"

"I'm not lying to you, Keith. I didn't call nobody. The guy who brought the mattresses used to get high with me. He came back after he finished his deliveries and had some stuff with him. I tried not to take it, I really did, but he kept waving it in my face."

Keith turned the chair back over and sat down. He put his elbows on his thighs and his head in his hands.

Cynda ran to him. She sat on the floor and put her hands on his leg. "I didn't give him sex, Keith. I told him I wouldn't do that. You believe me, don't you?"

Keith couldn't look at his wife. He couldn't pretend that

he didn't see his mother in Cynda's eyes. Every time she opened her mouth he heard his mother's voice.

"You believe me, don't you?" Dorthea had asked when she promised that she was kicking the stuff for good, for the hundredth time. "You believe me, don't you?"

No, he didn't. But she was dead before he could tell her that.

"Why do you think he beat me up?" Cynda swept her hand around the expanse of the living room. "Why do you think he tore up the furniture? Because I satisfied his every whim?"

He moved her hands off his leg and stood. He needed to be alone. He had to get away from his "mother-wife." He needed to pray and ask his Lord how much more of this he had to take. In his throne room, Keith fell on his knees and moaned and moaned and moaned until his sorrow-filled heart was laid open before the Lord. He wallowed on the floor as he rolled back and forth. "Oh God, how long? How long?"

Cynda knocked on the door and begged Keith to open it. "Come on, Keith, don't be like this. Look, I'm sorry, okay. I really did try to be good. I just can't help it."

She heard him wallowing around on the floor and crying, "How long? How long?"

She stepped away from the door and yelled, "Go ahead. Cry to your God. Ask Him to deliver you from the likes of me. See if I care." She stomped into the bedroom, mumbling, "I didn't order those mattresses. Didn't ask that guy to bring those drugs over here. But everything is my fault." She took off her torn clothes. "I don't need this. I can make my own way."

She still had the money she'd earned a few weeks ago. She'd use it to catch a cab and get out of here. She put on a pair of jeans and one of Keith's button-down shirts. The shirt was much too big on her, but it didn't matter. She just needed to get out of there. As she walked away from the home Keith had offered her, she vowed that she would not go back to prostitution. She would show Keith. She could turn her life around just as well as he did. He wasn't better than her.

Halfway down the block she remembered that she was on house arrest and that her ankle bracelet was probably sending off signals of her escape, but she couldn't worry about that right now. No way was she going back to that house and listen to the wounded animal she'd left there. It was better for Keith that she leave. Time he faced the fact that she was no good. Love wasn't an option for her. Too much had happened. Too much hadn't happened.

She caught a cab over to Jasmine's place, figuring she would bunk with her for the night, then maybe go to one of them temporary places and try to get a receptionist job or something. She could handle a straight job. Little Miss Janet wasn't the only one that could type. And she could take messages in her sleep.

When she arrived at Jasmine's, a party was just getting started. Cynda told Jasmine, "I'm just going to go to your room and crash. I'm not up for a party right now."

Jasmine was shaking her moneymaker as the CD player told them, *"It's getting hot in here, so take off all your clothes . . ."*

"What happened to your face?"

"Long story," Cynda said as she headed upstairs to rest. "I'll tell you about it tomorrow."

"Go on, make yourself at home, girl. I'll talk with you in the morning."

Cynda stepped over forty-ounces and chicken bones. Jasmine was a heck of a party planner. A slob, but a good party planner. As Cynda walked upstairs, a couple of the men leered at her, ogling her front and backside. She wanted to scream at them, tell them that she wasn't a piece of meat, that she had emotions and feelings just like anybody else, but they were all too high to care.

She hadn't brought a gown with her, and there was no way she was sleeping in those rouged jeans. She pulled them off, unbuttoned Keith's shirt, and climbed into bed. The sheets were soiled. Cynda wanted to climb out of that bed and go home. She'd just had a nice new mattress delivered and was sure it was comfortable. But then she heard Keith's moans of agony, his praying, and knew that she couldn't go home.

She shifted her position on the dirty sheets and drifted into her nightmare. It was the same one that plagued her since she was a child.

Uncle Romie was standing over her bed. "Hey, pretty one," he said. "Your mama's out whoring around so you've got to handle her business tonight."

Young Cynda smiled. "Stop joking around, Uncle Romie. Where's my mom?"

"I already told you, your mother is out making my money, so I'm going to show you how to make Uncle Romie happy." He pulled the covers off her bed and leaned into her, his hot breath beating down on her with the familiar smell of burnt licorice and his sour breath.

"Uncle Romie, you've been drinking, that's all. Go back to your room. I won't say a word," a scared Cynda said with a nervous chuckle.

"I've got to teach you." He took off his clothes and climbed into bed with her.

Cynda screamed and screamed, but her mommy wasn't there to hear her, wasn't there to protect her.

Someone was jerking Cynda out of her sleep, from one nightmare to another it seemed. They were breathing alcohol into her face.

"Leave me alone, Uncle Romie!" Cynda screamed.

Shoving her, the male voice said, "Baby, I ain't your Uncle Romie, but if that's who you want me to be tonight, I'm okay with that."

Cynda's eyes flew open and beheld the rotten-toothed man grinning down on her. She sat up in bed. She wasn't eight years old, and Uncle Romie wasn't raping her. She was at Jasmine's house. "What do you want?"

He offered her a swig of the forty in his hand. "Thought we could create a party of our own up here, just you and me."

"Not interested." Cynda then pulled the covers over her head and tried to turn away from him, but the bedroom door opened again, and another guy from downstairs walked in and shut the door. She rolled her eyes. "What do you want?"

He smirked. "I want to play too."

Hungry, sex-craved eyes devoured her. They'd take it if she didn't give it to them. And she wasn't about to let them rape her. No one would ever rape her again. She looked the men up and down. "Let me see your money?"

22

Three days later when Keith found Cynda she was higher than the Sears Building, standing on the corner in broad daylight, telling anyone who would listen that if they had fifty bucks they could get an hour of ecstasy. And all this time Keith thought he'd been given the "old friend discount" that day he took her to lunch.

Her brown leather mini-skirt looked more like a second skin than clothing. She'd obviously found someone to take the monitor off her ankle because it was gone.

Keith was in the back seat of the unmarked police car. He pointed Cynda out to Officer Darryl and then got on the floor and put a blanket over his body. Officer Darryl was one of Keith's church members. That's why Keith called him. He knew that he could trust Darryl to help him out with this situation.

Officer Darryl then slowly drove in front of Cynda and rolled down the window.

She leaned her head into the window. "Hey, daddy, what ya know?"

"I know I like what I see," Darryl told her.

"You want to spend some time?"

"How much time you got?"

Cynda looked around. Then she leaned her head back in the car. "How's an hour sound to you?"

"Hop in."

She opened the door and slid next to him. "So where we going, baby?" she asked when the car started moving.

"That depends. How much?"

She put her hand on his leg. "You can afford it."

He smiled. "That depends on whether I have to pull it out of the grocery money or the house note. So give me a price and I'll know if I can afford you."

"Fifty bucks, baby, that's all."

Officer Darryl pulled out his badge, and Keith popped up from the back seat.

Cynda screamed. She looked at the person in the back seat. "Keith, you almost gave me heart failure. What's wrong with you?"

His eyes bugged out. He had to restrain himself from shaking her. "What's wrong with *me*? I think we need to discuss your issues before we worry about mine, don't you?"

She sneered at him. "I ain't got no issues, just minding my own business and wishing you'd do the same. Why are you bothering me anyway? I already heard that Linda is in jail. She confessed to killing Spoony, so the cops can't be looking for me."

Officer Darryl said, "That shows how much you know about the law. You can't just up and leave when you're on house arrest. *We* have to release you."

"You talking about that monitor? That thing fell off. I don't even know where it's at."

"You've got bigger problems right now anyway, Cynda," Officer Darryl told her.

"Like what?"

"Like the warrant that's out for your arrest for skipping

out on house arrest. Like prostitution and the fact that you just solicited a cop."

"This is entrapment."

"Shut up, Cynda. Right now you've got two options— You can go to jail, and maybe those same women who beat on you before will be there to finish you off this time."

She sneered. "What's my second option? Go home with you?"

"No. You're going to sign yourself into a rehab program today."

"Ah, Keith, rehabs don't work. Most of the junkies out here have been to rehab."

"You'll make it work. I'll help you."

Cynda turned to Officer Darryl. "How long would I have to stay in jail?"

He kept his gaze on the road. "When we throw in the tampering charges, you could be looking at a couple years."

She closed her eyes and exhaled. "Keith, why do you waste your time on me?"

"I don't consider it a waste. Now what's it going to be?"

Rolling her eyes she asked, "What are my choices again?"

Standing at the intake desk of the rehab clinic Cynda disgustedly gave the place the once-over. It smelled like old people. Like old people with cats. The walls were dirty white, not a spark of color anywhere. "Do you really expect me to stay here?"

Keith didn't respond.

"What about Iona? How am I going to see her if I'm locked away in this place?"

"You didn't seem that interested in seeing her while you were selling yourself on the street."

"I was trying to earn the money to get an airline ticket to Dayton."

"What happened? The money kept going up your nose rather than in your piggy bank?"

Cynda banged on the bell at the intake desk and rolled her eyes. "Why don't they have someone out here?"

A lady with long micro braids and wearing an irritated I've-had-about-all-I-can-take-today expression came toward the intake desk and snatched the bell. "What can I do for you?"

"Give me a Big Mac and some fries. What do you think I want, lady? I'm a junkie, okay. Open up your prison doors and let me in."

The woman glared at Cynda then turned to Keith. "Sir, is she requesting treatment from this facility?"

"Yes. She very much wants to get clean. Isn't that right, Cynda?"

"Based on the alternative, yeah, I want to get clean."

The woman kept her attention on Keith. "Has she ever attended this program before?"

Cynda leaned against the counter and waved. "Hey, I'm right here. You ain't got to ask him nothing. Don't I have to sign myself into this place? Well, then ask me some questions." She stepped back and almost fell.

"I would, ma'am, but you seem intoxicated."

Cynda turned to Keith. "I'm not going to be able to get anything past her, am I?" She turned back to the woman. "Just get me a bed, okay." Cynda sat down and let Keith handle the paperwork. She signed the pages and indicated that she understood everything that was on them.

When Cynda was finally admitted, Keith was told that he wouldn't be able to see her for the first two weeks of the program.

He hugged Cynda. "I'll miss you. Get better, okay."

As she was carried away, she told him, "I'm not going to miss you. I'd rather be in this place than to live with you and that Bible you read every single night."

23

By the end of the first week Cynda had the chills. She vomited three times and started having delusions of visitations from her grandmother and mother. One time when Cynda's mother appeared, Cynda had to be restrained to her bed. On numerous occasions she screamed, "You let him touch me. I hate you!" Then she would chant, "Whore! Whore! Your mother's a whore!"

"I want to be good, Grammy. I just don't know how," she cried one night while a man sat next to her bed, wiping sweat and tears from her face.

He whispered into her ear, "You're going to be okay. Just have to let these old demons go."

Cynda thrashed around the bed, then she heard the man say, "Trust God. And lean not unto your own understanding."

"Huh?" she asked, opening her eyes. She put her hand over her face. "Turn that light off."

"Sorry," he said.

Cynda brought her hand down and looked into a familiar face. "Hey, I remember you." Then she smiled as a puzzle piece fell into place. "You were at Spoony's house that day, weren't you?"

He nodded.

"Why'd you resuscitate me?"

"You have much to live for."

A nurse pulled back the curtain and walked toward Cynda's bed. "Who are you talking to in here?"

Cynda nodded. "My friend. He's sitting right here. Don't you see him?"

The nurse chuckled. "Nobody is sitting in that seat."

Cynda turned toward the seat and saw that it was indeed empty. "He's always doing that."

"Doing what?" the nurse asked as she checked Cynda's vitals.

"Disappearing."

The start of the next week brought psychotherapy. Dr. Philmon, the staff psychiatrist, told Cynda that she had to participate in group sessions with the rest of the drugheads. Cynda wasn't having it. They weren't just going to pick her mind apart and leave her open and unfixed. She sat in the session, listening to the other dopeheads confess their transgressions.

Afterwards, another participant walked over to her. "You need to loosen up, girl. How do you think you're going to be free from whatever is eating you up inside if you don't talk about it?" the woman told Cynda.

"Ain't nothing eating me up inside," Cynda replied.

The woman put a cigarette in her mouth and extended her hand. "I'm Maggie."

Cynda shook her hand. "I'm Cynda."

"Look, Cynda, if you want out of this place, the best thing to do is cooperate. Open up when the doc has us in group sessions."

Shaking her head, Cynda said, "I'm not spilling my guts to him or anybody else in this group."

"Suit yourself, but I spill my guts every chance I get. That's why I'm going home next week." Maggie then rejoined the group and left Cynda standing alone.

"Iona, this is Dr. Bozeman, the Christian counselor I told you about," Isaac told his daughter.

"The one you want me to talk to?" Iona asked.

Isaac nodded.

Dr. Bozeman held out her hand. "Hello, Iona. You can just call me Beverly. I'm real happy to meet you."

Iona shook Dr. Bozeman's hand and said, "I guess you can call me Iona."

Nina and Isaac laughed.

"I've cleaned off my desk," Nina told her. "The office is yours if you'd like to speak with Iona in there." Nina showed Beverly to her office after Beverly took her up on her offer. "Just make yourself at home. We really appreciate you doing the sessions at the house."

Beverly walked around Nina's desk. She picked up the tattered orange stress ball. "Yours?"

"I've needed it a lot lately," Nina admitted.

"Really?" Beverly asked with questioning eyes.

Iona slowly walked into the room, and Nina backed out.

"Well, Beverly, I'll talk with you after your session with Iona. Maybe I'll lie on the couch and let you analyze me."

"Where do you want me?" Iona asked when Nina closed the door.

Beverly pointed at the black leather chair in front of Nina's desk. "How about right there?" Then she scooted Nina's leather recliner in front of the desk, so she and Iona sat facing one another with nothing in between. "How's that?"

Head bowed low, hands in lap, Iona said, "Fine."

"I agreed to meet with you here because I thought you

would feel more comfortable talking with me in your own home."

Iona looked up. "This isn't my home."

"Oh, really? Well, where do you live?"

Iona hunched her shoulders. "I used to live with my mom, but that wasn't our house either."

"Would you like to talk about your mother?"

Iona shook her head.

"What would you like to talk about?"

"Nothing."

"If we're going to sit in here, we have to talk about something."

"All right," Iona said. "Why don't you tell me about your family?"

When Keith arrived for his first visit, Cynda told him, "They're trying to kill me in here. You've got to take me home with you."

Keith put her hand in his and gently stroked it. "I can't, baby. This program is going to help you kick the habit. If you would just work with the people, it'll be over before you know it."

She pulled her hand from his. "Get out of my face. I don't want to see you anymore!"

He sat down and began to eat one of the sandwiches he'd purchased out of the vending area as Cynda stood with arms folded.

"You want something out of the vending machine?"

"No." Cynda then sat next to him and lifted his chin. She glared at him. "Can't you tell when you're not wanted? Are you really this thick, or are you just pretending to be stupid?"

Sadness crept into Keith's eyes as he rewrapped the uneaten portion of his sandwich. "I've got to get back to work anyway. I'll stop by tomorrow. If you want company just let me know. If not, I'll get out of your way." He stood. "I brought something for you." He handed her a piece of paper then turned and left.

At first Cynda wasn't going to read it. She was going to ball it up and put it in the trash, but then she decided it wouldn't hurt to read the note before throwing it away. She opened the paper and read the words: *Trust in the Lord with all thine heart; and lean not unto thine own understanding.* She smiled at the note. Her visitor had said the same thing to her just the other night. She would have to tell Keith about him.

24

The day before Maggie was released, Dr. Philmon brought the group together for another fabulous "why I am a loser" session. Cynda sat in the back with her feet in the chair, her knees pushed against her chest. She wanted to throw up when Maggie told the group that she'd made amends with her mother and would be moving back to Cleveland to live with her.

"That bus can't leave this town fast enough for me," Maggie told the group.

Dr. Philmon said, "That's good news, Maggie. You're taking a step in the right direction."

"Yeah, I figured it was high time I reconnected with my mother. She's not getting any younger, and I miss the old girl."

Cynda rolled her eyes, put her feet down, and stood up. "What if you get home and your mother has a new man and can't be bothered with you? Then what you gon' do, huh? Where will all your big plans for starting over with your mother be then?" Cynda then stormed out the room.

*   *   *

Iona and Beverly were in Nina's office for the third time in two weeks.

Iona screamed, "I'm tired of talking. Why don't you stop coming over here?"

"I just want to help you, hon, that's all."

"But I don't want your help. I don't want you asking about my mother or about Uncle Spo—I mean Spoony. I just want to forget, but you won't let me." Iona got up and ran out of the room and into the kitchen, where Nina was putting away the dinner dishes. "Where's my dad?"

"He's at the church, attending a men's Bible study tonight," Nina said. "How is your discussion with Beverly going?"

Iona folded her arms across her chest. "Make her stop asking me how I feel about my mother."

Nina picked up the dishtowel and dried her hands. "She's just trying to help you explore your emotions."

"My mom was a whore. How am I supposed to feel about that?"

Beverly came into the kitchen and put her hand on Iona's slumped shoulder. "I'm sorry, Iona. We can find something else to talk about if you're not comfortable."

Arms still folded, lip poked out, Iona jerked away from Beverly's touch. "Just stay out of my face."

Nina put the dishtowel down. With a long-suffering sigh, she asked, "Why do you have to be so defiant? We're just trying to help you."

"I don't need your help," Iona yelled as she turned and ran out of the house.

"Great! Another wonderful night at the Walker residence." Nina threw her hands up. She then turned to Beverly. "Thanks for coming tonight." She looked toward the front door. "I've got to go get her."

Beverly patted Nina on the shoulder. "Just call me when she's ready to talk again."

"Will do." Nina stepped onto the porch to confront Iona, but she wasn't there. She squinted in the darkness but couldn't make out Iona's form on either side of the street. Hyperventilating, she put her hands on top of her head and screamed, "Oh God, please help me!"

Beverly stepped out onto the porch with her briefcase and car keys in hand. "What's wrong, Nina?"

Frantically pointing into the darkness, she told her, "Iona's out there." Bad things happened at night. The Mickey Joneses of this world lurked in the night waiting for the opportunity to put a bullet in unsuspecting kids like Donavan. The Charlie Duprees beat and pimped girls like Ebony. "I've got to find her." Nina ran off the porch, screaming for Iona.

"I'll help you look," Beverly said.

They jumped in Beverly's car, and then Beverly drove down Superior, Grand and Lexington. Nina scoured the streets. As far as she knew, Iona hadn't made friends with any of the neighborhood girls, so she didn't have a house she could walk up to and ask, "Is Iona here?"

Beverly stretched out her arm. "Look, is that her?"

They were driving by Broadway Park, the same park where Donavan almost got himself killed. "Stop the car!" Nina got out and ran toward the little girl seated on the lopsided swing. She had to tread a hill to get to the swing sets. Sand and gravel cut into her bare feet. That's when she realized she'd left her shoes at home. The grass had been worn down in most spots. All that remained was dirt and concrete. The concrete was, of course, where the basketball rims and picnic tables were. So, Nina endured the pain as she treaded through dirt and rocks toward Iona. It had to be her. The little girl had on the same white cotton T-shirt that Iona had on. Her hair was in two ponytails like Iona's. *Dear God, let it be her*, Nina thought.

Out of breath, Nina bent down, hands touching her

kneecaps as she stood in front of Iona. When she caught her breath, she asked, "Why'd you take off like that?"

Iona didn't answer.

Beverly came up the walk. "You got her?"

"Yeah," Nina said, and then held out her hand to Iona. "Come on, honey, it's not safe out here at night."

Iona took Nina's hand and they went home. They didn't go inside though. Sitting on the porch, Nina talked with her about the things that could happen to a little girl at night. Little girls that get away from their parents.

Iona listened, and as her shoulders began to shake from the current of her tears, she confessed, "I was going t-to run away, but I didn't have anywhere to go. Nobody likes me."

At that moment, Nina forgot about Iona's earlier defiance and hugged her, thanking God that Iona hadn't gone far. She wiped the tears from Iona's face. "Let us help you, baby. You can't live with all this stuff bottled inside."

"But I don't want to hate my mother," Iona cried.

Surprise registered on Nina's face. "We don't want you to hate your mother. We're just trying to help you deal with some of the things you've gone through."

Frustrated, Iona hit her legs with her fists. "You want me to say that what my mother did was wrong. But if she was wrong, I should hate her, right?"

For the first time since Iona came to stay with them, Nina felt pain that wasn't her own. Tears formed in her eyes, and she wiped them away. She hugged Iona again. Then, as they parted, Nina asked, "Can I tell you a story about a Man who loves us, even though we continue to do wrong things?

The following day when Keith came to see Cynda, she was insulting and cantankerous. "You're not a man," she said, laughing at him. "You don't even know how to take what you want."

Keith rubbed her arm. "How are the sessions going?"

She pushed and cursed him. "Does that tell you how the sessions are going?" She pushed him again. "You make me sick. I'm serious. I vomit every time I think about you."

When Keith arrived the following day, she ran to him, gave him a hug. "I didn't think you were going to visit me today." She hugged him again. "I missed you so much."

Keith knew that this was all a part of the mood swings he would have to endure while Cynda came down off the drugs. One day she'll love him, the next day she'd hate him. He was prepared to go the distance with her.

They sat down at one of the tables in the visitation area. "I brought you another scripture."

Cynda took the paper from him and read: *I have loved thee with an everlasting love: therefore with loving kindness have I drawn thee. I will build thee, and thou shalt be built, O virgin of Israel: thou shalt again be adorned, and shalt go forth in the dances of them that make merry.* She smirked. "I hate to break it to you, Keith, but I haven't been a virgin since my mama's boyfriend had his way with me when I was eight years old."

Keith saw the pain in her eyes. "God will rebuild you. You will become like new again," he said with conviction.

Cynda shook her head. "I don't understand you. How can I become new when I'm already twenty-nine? I've seen and done too much to ever be new again."

Keith took her hand in his and squeezed. "Trust God, Cynda. He is the Maker and Giver of all good things."

She pulled her hand from his grasp. "I can't trust in a God that has never done anything for me." She put his face in her hands "You, Keith, you have been good to me. But I can see you. I can touch you." She explored his brownish-grey eyes, his flat nose, and the high set of his cheekbones. "Don't ask me to believe in a God I can't see."

"That's just it, Cynda. When you see me, you're looking at my God. Everything I am is because of Him."

She let his face go. "Well, I don't want to become like your God."

"Why are you putting yourself through this, Keith?" Janet asked him as he prepared to leave work to go see Cynda.

"What else am I supposed to do?" He put a stack of papers in his briefcase.

Janet put her hand on his arm. "Let her go. She's no good for you." She brushed her hand across his face. "Look at you. You never used to come to this office unshaven and unkempt."

He looked at his clothes. They were a bit wrinkled, but he wouldn't say that he was unkempt.

"Don't destroy yourself for this woman. She's not worth it."

Keith removed Janet's hand from his face. "I took vows before God with her."

Janet smirked. "Shoot, as far as I'm concerned, you and God are even. He can't expect you to stay with a woman like that."

Zipping his briefcase, Keith told her, "That woman is my wife, Janet. And I owe her my loyalty and love. I'm going to be there for her, and that's final."

He heard the harshness in his voice and regretted it when Janet backed away from him like a wounded animal.

"Look, Janet, let's just keep my wife out of our discussions, okay."

During Cynda's fourth week she asked to see Iona. Keith told tell her that Isaac didn't want her coming to the rehab facility and that he did indeed receive full custody of Iona.

"He's a pig! He ruined my life, and now he's keeping my daughter away from me. And the courts are just going to let him do it."

"Iona's in therapy," Keith explained. "Isaac doesn't want anything to set her healing process back."

"If he hadn't treated us so carelessly, she wouldn't need therapy."

"Be reasonable, baby. You can't blame Isaac for how your life turned out."

Huffing, and screaming in Keith's face, she told him, "He sold me to Spoony."

Keith leaned back as his wife pulled at her hair and then angrily let it flop down around her face.

"That's right," she continued as she strutted around in front of him, her blue jeans swishing with each angry step. "Your precious preacher man gave me to Spoony and let him do whatever he wanted with me. Do you want to know how much I was sold for?"

Keith didn't respond.

"Fifty cents."

He tried to pull her to him. "Sit with me, Cynda."

"No, no." Her hair was wild as she jumped around in front of him. "How does that make you feel, Keith, knowing that you married a woman who is only worth fifty cents?"

"No, baby, you're worth far more. You are precious to me."

She sat down next to Keith, eyes distant. "I heard everything. They didn't think I was listening, but I was at the top of the stairs when he sold me." She looked at Keith. "I knew I was pregnant too. I was going to tell him, but when he did that, I vowed he would never have a chance to discard my child as he'd discarded me."

* * *

At home Keith prayed and fasted, fasted and prayed for Cynda. It drained him to see her. Her life was full of so much pain that he didn't know how to help her heal. But he knew the One who could heal her. It was his job to pray and ask the Father to have mercy and deliver her. "Show her Your great love, Father."

25

Cynda barked at Dr. Philmon, "He raped me, okay. Are you happy now?"

"Why does it still hurt so much?" Dr. Philmon asked.

Her eyes turned cartwheels. "Duh. Because eight-year-olds aren't supposed to have sex. They're not supposed to know that life hurts."

"What are eight-year-old little girls supposed to do?"

Cynda closed her eyes. She blocked out Dr. Philmon's mahogany desk and the uncomfortable wooden chair she was sitting in and drifted.

Dr. Philmon persisted, "What are eight-year-old girls supposed to do, Cynda?"

"They're supposed to have tea parties with their friends, play hop scotch, and double Dutch. They're supposed to have fun at the park. They're supposed to have a mommy who'll protect them."

"Did you do any of those things when you were eight?"

"No!" she screamed. "The kids didn't want to play with the child of a whore. And my mother was too busy whoring to protect me."

"What happened when you were nine? Did things change?"

Her chin quivered as tears cascaded down her face. "When I turned nine, my mother's pimp raped me again. He said it was my present for being such a big girl."

"What did your mother do about it?"

A bitter laugh escaped Cynda's lips. "Nothing. She didn't care about me. She loved that pedophile enough to let him have her only child. Then she let him kill her."

"Do you miss your mother?"

"Nope. I hate her. If she was still alive, I probably would have killed her myself by now."

Dr. Philmon opened his mouth to ask another question.

Cynda raised her hand, halting him. "Look, can we talk about something else? My mother is a non-issue. I hate her, but she's dead. Move on."

He took a moment to write in his notepad. He looked back at Cynda. "Should we talk about your husband or your daughter?"

"Leave my daughter out of this too. I ruined her life just as much as my mother ruined mine. She's in therapy now herself, did I tell you that?"

"No, you didn't, but it's probably a good idea to have her see someone. How does that make you feel?"

Rubbing her hands on her pants leg, she said, "Like I want to get high. Just get so buzzed that I don't care how bad I've messed her life up."

"Do you think you'll do that when you get released?"

"To tell you the truth, doc, I don't know."

During their next session, Dr. Philmon tried to pull more information out of Cynda. She wasn't as talkative this time. He asked, "What's bothering you today?"

Cynda sighed. "I've got some things on my mind, doc."

"Would you like to share?"

"Just been thinking about all the stuff I've done to Keith."

He looked at his notes. "Keith is your husband, right?"

"Don't ask me why, but yes, he is." Cynda shook her head. "I never lied to him. He knew exactly who I was when he married me, but sometimes I feel like he drew the short straw. You know what I mean?"

"Does he feel that way?"

Cynda rolled her eyes. "Keith is not normal. He's got to feel like God and Satan are playing head games with him, but he rarely acts as if he regrets marrying me."

Jotting in his notepad, Dr. Philmon said, "Maybe he doesn't."

"He will, doc. Believe me, he will."

The week that Cynda was to be released, Keith sat with her in the visiting room. "So are you excited about coming home, sleeping in your own bed?"

She put her hands in her lap and twisted her gold wedding band. "I might as well tell you now."

Keith smiled. "Tell me what?"

"I'm pregnant."

The smile faded, and the wind gushed out of him.

"So if you don't want me to come home with you, I'll understand."

He was too numb to speak, too beaten down to get right back up.

"Before you ask, I'm three months pregnant so I conceived since we were married. And we both know there's no chance of you being the father."

When Keith didn't respond, she said, "You want me to have an abortion or what?"

"What kind of monster do you think I am?"

She shook her head. "I don't think you're a monster. You're good. Too good for me, that's for sure."

"Then how could you ask if I want you to abort our baby?" It hurt him to use the word *our* for a baby that could have been fathered by any number of men, but he'd taken vows, married this woman, and he would accept this baby.

"First of all, this isn't *our* baby. I have no idea who the father of this child is. And secondly, having an abortion is no big deal. I've had about three or four already. It's a thirty-minute procedure, tops."

Keith looked to his Heavenly Father. *Is there anything this woman hasn't done?*

No, my son, her sins are great.

"We're keeping our baby, and that's final."

She rolled her eyes. "Whatever, man. I just don't understand how you can say that this baby is yours."

"Because I married you. In doing that I accepted the fact that what you have is mine and what I have is yours."

When Keith left the rehab center, he got in his car and sat there without putting the key in the ignition, without putting his seat belt on. He cried for Cynda, for the life she'd led. Cried for himself.

Over a decade ago, before he knew the Lord, he'd actually escorted three different women to the abortion clinic and paid for them to have his children sucked out of their bodies, not wanting to be tied down to women he didn't love just because they had a child together. He'd only confessed this sin to Nina. And she lovingly told him about God forgiving murderers like Moses, and King David. Now he was tied to a woman who was carrying someone else's baby. The pain she caused him felt like being gutted. The ache was soul deep. How he wished God had chosen someone else. He put his head in his hands, ashamed of the fact that he didn't want this burden. Didn't think he could endure much more. He remembered reading a scripture that said, *If you suffer with Jesus, you shall also reign with Him.* How puffed up had he been when he told the Lord he would gladly suffer for him.

"Take it away, Jesus," Keith begged. "This is too much

for me. I'm not as holy as You are." He rocked in his seat. Blinding tears hindered his vision.

Someone knocked on the window. "Hey, buddy, you're in a public parking area. Quit acting like a punk."

Another tap on the window. "Go home and do all that crying."

Another said, "Yeah, we visit our dopehead relatives without falling apart. What's his problem?"

Keith wanted to get out of his car and beat them to a pulp, show them how much of a man he was, but he didn't feel very manly with this ache in his heart. He told his Lord, "This woman causes me to feel every emotion but love. I don't suffer well, Father." He lay on the front seat of his car and wailed. People passed by pointing and laughing at him, but he didn't care. He had to get through to his "Daddy." Had to let Him know how he was feeling. "This hurts."

I know it does, son. I feel that kind of pain everyday.

Keith found a handkerchief and blew his nose. He allowed God's words to sink into his spirit. And then he realized an immeasurable truth: God chooses to love us anew everyday, even after we break His heart by doing our own thing and ignoring His will for our lives.

For God so loved the world that He gave His only begotten son. That whosoever believeth on Him should not perish but have everlasting life.

Jesus became the ultimate sacrifice. That was God's great love. "Strengthen me, Father. So that I might be able to do Your will." And with that he put the key in the ignition and drove home to fast and pray some more.

26

"Have you lost weight?" Cynda asked when Keith picked her up from the rehab.

"Maybe a little."

She hesitated. "You came to take me home? Even with the baby?"

He reached out a hand and took her bag. "Let's go, lady."

Cynda put her arm in his. "Well, when I get you home I'm going to fatten you up. I have a few recipes that my grammy taught me. You'll be back to your normal weight in no time."

He smiled.

When they arrived home, Cynda went to their bedroom and started unpacking the clothes she brought from rehab—conservative, non-street walking clothes. The last item in her suitcase was the brown leather mini-skirt she'd worn the day she checked into the rehab. She lifted it out of her suitcase, studied it and frowned. She couldn't fit this thing the day she had it on, and with the ten pounds she put on with her pregnancy, there was no way she was getting in it again. But would she want to wear something as itsy-bitsy as this butt-cheek-showing skirt if she could still fit it? She showed the skirt to Keith as he walked in. "What do you think, keep it or trash it?"

He laughed. "Oh, I get a choice?"

"Yeah. Would you want me walking down the street with you in this skirt, yes or no?"

Keith twisted his lips. "No, sorry. I just don't like it."

She threw the skirt on the floor. "I don't like it either. It's going in the trash."

He grabbed her hand and pulled her out of their bedroom. "I've got something to show you." He opened the door to the guest bedroom next to their room.

Cynda walked in and immediately turned to Keith with an open mouth. In astonishment she asked, "How, I mean, why would you do this?"

The guest bed had been taken out of the room, and in its place was a solid oak crib. A changing table sat against the wall next to the bed, and a rocking chair stood in the middle of the room.

Keith said, "I figure we'll paint the room once we know if it will be a girl or boy."

Cynda turned and ran out of the room.

Keith caught up with her in the hall and made her face him. "What's wrong?"

She yelled at him, "Why are you so good to me? Why don't you just treat me how I deserve to be treated?"

He brushed back her hair and placed a gentle kiss on her neck. "God didn't do that to me, Cynda. He loved me even when I did things He didn't condone."

Her eyes filled with tears. "Is that what you're doing, being like God again?"

"I am called to be Christ-like, so yeah, I guess that's what I'm doing again."

She couldn't take it anymore. There was no way she could be with a man like Keith. She was going to the Devil, and he was ascending to that holy place her grandmother used to talk about. All that lip service about how opposites attract was bull. Opposites repelled, grated on each other's nerves until one of them bought a gun and ended up on News at Eleven.

"Get away from me, Keith." She was shaking as she screamed. "I can't stand being around you."

He backed up, lifted a hand to halt her tirade. "Calm down. I have a couple things to finish up in the baby's room. I'll just work on that, and we can talk later."

She watched him go into the baby's room. *Why would he make a baby's room? This isn't his baby.* She put her hands to her head. She could feel the onslaught of a killer headache. *Get away from him.* Yes, that's what she needed to do.

She grabbed his car keys off the kitchen counter and got in his truck and took off with a half tank of gas and no idea where she was going, leaving her purse behind, not that she had any money in it.

The only friend she had in this town was Jasmine. But she was clean now, and Jasmine wasn't. Dr. Philmon told the group that they had to stay away from the places they used to haunt if they wanted to stay clean, but where else could she go? Certainly not back to that Good Samaritan husband of hers. She would just tell Jasmine the deal up front. No more drugs, but she needed a place to crash for a couple of weeks while she figured out what she would do with her life. She didn't want to go back to tricking, but in reality, that was all she was ever good at.

Cynda pulled up in front of Jasmine's place. The door was ajar at Jasmine's place, and loud rap music blared from the house. That Jasmine was always partying. Probably had a house full of people in there, every last one of them high as a kite. Not one of them had the good sense to close a door. Cynda clung to the steering wheel. The last time she'd visited Jasmine she had to sell her goods to keep from getting raped.

Keith sat in his kitchen listening to the dripping of the faucet and decided that he'd had enough. How much could one man take? He'd let her stay when he caught her selling her body. In his house. He'd gone to get her after she let someone tear his house up, found her on drugs and selling her body again. Accepted the baby she was carrying. Keith looked to Heaven.

To thank him, she ran away again, but this time she stole his car. Well, he'd get his car back, but if she was out whoring again, she could stay on the corner of her choice. He was done.

He picked up the phone and called Officer Darryl. "Hey, man. How's it going?"

"Things are good. What's up with you?"

"Look, man, I'm not going to play games with you. Cynda just stole my car. I was hoping you could help me get it back."

"That blue Ford Ranger you drive to church?"

"It's the only car I have right now."

"I'll see what I can do."

Cynda sat in the truck for an hour waiting on some of the crowd to leave, but no one had gone in or come out of Jasmine's since she'd pulled up. Maybe they had gotten so zooted out that they'd fallen asleep. Right now, sleep sounded like a real good idea. For the last month the baby had been making her drowsy, forcing her to take naps in the afternoon and evening. If she wasn't going to stay with Keith, she'd have to figure out what she was going to do with this baby. She'd think about that tomorrow. After a good night's sleep.

She decided to just go ahead and get out of the truck and go into Jasmine's house. "Go Head" by Gucci Mane was blaring through the house as she entered. A pizza box with half-eaten pepperoni and ham pizza lay open on the table, and cans of Miller Lite, Budweiser, and several forty-ounce bottles were strewn across the dirty hardwood floor. A dark-skinned, scraggly-haired man was on the couch passed out, and a white woman with blonde hair lay comatose on the floor next to the couch.

Cynda yelled for her friend several times. "Jasmine!" When she didn't get an answer, she stepped over a KFC box and two bottles of beer to get to the stereo to shut Gucci Man up. "Jasmine!" She headed up the stairs, here more beer bottles and a couple of McDonald's bags lined the stairway. Jasmine needed her butt kicked for letting people destroy her place like this. "Girl, where you at?" She pushed open her friend's bedroom door. And that's when the wave of terror she'd only felt one other time in her life hit her. Somebody had done more than kick Jasmine's butt. They'd cut up her face and slit her throat. The cut line ran in-between the flaps of fat around her neck. The blood on her body was her only covering.

Cynda backed into the corner across from Jasmine's bed. She opened her mouth, but she couldn't scream. She crouched on the floor, her arms wrapped around her legs, and kept her mouth open, waiting for her vocal cords to work.

"We found your truck, man," Darryl said when Keith picked up the phone. He gave Keith the address. "You might want to bring Cynda's lawyer with you."

Keith was tempted not to call Jim. He wanted to just go get his truck and let Cynda dig her way out of whatever she'd gotten into the best way she could. But no matter how much Keith lamented the fact, that woman was still his wife.

When Jim picked him up, Keith couldn't look him in the eye. He'd endured a lifetime's worth of humiliation and didn't have strength for another blow. He'd asked for Paradise, but God had given him swampland. He was tired of trying to swim through the muck and mire.

Jim opened his car door and stepped out. "Are you coming in?"

"No. Just ask Darryl to bring my keys so I can go back home." Keith watched a police car pull up next to the ambulance, as if the three police cars already there weren't enough. What had Cynda done now? Nope, he wouldn't go there. Wouldn't ask questions. This was no longer any of his business. She'd proved to him today that she wanted nothing to do with him.

Jim walked into the house as two medics came out carrying a body bag. "What? Do body bags follow this woman around?" Jim said under his breath.

Keith put his hand on the door as two more medics appeared with another body bag. Bile rose in his throat as he went back twenty years thinking about standing outside watching his mother's body being carried out of one of the rooms of a rundown motel. He remembered asking the paramedics, "What happened?"

"Another whore got her throat slashed," the pimple-faced medic told him, unaware that whore was Keith's mother.

"Lord, please tell me Cynda is not in one of those bags," he pleaded as he got out of the car and ran to the door. What was going on here? Why hadn't Darryl said more than, "Bring Cynda's lawyer with you." Had she killed someone and then died herself? His eyes were wild with questions. He ran straight into Darryl.

Darryl said, "I'm glad you got here as quick as you did. I think we're going to need your help."

Keith scanned the room. He saw food, cans, and bottles

strewn around the place, but no Cynda. The two medics he saw carrying the first body bag were now descending the stairs with a third. "Where is Cynda?" Keith demanded.

"Relax, man," Darryl said. "Cynda's not dead, but she's really out of it. We're going to need you to calm her down,"

"What do you mean? What happened?" Keith asked as Jim walked over to him.

Darryl shook his head as he surveyed the room. "When we got here, we found a body on the couch and one on the floor. They'd both been shot in the head. We found the third body upstairs, throat slit."

"Good Lord," Jim said.

Darryl grabbed Keith's arm and pulled him forward. "Come with me. Your wife is up there. She's been screaming her head off since we got here."

That's when Keith heard the guttural sound of a trapped animal.

"She's hoarse now. If she doesn't stop soon, she won't be able to speak for a month," Darryl said as they mounted the stairs.

When Keith, Jim, and Darryl stepped into the room, he first saw the blood-soaked sheets. He then turned and saw his wife crouch in the corner, screaming and clawing at two officers trying to get her out of that corner. She had this dazed, out-of-it look in her eyes, like she wasn't really sure where she was or what was going on.

"What happened to her?" Keith asked Darryl.

"I think she got the scare of her life when she found that woman." Darryl pointed to the bed.

Keith stepped forward. "Cynda."

She didn't respond.

He tried again. "Cynda."

She put her arms down, turned toward him. Slowly she stood, back against the wall. Her eyes came into focus. "Keith?"

"It's me, Cynda."

On wobbly legs, Cynda made her way to her husband. She clung to him and sobbed. "Help me, Keith. I don't want to die like that."

They stayed at Jasmine's house for several hours as the police questioned Cynda about the bodies found in the house. She answered their questions as best she could.

"If there's nothing else, my client needs to get some rest so she can recover from the shock of this incident."

The police let her go, with a not-so-polite reminder not to leave town anytime soon.

Keith put his jacket around Cynda and walked her to the car. She had this terror-stricken expression on her face as she sat next to him. He didn't know what to do for her, didn't know how to make it better.

"My mother died just like Jasmine. I was the one who found her body. She was naked and cut up." Cynda laughed. "No wonder I grew up so screwed-up in the head, right?"

Again, he didn't know what to say, but he felt like kicking himself. Here she was going through an ordeal like this and he was wondering how fast he could get the divorce papers. *How could I have given up on Cynda, like I did with my mother? Forgive me, Lord.*

"My grandmother had an open casket funeral anyway," Cynda continued.

"Your friend's face was slashed, right?"

"Yeah."

"Was your mom's?"

She nodded. "And her throat. The death of a whore."

He sidestepped that comment. "Why was the casket open, if your mother's face was slashed?"

Cynda closed her eyes to shut out the pain. "My grandmother wanted the world to see what that monster did to her baby, but I don't think she ever considered what it did to me."

"I'm sorry."

When they arrived home, Keith helped Cynda out of her clothes, put her in the shower, and gave her a clean nightgown to put on. He rocked her to sleep that night. And as she lay cradled in his arms, Keith thanked God for the woman he'd been given and asked the Lord to give him the strength to help her find her way home.

He had a lot of paperwork to catch up on, so he stayed home with her the next few days and worked in his office while she slept and cried. Cried and slept. In between, Keith fed and bathed her, just as he'd done the first time he'd brought her home. Only, this time it wasn't physical bruises that incapacitated her. The wounds she was dealing with cut way down to the soul.

Jasmine's funeral was the following Thursday. It was closed-casket. As Keith sat comforting Cynda, he said a silent thank you to his Lord that Cynda didn't have to view her friend's body.

When the service was over Darryl approached them as they were standing outside. The wind was blowing, causing Cynda's navy blue swing dress to swing up.

"Keith," he said with a nod. Then he turned to Cynda. "How are you doing?"

Holding her dress to her leg, she said, "I've been better."

"Well, at least you don't have to worry about the police interrogating you about your friend's death any more," Darryl told her.

Keith put a protective arm around Cynda. He asked Darryl, "You found the guy who did it?"

"We believe so." He turned his attention back to Cynda. "Do you know Jimmy Cooper?"

"Yeah, I know him."

"Evidently Jasmine and the white woman we found dead at the residence were running drugs for Mr. Cooper. Word is, they were helping themselves to an unearned commission."

Cynda's face was without expression. She didn't respond to any of it.

"What about the man?" Keith asked. "Why was he shot?"

"Wrong place, wrong time is my guess," Darryl told him.

"Thanks for letting us know," Keith said, shaking hands with Darryl. "I'll see you at church on Sunday."

They parted company, and Keith took Cynda home.

Shortly after they arrived home Keith found his wife sitting on the floor with her back against their bed.

He sat down next to her. "A penny for your thoughts."

She looked at him. There was still so much sadness in her eyes. "I just don't understand people sometimes. I mean, Jasmine and Cooper really enjoyed being around one another." Her brows furrowed. "And he kills her over a few dollars?"

Keith stretched out his leg, got comfortable on the floor. "If God isn't in the middle of the relationship, it's easy for evil to creep in."

Her eyes took on this look of wonderment. "I don't understand you either."

The pimples on her face were gone. Most of the dark splotches had disappeared also. He traced the lines of her face with his finger, taking in every perfect piece of her.

She let out a deep sigh. "How can you look at me like that?"

"Like what," he asked, removing a few strands of hair from her face.

"Like I'm beautiful . . . when God knows I've exposed you to so much of my ugliness?"

Running his fingers through her hair, he said, "I look at you through eyes of love, my dear. There is no flaw in love." With that, he kissed her.

She threw her arms around him and pulled him closer. He lifted her and laid her on their bed. Undressing her between kisses, he said, "I love you, Cynda Williams."

And as they joined together, she allowed him to love her. Allowed herself to imagine that what she and Keith were doing was different from what she'd done so many times before. This was special.

Wrapped in his arms later that night, she told him, "I wish I'd met you before Isaac. I wish you had loved me before so much of life happened to me."

"Why can't we start from here and forget about the past?"

His arms were around her, and she let her fingers trace the veins in his hand. "Even if I wanted to forget, there are too many people out there that won't let me."

He leaned over and kissed her on the forehead. "Just take baby steps. Forget who you used to be when you're with me."

She smiled at that thought.

The next morning she got out of bed and fixed Keith some bacon and eggs with toast and jelly, just as a normal wife would.

Putting eggs on his toast, he said, "I'm only going to work a half day today, so I'll see you at lunchtime."

She put her fork down and mumbled, "Mmmph," while rolling her eyes.

"What's that supposed to mean?" he asked, eyebrow arched.

"Don't trust me in your house alone, do you?"

He put his hand over hers, his eyes imploring her. "You don't have a past with me, Cynda. I was coming home to take you shopping for some more clothes and baby furniture."

"Oh"—She held up her hands in surrender—"I'll be dressed and ready to go when you get here."

He smiled at her. "See that you are, or I'm going to pick out your maternity clothes myself."

She walked him to the front door. "Oh no, you won't. I'm barely able to tolerate the other clothes you picked out for me."

"Hey, I'm a man. I figure, if it's clean and it fits, what's the big deal?"

"Exactly. That's why I'm going to be ready when you get here." She kissed him and shoved him out the door. When he was gone, she leaned against the door and reminded herself to forget.

27

At the mall, Cynda didn't find anything she wanted. The clothes were just too expensive for something she'd only wear four or five months. She told Keith about a second-time-around shop, which just happened to be in her old stomping grounds. At first, Keith objected to taking her to that area, but Cynda convinced him that this shop had the best prices.

She walked through the store picking up cotton stretchable shirts and pants with expandable waists, no zippers. Keith found a top that said, *Baby down here*, with an arrow directing the way to the baby. She smiled. "I like it."

They were headed to the checkout line when she noticed a woman standing outside panhandling. Cynda handed Keith the cart. "Can you take care of this? I see somebody I know."

"I'll meet you out there." Keith pushed the cart toward the checkout line.

Cynda stepped outside the store and called out, "Maggie?"

The woman looked to Cynda and grinned. "Hey, girl. When did you get out?"

Cynda wanted to cry for her. Her clothes didn't look as if they'd been washed since she left the rehab a month ago, and her face had the ashen look of a crackhead. "A week ago," Cynda answered.

"Girl, I am so glad to be out of that place. Them fools was strict."

Not strict enough, obviously. "I thought you were going to stay with your people in Cleveland when you got out?"

Maggie shrugged. "You know how it goes. They sent the money, and before I got on the bus, I decided to get one last high."

Keith walked out the door with Cynda's bags in hand.

She told Maggie, "Why don't you let me drop you back at the hospital?"

Maggie shook her head.

Cynda turned to Keith then back to Maggie. "Well, can we at least take you to dinner?"

She shook her head again. "You go on with your new life, Cynda. Don't waste your time on people like me."

They drove home in silence. Cynda leaned against the window, moving herself away from Keith. When they arrived home and were in their bedroom putting Cynda's new clothes away, Keith finally asked why her mood had changed.

"Don't you get it, Keith? Maggie told me to stay away from people like her, but I *am* people like her," she said with tears in her eyes. "So maybe you should stay away from me." She started throwing her new clothes across the room. "Maybe I will suck all the goodness out of you. Did you think about that?"

"What do I have to do to convince you that I don't care what you used to be? I love you, right here and right now. That's all that matters to me."

She threw her hands in the air. "Did you see Maggie, Keith? Did you see what I'm likely to be like in the next few weeks? Who are we kidding? You can't change a hooker into a housewife. Well, I'm living proof of that." She flopped down on the bed. "I just wish you'd stop trying."

"Never."

"Well, then you're crazy."

He walked over to her and put his hands on her shoulder. "Why don't you go see Iona? Don't you think that will make you feel better?"

She brushed his hands off her shoulder. "I don't want to mess Iona's life up anymore than I already have. I've decided not to interrupt her life unless I know for sure that I can stay clean."

"Suit yourself," he said as he turned and left the bedroom and went into the kitchen.

Cynda had taken some chicken wings out and left them to thaw in the sink while they were gone. He took the wings out of the pack and rinsed them. He pulled a skillet out of the cabinet.

She came into the kitchen. "What if you're wrong? What if I can't change?"

"Baby, with God, all things are possible."

"I'm not talking about God. I'm talking about trick-turning, crack-taking me." She jabbed herself in the chest. "Do you think I can change?"

Their gazes locked.

"Yes."

Eyes downcast, she said, "Do you remember what I said when you picked me up from Jasmine's?"

He put the skillet on the stove. "Yeah. You said you didn't want to die like that."

She looked up. She saw tenderness in his eyes. No one had ever looked at her the way Keith did. "I don't want to live the way Maggie does either. You've shown me a different way of life, and I want so desperately to be a part of it. But I keep thinking that I'm going to wake up tomorrow and you'll be gone and I'll be who I used to be."

"I'm right here, Cynda. I'm not going anywhere."

She gave him a half-smile, took the Crisco out of the cabinet, and poured it in the skillet. "Go pay some bills or send letters to late-paying clients. This is my job, remember?"

He walked toward his office. "Call me when dinner is ready."

Within an hour, they were seated across from one another enjoying broccoli, scalloped potatoes, and fried chicken.

Keith licked his lips. "These scallops taste too good to have come out of a box."

"They didn't," Cynda told him before biting into a chicken wing.

"How'd you get them done so fast?"

"I sliced and boiled the potatoes before we left this afternoon. I don't just sit in the house watching talk shows while you're gone, you know."

Keith put his hand over Cynda's. "I wasn't implying that you don't work around the house."

She snatched her hand. "Well, that's how you act sometimes."

There were days when Keith wasn't sure how he would find his wife when he arrived home from work. One day she would greet him with a smile, and hug and kiss him at the door. Another day, like today, he would come home to an eye-rolling, head-spinning Cynda.

"You think I'm your maid or something?"

"No," he answered as he shut the front door behind him.

Cynda threw a pile of clothes at him. "Then why'd you leave these on the bathroom floor?"

He picked up the clothes that fell around his feet. "I didn't know it was a big deal."

Hands on hips, neck jerking, she said, "Well, it is. I've got enough to do around here without having to pick your dirty underwear off the floor."

"I can get my stuff off the floor before I leave in the morning. No big deal." He walked by her, headed to their room, so he could change and pray for a peaceful evening. He knew that her mood swings came from trying to stay clean, so he tried not to get on her case too much about her rotten attitude.

Cynda followed him, head still spinning. "I suppose you think that because you've got the big important job and I'm stuck here all day with nothing to do but clean your house that you can treat me like some indigent worker?"

He threw his clothes in the laundry room and then turned to face his wife. "Can I take a shower and get out of these grungy work clothes? We can discuss your issues at dinner, all right?"

She put her hands up as her neck did the "sista-sista" jerk again. "Don't let me stop you. Go on. Take your shower. I'll be sitting in the kitchen when you're done just waiting to serve you, since I don't have a car and can't just come and go as I please like some people."

He didn't have the mind of a woman, and he certainly didn't understand the one in his house, so he retreated to his bathroom.

At dinner he said, "You know, I was thinking . . . the furniture and everything in this house was put here before we got married. You might not like the way I decorate, so why don't you fix the place the way you'd like to see it?"

She jumped in her seat. "You really mean it? You're not going to change your mind? I can fix this place the way I want it?"

He squeezed his eyes shut and rubbed his temple. "Yeah, do whatever you want to the place."

She jumped in his lap and kissed him. She got up and ran

into the living room. Inspecting it, she said, "Those played-out suede curtains have got to come down."

He soon followed her. "What's wrong with those curtains? One of the women from my church picked those out for me."

Cynda smirked. "Is that why you didn't marry her?"

He had the good sense to look away. "It wasn't like that. Janet was just being nice."

Her eyes flashed with a hint of jealousy. "Boy, please . . . ain't no woman hanging curtains in a house she don't want to live in." She gently touched his face. "That baby face of yours is just too gullible where that woman is concerned."

Guilt ate at him. "Sit down for a minute. I need to talk with you about something."

"Woo! This must be serious. I've never seen you look so somber."

They sat across from one another. "I want to tell you the truth about my relationship with Janet."

"Confession time, huh?" Her lip curved into a nasty snarl. "So all this time you've been trying to make me feel guilty about what I've done to you, and you've been carrying on with that woman?"

He put his hands up. "Will you allow me to speak?"

She waved her hand. "Go on, you've got the floor. Confess your sins."

He hesitated, then blurted, "Before I married you, I was interested in Janet. I thought that if she and I got to know each other, our relationship would develop beyond friendship."

"Mmm. I bet you wish you had gone on and married her now, don't you?"

He held up his hand again. "But when I married you, I knew that no other woman would be able to take your place. To put it in simple terms, Mrs. Williams, I fell in love with you, girl."

She smiled and nudged his shoulder. "You say that to all the girls."

"So are we okay? Do you trust me?"

"Yeah, I trust you, but that Janet is another story. I knew the day she came over here that she had it bad for you. She actually yelled at me and started crying. Told me I was no good for you."

Keith saw the look of sadness on Cynda's face and wanted to make her feel better. "Look, Cynda, I'm sorry about that. Janet was just looking out for me."

Cynda waved him off. "Don't worry about it. I'm just going to get on the bus and make some unannounced visits to your office."

They laughed.

She turned back to her new assignment. "And don't think this big old couch is staying in here."

He held up his hands. "Hold on now, I do have to make one stipulation. You have to come up with a budget and stick to it. And, to be truthful, I don't think our budget can handle a new couch right now."

She put her hands on her hips. "Don't you own that construction company?"

"Well, yeah. But, like I told you, the business is doing okay. That's it. One wrong move and we could lose this house."

"Okay, mister low money-bags, what can our budget afford?"

He smiled. "Slipcovers."

She cringed. "All right then. I'll look at some of the things I want and come up with a budget and present it to you. How's that?"

"Sounds good."

"I was watching HGTV last night. They did a living room remodel that was off the hook, but I can do better."

He smiled.

They talked some more about her ideas for the house, watched a movie, and then turned in for the night. They drifted into a world where nothing else mattered, except the way they felt in each other's arms. Contented with the comfort they found in one another, they lay together in silence. Cynda was against Keith's chest while he put his arms around the small bulge of her belly.

"Can I ask you something?" Cynda said, cutting through the silence.

He rubbed her stomach. "What is it?"

"This God of yours, He loves you, right?"

"Yes, He does."

She put her hand on his as he rubbed her belly. "Then why do you think He would make you marry a whore?"

Keith turned Cynda around and looked her in the eye. "I'm not perfect, Cynda. I've sold drugs, I even murdered a man before God saved me. Why do you think His love is big enough to cover my sins but not yours?"

Putting her hand on his cheek, she leaned up and kissed his chin, then his mouth. "I just don't understand your God, Keith. You've been good for so many years, and He punishes you by having you marry someone like me."

"I'm not so special, baby. God had a prophet in the Bible marry a prostitute."

"No way!"

"Yeah, He did. The act of marriage between the two was a symbol of God's great love for us. It showed how God continues to love us even though we stray away from Him."

She played with the hairs on his chest. "I bet this prostitute was so grateful she was saved from a life of sin that she did everything this prophet told her to. She bowed and scrapped at his feet, right?"

Keith frowned. "No, baby, she didn't. She ran away from him. He had to go find her and bring her home again."

"So he could beat the daylights out of her, I bet."

"The prophet loved his wife. He didn't want to harm her."

"Well, did she stay with him after he brought her back home?"

"No. She kept running back to her old life. She had children with other lovers, and Hosea took them in."

Cynda turned to the wall. "I don't understand this God of yours, Keith, and I don't like this story."

At four o'clock in the morning, Keith woke and reached for Cynda, but she wasn't in bed with him. Frantic, he jumped up. He was kicking himself for telling her the story of the prophet and the prostitute. He opened the door to the baby's room and found her seated in the rocking chair.

He took a seat on the floor next to the chair. "Couldn't sleep?"

"No."

"Is the mattress still too hard?"

"It wasn't the mattress, Keith. I was having another nightmare. I just needed to get out of the bed."

"You want to talk about it?"

She put her feet in the rocker and let it glide back and forth. "It's the same dream I always have. My mother's pimp is raping me, and I'm trying to tell him that I'm too little to take my mama's place, but he won't listen. The whiskey on his breath makes me want to vomit, but I'm too scared to do anything but lay there and let him take my innocence. I probably could have dealt with him taking my innocence. It's just sex, right? But why did he have to take my mother away from me?" Cynda's lip quivered as she looked at Keith. "You want to know something funny? I'm upset about him taking my mother away from me, and I hated that woman."

"Maybe *hate* is too strong of a word, huh?"

She shook her head. "No, I hate her. From the day I looked into her coffin and knew that she had allowed that monster to take something else from me, I've hated her."

Cynda said the words with such venom that Keith didn't know what, if anything, he could say in her mother's defense. "Where is this man now?"

"Dead," she told him without emotion. "Somebody stabbed him in the heart in prison."

"The dead can't hurt you, baby. It's time to move past that pain."

"They don't seem dead to me, Keith." She pointed at her heart. "In here they're still alive. Still got my heart so clenched with hate that I can't find room to love."

He understood where Cynda was coming from. His mother hadn't caused his heart to fill up with hate, but his inability to forgive himself for what happened to her had paralyzed him. Made him want to keep Cynda a prisoner in their home so she would be safe. "Can I tell you something?"

She leaned her head against the rocker. "Yeah. What?"

"My mother became a whore."

Cynda's lifted her head off the rocker and stared at Keith. "What did you say?"

He picked some lint off his pajama pants. "You heard me."

"Why didn't you tell me this before?"

"I didn't want to talk about her."

"And now you do?"

He put his hand on her leg. "She wasn't always a whore. She was a junkie first. Then I told her I wouldn't help her to get high any more. Told her I didn't want to see her until she got clean. So she started turning tricks to get what she needed. She died a week after I told her I wouldn't help her any more." He shook his head as tears swam around the base of his eyelids. "She was murdered by a john. And I have blamed myself for her death for twenty years now."

Cynda lifted Keith's head and wiped the tears from his eyes. "That's pointless, baby. You had nothing to do with her death. You can't blame yourself for what someone else did to your mother."

He nodded. "I'm starting to see it that way. But don't you think it's equally as pointless to blame *your* mother for what someone did to her? I mean, come on, Cynda, do you really think she wanted to be murdered?"

When she didn't respond, he stood up, reached out his hands and pulled her out of the rocker. "Come on, let's go back to bed."

She leaned against the wall in the baby's room and looked around. She turned out the light in the baby's room. "We had some lousy parents, didn't we?"

Nodding, Keith told her, "We don't have to be like them, Cynda."

"Do you really think it's possible for me to be a good mother?"

"All things are possible, babe. Believe in yourself."

The next day, Keith bought Cynda a used Honda Accord.

She ran out the house, cheesing from ear to ear. "You got this for me?"

"So you won't have to catch the bus to make those surprise visits to my office."

She squealed.

"Now it's not new, but I paid cash for it."

She took the keys from him. "I'll be back. I'm going to the grocery store."

Keith sat in the house nervously waiting for her to return, chiding himself for being the dumbest man on earth. Now she didn't have to steal his truck if she wanted to leave him. He'd provided her a getaway mobile. But he wouldn't have his wife feeling trapped. She needed to know that she was free with him.

Cynda arrived back home an hour later. "Traffic is awful around here. I don't know how you put up with it day after day," she said, entering the house with grocery bags in hand.

Keith grabbed the bags out of her hands and put the milk and cheese in the refrigerator. "You get used to it."

As he was putting a bag of rice in the cabinet, Cynda touched his arm and turned him around to face her. "Thank you."

In the following weeks they grew closer, began to understand each other a little better. They desired each other and wanted to be together. She even visited him at work, brought him lunch, and glared at Janet. When she wasn't glaring at his receptionist, Keith began to wonder if he was seeing sparks of love in his wife's eyes.

One night they were discussing the baby and making plans for future vacations when Cynda said, "I want to see Iona. Can you take me to her, please?"

28

The revival, the event that Isaac had been planning for the last five months, was upon them. Nina sat the children down in her home office and encouraged them to be on their best behavior during the revival that evening.

Donavan pointed at his little sister. "I don't know about Iona, but I know how to act."

Iona got in Donavan's face with a sista-sista roll of the neck. "And I don't know about Donavan, but I know how to act better than he does." She stuck out her tongue, and he pushed her.

"Donavan, stop it right now," Nina said. "This is the type of stuff I'm talking about. Can the two of you sit by each other without it coming to blows?"

"No," they answered in unison.

Nina lifted her face to Heaven then looked back at her wayward children. "That's just fine. You're not going to be allowed to sit together during this revival. You'll sit on opposite sides of me."

"Can we go now?" Donavan asked.

"Yeah, go on. I've got a lot of work to do before we leave the house," Nina said.

Iona and Donavan ran out of Nina's office, but then Nina remembered something and called Donavan back to the room.

He walked back in. "Yes, ma'am?"

"Sit down for a minute, Donavan, I want to speak with you about something."

Sitting down, he raised his hands in the air. "I didn't do it. Swear I didn't."

"No one's accusing you of anything, but now you've got me wondering."

He grinned at her. "What did you want to see me about?"

"I've been a little worried about you. You just haven't been acting yourself around me lately. Are you upset because Iona is here?" She'd been on a girl's day a few more times with Iona since the first day they'd spent together, Donavan only tagging along once.

"No way. I prayed that another kid would come live with us. You need her."

Nina closed her eyes. Why hadn't she seen this coming? It was back to this, Donavan blaming himself for her inability to have more children. Calmly, she told him, "I'm glad Iona is here too, but you do know that I would've been okay if I'd only had you to pal around with, right?"

"Yeah, Mom. I just think it's great that you don't have to wonder what the house would be like with more than one kid in it."

"Is that why you keep hitting on Iona, because you're so glad she's here?"

He hung his curly head low. "I don't know. She bugs me sometimes."

"Why? What's going on?"

Fire shot through his eyes. "I don't like the way she talks to you, okay."

She hugged her son. "I don't like the way she acts sometimes either, baby, but you know what . . ."

He pulled away, wiping his eyes as they began to water.
"What?"

"My mother gave me away when I was a small child, and
I never knew who my father was."

"I know. You told me."

"Well, let's just say, I'm familiar with a bit of the pain
Iona is dealing with. And if God had not given me two loving foster parents, who knows where I'd be today?" She
scruffed up his hair. "So can you help me love Iona through
this?"

"I'll try, but I can't promise not to get mad if she keeps
flapping that smart mouth."

"Just try to control yourself, okay."

He nodded.

"And you do know that your father and I don't love you
any less since Iona came, right?"

Donavan shrugged.

The doorbell rang, and Iona ran to it screaming, "I'll get
it!"

Nina got up. "How many times have I told that girl about
opening the door for strangers?"

As Nina and Donavan walked toward the front door, they
saw a woman bend down, and Iona ran into her arms.
When Keith stepped in, Nina knew exactly who Iona was
hugging. Cynda Stephens, her nemesis. A woman who
hated her and wanted nothing more than to pull her and
Isaac apart. And had almost succeeded.

"Hey, baby, your mama's been missing you," Cynda said
to Iona.

"I missed you too," Iona said. "Are you going to stay here
with us?"

Keith stepped to Nina, and they embraced. He told her,

"I called Isaac. Told him we were coming to town for the revival."

"I'm glad you could come. Where will you be staying this weekend?"

"We've got a room at the Doubletree," Keith answered.

Cynda stood up, and Nina's gaze fell to her stomach. She wanted to scream and ask the Lord if this was some cruel joke. How could He allow a woman who couldn't even take care of the child she had to conceive another? *Please remember me, Lord.*

Cynda patted her belly. "The baby's due in August."

Iona put her hands on her mother's stomach. "No way."

Smiling, Cynda said, "It's true, honey. You're getting ready to have a brother or sister."

"Will the baby be Donavan's brother or sister too?" Iona asked.

The room grew silent.

Then Nina said, "I really wish you had called me instead of Isaac, Keith. We were getting ready for the revival. We've really got a lot to do before heading out, so—"

"Here's the thing, Nina," Keith said. "We were kind of hoping that you'd let us take Iona for a couple of hours, and then we would bring her to the tent revival with us."

"I don't know, Keith," Nina said, thinking Isaac would be ticked.

Iona glared at Nina. "You can't stop me from seeing my mother."

Was she going to say, "No, Iona, you can't spend time with your *real* mother?" Nina wasn't the vindictive type. Never had been. She stepped back. "Go ahead, Iona. Enjoy yourself."

Keith said, "Nina, if you already had something planned, we can wait until tomorrow."

Hands on hips, Cynda asked, "Why we gotta wait?"

When Keith opened his mouth to respond to Cynda. Nina held up a hand and said, "That's all right. Go ahead and take Iona. Just bring her to the revival."

Nina and Donavan arrived at the revival meeting an hour before service was to begin. They walked the expanse of the tent and prayed over each seat. Since God was going to show up and show off in this place tonight, Nina didn't want Him to miss one person in need of healing or deliverance. "Pour out Your anointing," she prayed. "Give these people the power to live this thing the way You desire for us to live it. Open their eyes, Lord. May they begin to see it how You see it. No more living by our own rules, in Jesus's unmatched name I pray."

Isaac was behind the pulpit on his knees, calling out to God. When he finished, he, Nina, and Donavan linked arms and prayed once again. They sat down and waited for the volunteers and his street congregation to arrive.

Nina waved at a few of the volunteers as they arrived and began setting the food up on the long tables provided for social hour before Isaac would preach that night.

"Why'd you let Iona leave with Cynda?" Isaac finally asked.

"I can't very well stop Iona's mother from seeing her own child, now can I?"

"The courts stopped her. Why do we have to allow her to contaminate our daughter, when no judge in his right mind would give her that right ever again?"

Donavan stood. "I'm going to help them bring in the rest of the sandwiches."

"Go 'head, baby. I'll come help in a minute." Nina then turned back to her husband. "They should be here with Iona in a little while. They wanted to attend this revival to support you. Will you allow them to do that, honey, please?"

Nina got up without waiting for a response. She gave the ushers and greeters instructions for the evening.

The volunteers were out in the neighborhood passing out more flyers, letting the people know that Pastor Isaac Walker would be speaking tonight and that free food and games would be offered each night of the revival. Neighborhood crack-heads, drug dealers, and hard-working residents began to show up to eat, laugh, and enjoy themselves with other neigh-bors.

Nina was reviewing last-minute serving instructions with the food service volunteers when Keith, Cynda and Iona showed up. She watched as Isaac walked over to his friend, his enemy, and his child, and prayed that her husband wasn't about to act a fool.

Isaac told Iona to go help Nina then turned back to Keith and Cynda. "Don't take my child out of my house without my permission again."

Cynda put her hands on her hips. "I don't need your per-mission to see my own child."

"The courts would disagree with your negligent, unfit self," Isaac said, not caring about the people starting to gather around to listen to their conversation.

"Be reasonable, Isaac," Keith said. "Cynda is not the same person she used to be. Everyone deserves a second chance."

"How many chances are you going to give her? What does this woman have to do before you give up?"

"How dare you judge me. What you need to do is turn that signifying finger of yours on yourself," Cynda said.

He moved closer to her and put his finger in her face. "Judge you?" Isaac laughed cruelly. "I don't even think about you. And I'll tell you another thing—My daughter is just fine without you. She doesn't need your kind of drama."

"*Your* daughter? *Your* daughter?" Cynda screamed, arms flailing.

People around them whispered, laughed, and pointed.

"You never knew her. That's *my* daughter."

"Why didn't I know her, Cynda? Because you never opened your trashy mouth to tell me about her."

Keith tried to pull Cynda away. "Let's go, Cynda. We don't need this."

She shoved Keith. "I'm not finished talking to the great Isaac Walker." Then she turned back to face Isaac. "I didn't tell you about Iona because you sold me to Spoony."

Isaac glared at her, lip curled.

"Remember that? How much was I worth back then, Isaac?"

Arms folded, lip twisted, Isaac said nothing.

"Fifty cents is what I went for, right?" She was in his face, fire in her eyes. "And you have the nerve to judge me for being a prostitute when you're the one who made me one."

"You can't blame me for what you did to yourself."

"I had help, you hypocrite!" Her lips tightened.

"If you even think about spitting on me, I will knock you across this room."

She'd spat on him before, and he'd just let it go. Back then she was just an embittered ex-girlfriend. Today, he knew her to be the betrayer who snitched on him and kept his child a secret for ten years. If even a drop of spit left her mouth while she spoke, he'd knock her out, and repent later.

Iona pushed her way through the crowd and yelled at Isaac, "Don't hit my mom, Daddy."

Keith moved Cynda out of the way. He and his old friend stood glaring at each other.

Isaac said, "What?"

"That's my wife, man," Keith said.

"Well, your wife looks like she's pregnant again. Who's the daddy this time?"

Eyes downcast, Keith said, "We don't know."

Cynda marched away from the scene, huffing and cursing.

Nina told Donavan to grab Iona and take her into the tent area. She then walked over to the two men and told Keith, "You need to go check on your wife."

"He better rush," Isaac said. "There's a lot of men out here with money to burn."

"Isaac, that wasn't called for," Nina said.

Keith clenched his fists and hit Isaac in the mouth.

Isaac stepped back and put the back of his hand to his mouth and wiped the blood from his lip. "You puffed up, huh? Ready to get knocked out?"

Keith's fist remained clenched, his legs spread apart, ready to spring. Isaac's fist tightened.

Nina grabbed Isaac's arm. "Don't do this, I'm begging you."

Isaac stepped to his old friend, ready for a brawl.

Nina stepped between them. "Don't do this."

Isaac stopped. "I'm cool, Nina." He unclenched his fist and smiled at Keith. "Hey, after all these years of friendship, if you can't get one punch off, then we've never really been friends, right?"

Keith wasn't smiling. "You're a hypocrite, Isaac, just like Cynda said, and I don't want anything else to do with you." He turned and walked away as Isaac tried to call him back.

Even with all that had happened, Isaac still felt that he should preach the word that night. Before the event, he labored over the message that he would deliver to these people who'd lived without God as he once did. God had given him a message of love. He would tell the people about God's compassion and His long suffering.

But Isaac could not get past the ungodly anger he felt towards Cynda. He needed to convince himself that his feelings were justified.

When he opened his mouth, the message of love he'd

prepared got lost in legalism and rules. Isaac preached about the woman at the well, but he didn't preach about God's compassion for her. The way Isaac explained the scene at the well was that Jesus told the woman how treacherous she was and how many men she'd had, and instead of the woman repenting for her sins, she brought others to hear what the Lord had to say, as if He were some sort of traveling road show.

"That's why," Isaac continued, "the Bible admonishes us not to be unequally yoked together with unbelievers. But you can't tell some Christians nothing. They want to make their own rules." He stumbled around scriptures such as, "don't cast your pearls before swine," and he told them, "God is not mocked. What a man sows he shall reap."

Needless to say, by the time he closed his message and made an altar call, his congregation was too confused to know whether or not they wanted the God Isaac had offered them, so they stayed in their seats.

29

Keith broke the speed limit, barreling down I-70, trying to put as much space between him and Isaac as possible.

Cynda was captivated and bewildered all at the same time. "Why do you love me?"

"Huh?"

She turned sideways in her seat to face him. "Look, Keith, you just threw away a twenty-five-year-old friendship with someone that I know you would have died for. If that doesn't convince me that you love me, nothing will. But I just don't understand why."

Taking her hand in his and squeezing it, he said, "I love you because of your sweet disposition."

Cynda shoved him. "I'm serious, Keith. Why do you love me?"

He let go of her hand and put a Smokie Norful CD in the player. "You're my wife. Who am I supposed to love, if not you?"

She turned away from him, eyes downcast. "But I'm all

wrong for you. I don't know how to give or receive your love."

His thumb gently stroked her hand. "Why don't you rest your mind and let your heart take over?"

"Because I don't want to love you," she said, tears welling up in her eyes. The man was insufferable sometimes, the way he held onto things. "Isaac is right, Keith. If you stay with me, I'll just ruin your life." She turned back toward him. "What about the women at your church? Before you decided to marry me, you were interested in Janet, right?"

He laughed. "I plead the fifth."

"I'm serious. She would jump at the chance to be with you. I saw it in her eyes that day she came to the house."

"Janet is not the woman for me. You are, and I'm okay with that. More than okay."

She shook her head. "This thing between us isn't going to work. You're a good man. But a few months with me and I've got you ready to fight your best friend and throwing away a chance to work in the ministry you told me you wanted to be a part of."

"There are other street ministries that I can work in."

"But you wanted to work with Isaac."

He held up his hand. "End of discussion. I won't work with a man who doesn't respect my wife."

"I don't need you to defend my honor. You're not my protector, Keith."

Keith shushed her as the wondrous sound of Smokie Norful's "In the Middle" filled the car. *When you were in need I provided, when you couldn't see I led the way.*

Keith brought her hand to his mouth and kissed it. "I might not be your protector, baby, but God is, and He provided me for you."

I was there in the middle of your pain, I was there when they tried to take your hope away.

Fuming, Cynda ejected the CD. "*You*'ve been here for me, Keith. You, not God."

Keith shook his head. "I'm no substitute for God, baby."

Her head started bobbing. "If God has been with me through all of the things I've been through, then I'd hate to see how my life would have been if He wasn't here."

He put her hand in his. "Sometimes God has to allow us to go through the storm so that we can appreciate the blessings on the other side."

She turned and glared out the window, still holding onto Keith's hand. She could barely see where they were going, as darkness had settled in and the rain beat against her window. *They should put more lights on highways.* Or maybe she needed more light in her. Needed to see her way through.

When they reached the house Cynda pulled Keith into the bedroom.

"What you got on your mind, woman?"

She closed the door and sat him down on the edge of the bed. Bending down, she kissed him. Then she began unbuttoning his shirt.

"What's gotten into you?"

"I'm doing what you said. I'm loving you. Now just sit back and receive it."

This wasn't the kind of love he was referring to, but he wasn't about to turn it down. Smiling, Keith helped his wife undress.

They mingled together as God intended, and as they were swept into a vortex of passion, Keith blurted out, "I love you. Oh God, I love you, girl."

He saw her tears, then heard the pain in her voice as she declared, "You're the best thing that's ever happened to me."

Those words should have brought him great joy, but they weren't the ones he longed to hear. The words that he knew were locked in her heart. The pain he heard in her voice let him know that she was pulling away from him again. *Help me, Lord. I can't survive without her.*

Pastor Paul O. Mitchell was scheduled to preach the second night of the revival. The news of the fights that broke out after Isaac preached the night before spread across the city. Isaac prayed that Pastor Paul would not back out. Tonight dignitaries and pastors from all over the city lined the front row of the pews and the pulpit area. The individuals this revival was meant to reach were able to sit anywhere they wanted, just as long as they didn't come near those reserved VIP seats.

When Pastor Paul arrived during praise and worship, Isaac let out a sigh of relief.

Once Pastor Paul was introduced, he opened his Bible and preached out of Matthew 7:15-27. His text also came out of Mark 7:1-15. Finally he read Matthew 12:33: "Make a tree good and its fruit will be good, or make a tree bad and its fruit will be bad, for a tree is known by its fruit. In other words, either get all the way in, or get out. Either be hot or cold. But don't play games. Religious people are lukewarm. That's why Jesus called the Pharisees hypocrites."

Isaac squirmed in his seat. He remembered Keith calling him a hypocrite yesterday.

"See," Pastor Paul continued, "when you really get a word from God, it will deal with your devils. And the real devil we have to fight today is that demon of religion where people think they can go to church two days a week, but still treat others any kind of way. That's why I came tonight. The Lord told me to talk to the people who don't understand why their actions of wrongdoing still exist even though they faithfully attend church." He pointedly scanned the room. "My brothers and sisters, going to church won't save you. It is the Word of God that will deliver you . . . because the Word goes where the defilement is.

"I don't know about you, but I'm tired of seeing the so-called saints of God speak in tongues, dance, and shout, and then curse their brother or sister out. Always judging people for not being the way you think they should be."

Isaac squirmed in his seat a little more. He looked over at some of the other pastors and saw that they had a little squirm going on also.

Strangely though, the congregation seemed to cheer on Pastor Paul, screaming, "Preach."

"You know you're telling the truth."

Looking directly at the pastors, Pastor Paul said, "You don't have to amen me, but I tell you this. God is so tired of what he sees in the church that he's about to go and pull his generals out of crackhouses. He's about to set some prostitutes free."

God had pulled Isaac out of a prison cell and anointed him to preach, so he was familiar with God using the uncommon. He looked to Heaven. *Have I misjudged this thing, Lord? Is Cynda—*

Before Isaac could finish his silent communication with the Lord, Pastor Paul's powerful voice boomed, "There is only one judge who is able to save and destroy. Who are you that judges another? If you truly understood the revelation of love, you wouldn't judge each other. You'd be there to help pull a fallen soldier up. James 1:26 says, 'If any man seems to be religious and does not bridle his tongue, but deceives his own heart, this man's religion is vain.' In other words, this man is a hypocrite."

As Pastor Paul closed down his message and made an altar call, the aisle became flooded. Isaac's altar call the night before had been empty, but tonight so many of the people he'd prayed for came forth. Even Charlie Dupree stood at the altar, tears staining his face.

Isaac felt compelled to step down from the pulpit area and bow down at the altar and ask God for forgiveness. Here he was a man of God, with a hard head and a hard heart. He couldn't let go of his pride. He couldn't let everyone know that he was in need of prayer himself. After all, this was *his* revival.

When service was over, he shook Pastor Paul's hand and thanked him for delivering the word. Then he went home and lay on his bedroom floor and wept.

Nina bowed down on the opposite side of the bedroom and prayed.

Isaac crawled over to her and buried his head at the base of her neck. He clung to her. "That was God speaking tonight, Nina. And it was loud and clear. I'm a hypocrite."

She gently stroked his back. "Cynda is a prostitute. All she's doing is messing Keith's life up. He could've had a peaceful life with Janet, but what does he do? He marries a whore." She rubbed her husband's wavy hair. "Baby, what do you think of Ebony?"

He lifted his head. "I see where you're going, and you can stop right there. Ebony is nothing like Cynda."

"She was on drugs, right?"

"Yeah."

"And she was prostituting herself to get those drugs."

He held up a hand. "But Ebony is just a kid. She got caught up in a world that took advantage of her."

"So did Cynda, baby. They are no different. I wanted to stay angry with Cynda myself, but she deserves the same mercy and forgiveness that we prayed God would give Ebony."

He plopped his head back into her lap. "I don't want to forgive her, Nina. She had me arrested. She kept my child from me."

She gently stroked his back. "You have to let it go, baby. You didn't do right by her either."

He lifted his head and looked Nina in the eye. "You don't

believe that mess about me selling her into prostitution, do you?"

"Back then, you were capable of anything. Ask God to let you see it the way she sees it."

His head flopped back down. "That's just it. I don't feel like God wants to hear from me any more."

"Isaac, have you forgotten who God is?"

He shook his head.

"Then don't you think God knew you would be at this crossroad when he called you to preach, just as He knew that Peter would deny Jesus? But He also knew that when Peter was restored back to God, he would lead a revival that would shake a nation. Keep the faith, baby."

30

At three in the morning, Cynda eased out of bed. She quietly opened and closed drawers, pulling out clothes and stuffing them in her bag. When she was finished, she tiptoed back over to the bed. Sniffling, she leaned over and planted a kiss on Keith's mouth. She whispered, "I love you, baby."

He reached for her. "What are you doing out of bed?"

"I'm just straightening up a few things. I'll be back to bed in a minute." She opened the bedroom door and walked out.

Once out of the house, she let the tears flow freely. Looking back on the house where she'd finally learned to love, she ached from wanting to die, or at least turn into a pillar of salt, before she could go one more painful step. But it didn't happen. She was forced to endure this pain as she'd endured all the rest of the hurt that had come her way.

For one brief moment she was tempted to take her car, but the smiling face Keith wore when he gave her the keys to the car flashed before her face. She heard adoration in his voice as he declared his love. She was taking his heart with her; she wouldn't take anything else from him. She opened the driver's side door and placed her keys on the seat. Keith had shown her a better way. Never had she felt dirty when they were together. She felt right and loved. And although she couldn't stay with him, she would forever cherish what he did for her.

She still had a couple hundred dollars of the money he had given her for shopping, so she took a cab to a small town on the outskirts of Chicago and rented a twenty-nine-dollar room.

Bright and early the next morning, Cynda got out of bed, showered, and set out to find a job. She'd never get a permanent position while she was pregnant, so she walked into the first temporary agency she could find.

"Hello, my name is Cynda Williams." She said the last name with pride. "I'm looking for a temporary assignment."

The receptionist handed her a clipboard with an application on it. "Fill this out and bring it back up when you're done."

Sitting down to fill out the application, Cynda got nervous. How could she explain that she hadn't held down a real job in ten years? Would they know what she'd been doing during that time? She wrote in her high school graduation information and her last job, from which she'd been fired for coming on to her boss.

She smiled sweetly at the receptionist as she read the nametag on her desk. "Where would you like me to put this application, Ms. Hodges?"

"I'll take it."

Cynda stood in front of the desk and watched the woman eye her application.

Ms. Hodges looked at her. "You haven't held a job in ten years?"

Cynda rubbed her belly. "Of course, I've worked. I've been a stay-at-home mom."

"Oh," she said. "Are you sure you want to go back to work with another one on the way?"

"My husband left me." She shrugged. "I don't have a choice." She hated lying on Keith like that. He wouldn't have left her in a million years, no matter what she'd done to him.

"Don't worry yourself. You're probably better off without him." The woman leaned closer to Cynda. "Mine left me after I had three kids for him. But I got the last laugh. The woman he left me for, her husband shot him."

Cynda laughed. "Nothing like that would ever happen to my husband." *He wouldn't leave me for another woman, not even if I gained two hundred pounds after having twenty kids for him.*

"I bet he's too cheap to pay child support, huh?"

Cynda couldn't defame Keith any more than she already did. "He actually wants to care for the children. He just doesn't need me around him, that's all."

"Mmm . . . just like a man." She put a piece of chewing gum in her mouth. "Look, we don't have any assignments right now, but we probably can get you in something within a week or two."

A week she could do, but any more than that and she was afraid of what might happen. She smiled. "Thanks, I'll check back with you next week." She left the agency and put in an application at the grocery store down the street. The coffee shop had a help wanted sign in the window, so Cynda trotted over and asked the manager for the application.

He wiped his hands on his dirty apron and pointed at her belly. "I don't hire pregnant women. The bigger you get, the slower you'll be."

"I have a right to work whether I'm pregnant or not! I could sue you for making a comment like that."

He laughed. "Go ahead, lady. All you'll get is the coffee shop and all my debt. Please, take me out of my misery."

A lecherous old man at one of the counter seats said, "As pretty as you are, I can put you to work. It won't take you but fifteen minutes to earn a day's pay with me."

Laughter filled the little coffee shop as she walked out, cursing their ignorance.

The baby was getting hungry, so she grabbed a couple of sandwiches from McDonald's and went back to her hotel room. She was tempted to call Keith but didn't have any good news to give him. She curled up on her bed and cried herself to sleep.

In the morning Cynda forced herself out of bed and back into her job search. Determined not to let Keith down by going back to her old ways, she stopped at five places before the baby demanded food again. She stepped into a little café and ordered a turkey club sandwich. The bread was soggy and the bacon half-cooked. Even the baby didn't want this sloppy mess.

She marched to the counter and demanded to speak with the manager. When he stood before her she blurted, "This is the worst sandwich I've ever had. What's wrong with your cook?"

He frowned. "He's my wife's cousin. I can't do a thing about it."

She pushed the plate toward him. "Well, I'm not paying for it."

"That's fine. Just leave your plate right here."

She turned to leave, but then a thought occurred to her. "Hey," she called after the manager as he was walking away, "I'm looking for a job. I can teach your cousin how to cook."

The manager's blue eyes brightened. Then the light went out, and his shoulders slumped. "No, it'll never work. You're much too pretty. My wife would skin me alive if I hired you."

She was sure that comment was worth some money in

court. Where was she, Hicktown, USA? Had these people never heard of employment laws and the things you just couldn't say to potential employees? Forget it. She didn't have the strength to exert her rights. Shaking her head, she put her purse around her shoulder and walked out of the café.

She was hungry. She had just a little over a hundred bucks to her name and still needed to pay the hotel fee for the following day and the rest of the week. She sat down on the bench outside of the café and wondered if she was meant to hold down a regular job. Maybe she was out of her element and just needed to go right back into town and pick a corner and start hustling.

The thought of that made her want to cry. With Keith, the act felt special and right, but if any other man should touch her, she would feel dirty and unclean again. Droplets of tears formed in her eyes.

A slender white man in a navy blue business suit approached her. "Excuse me, Miss, but can I discuss a proposition with you?"

Cynda looked down to check out her attire. She had on a pair of maternity jeans and button-down long-sleeved blouse. Only the top button was undone. She didn't have on anything revealing. Nothing that screamed, "I'm a whore, so show me the money."

"I beg your pardon?" she said in her most indignant voice.

"I'm sorry, I didn't mean to offend you. This might not be anything you're interested in anyway. But since I heard you tell that manager you could cook, I figured I'd at least ask." He held out his hand. "My name is Harlan Dobbs, and I am looking for someone to take care of my mother."

Was this man some sort of sicko? Was *mother* code for something else that he wanted her to take care of?

He took out a business card and handed it to her. "I'm an

attorney. I spend a lot of time at my practice, so I can't give my mother the kind of care she needs right now."

"How old is your mother?" Cynda asked cautiously.

He smiled. "She's ninety-two, but she doesn't look a day over ninety."

31

Ms. Geraldine Dobbs was a slender, blue-eyed, mild-tempered woman for whom Cynda enjoyed working and spending time. The youthful pictures that lined the walls of the home and sat on end tables declared the beauty this woman possessed before time won the battle and wrinkles creased her face.

Cynda enjoyed her job to the fullest. Well, actually, she did have one problem with her duties. She didn't have a problem emptying the bedpan. (Ms. Dobbs was sometimes too tired to get out of bed to take care of her business.) It wasn't the breakfast, lunch, and dinner that had to be cooked, or the cleaning between meals. Her only problem with this job was that Ms. Dobbs' eyesight wasn't as good as it used to be, which didn't stop her from spending the first hour of each morning with the Lord. So Cynda had to wake up each morning and read Ms. Dobbs's Bible out loud so that she could still get in her daily word.

As she closed the Bible for the third morning in a row, Cynda wondered what in the world was wrong with people like Ms. Dobbs and Keith. Why did they waste time on empty words and promises? Did they truly believe that the Lord was their shepherd? Or that when enemies come against them, God would protect them?

She put the Bible on the nightstand next to Ms. Dobbs's bed, right where Keith kept his, and stood, shaking her head.

"What's wrong, beautiful one?" Ms. Dobbs asked.

Since the day Cynda walked into the Dobbs's home, she took one look at her and refused to call her anything but *beautiful one*. Cynda didn't want to lose this job, so there was no way she was going to tell Ms. Dobbs her thoughts on the Bible, God, and all that other religious mess.

"I'm fine. Nothing's wrong."

Ms. Dobbs reached out to Cynda. "Come here."

Cynda moved closer to the bed and took her hand.

Ms. Dobbs patted Cynda's hand. "You don't believe in God, do you?"

What was up with this town and the violation of her employment rights? "I didn't know that was a requirement for accepting this job. If I—"

Ms. Dobbs lifted her green-veined hand and waved away her concerns. "I wouldn't have turned you away, beautiful one. I just can tell you've been hurt, and it seems as if you're taking it out on God." She glanced at Cynda's protruding stomach. "Was it your husband? Did he hurt you so bad that it's caused you to be angry with God?"

No. She wanted to scream, "It was my mother, her pimp, my pimp, and all those other men that didn't see any value in me."

"Keith was good to me. He would've never hurt me. I left him, because I was tired of seeing him hurt."

"He's probably hurting like crazy right now."

Cynda frowned. "Why would you say that?"

"If the man loves you, he probably hasn't slept for worrying since you ran away with his baby in your belly."

Cynda let go of the woman's hands and stepped back. "It's not his baby. I don't know whose baby I'm carrying."

Ms. Dobbs' eyes widened. "Well, call him anyway. Go ahead, I give you permission to use my telephone. Just don't call any nine hundred numbers."

Cynda walked out of the room laughing. But then she wondered if Ms. Dobbs was right about Keith not being able to sleep, or about him worrying about her and the baby. Knowing Keith, he was worrying. She couldn't allow that. Couldn't let him waste time thinking about her. She wanted his mind and heart free, so he could concentrate on finding a good wife, someone who would be good to him and attend church with him.

She sat down on the couch in the living room and picked up the phone. Keith answered after the first ring.

"Hi, it's me," Cynda said into the phone.

"Where are you? Baby, I've been so worried. I've searched everywhere."

Closing her eyes, she tightened her grip on the phone. She didn't know that hearing his voice would be like the taste of fresh-squeezed lemonade on a hot summer day. "That's why I called. I don't want you to worry about me. I'm fine."

"Where are you, Cynda? I'll come get you right now."

A tear rolled down her cheek. She knew he'd say that. "I don't want you to come get me. I just wanted you to know that I found a job. I'm getting paid to take care of this really nice lady, so you don't have to worry that I've gone back to my old ways." She wouldn't tell him that she came close to considering it. If Mr. Dobbs hadn't showed up when he did, who knows what she'd be doing right now.

"I want you to come home, baby."

She took a deep breath. "I also wanted to tell you that I'll be filing for divorce," she said, her voice breaking, "as soon as I earn enough money."

"Why do you love me?"

She took the phone away from her ear, stared at it, and then put the phone against her ear again. "I just told you I want a divorce. Does that sound like love?"

"I know you love me, Cynda. You kissed my lips and told me before you left. Did you think I'd forget something like that?"

She had hoped he'd slept through her declaration of love.

"So answer my question—Why do you love me?"

Her lower lip quivered. "Let me go, Keith. Find someone who is worthy of your love. Someone who deserves it."

"There will never be anyone for me but you. So if you don't come back, I'll be alone for the rest of my life. Is that what you want for me, Cynda?"

No. She wanted love, laughter, and happiness for him. She wanted to pull the moon down from its reserved spot in the heavens and gift it to him. She would give him anything but the lifetime of pain and misery being with her would bring. "You're too stubborn for your own good, Keith."

"I love you, baby. Come home."

Tears ran down her flawless face. She swallowed the lump in her throat. "Find someone else, Keith. I'm not coming back."

She hung up, confident that she'd done the right thing, but by the next morning, her pillow was drenched from the river of tears she'd shed.

It took Isaac a week and a half to disconnect from his pride and call Keith and Cynda to apologize. When Keith told him that Cynda was gone, Isaac felt worse than ever because he knew he was partly responsible for her departure from his life. Miserable, Isaac sat on the edge of his bed with his head in his hands when Nina walked in their room.

"Keith didn't want to talk to you?" Nina asked her husband.

Isaac pulled his wife onto his lap. "Now you know Keith.

He forgave me the moment I asked for it." He kissed Nina's forehead. "Why can't I be like that? What's wrong with your husband, and why haven't you fixed me yet?"

"Believe me, I keep praying," she joked.

He smiled then got serious. "I've messed things up bad this time, baby."

Nina put her finger under his chin and lifted his head. "What happened?"

Massaging his forehead, he told her, "Cynda left Keith. He has no idea where she is or what she's doing. Well, he thinks he knows what's she's doing, but that's it. He's hurting, Nina. I can hear it in his voice."

"Then why are you still sitting here?"

His brows furrowed in confusion.

"Your friend is hurting. If Kenneth had left Elizabeth and I knew she was in unbearable pain, I would be on the first plane out of here."

He lifted her off his lap and went to the closet to get his suitcase. "You're right. I should be with him."

"I'll let the kids know that Daddy won't be here to boss us around for a couple of days."

"Girl, you need to quit. Every time I'm gone y'all leave faceprints on the window looking for big papa."

32

"You need to eat," Janet told Keith as she stood on his porch with a plastic food container in her hand.

He opened his screen door and let her in. She wore a lime green swing dress that seemed to welcome spring as it swayed in the wind, brushing against her voluptuous hips. He should have stopped her at the door. Should have admonished her for bringing food to a married man. He wasn't proud of himself as he opened the container and savored the smell of oregano mixed in the tomato sauce, and the ricotta cheese blended into her famous chicken lasagna. But truth be told, he hadn't eaten much of anything since he'd heard from Cynda, and he was all fasted out.

"Thank you, Janet. I was just getting ready to go pick up something to eat." He inhaled the food. "This is so good." Lines of laughter formed on his face. "Girl, if I wasn't already married . . ." He put his fork down. "I'm sorry. I shouldn't have said that to you."

She slammed her fist against the hardwood of his kitchen table. "Why do you torture yourself? Why won't you just divorce her? God knows you have more than ample reason."

"She's my wife, Janet."

"But you deserve so much more."

"I took vows with her, and beyond that, I love her." He saw the hurt in Janet's eyes as his words registered. He wished he didn't have to hurt this woman in order to love another.

"I don't understand you, Keith. How you continue to love a woman who doesn't love you back is beyond me." Her brown eyes were moist as she stood. "I'm putting in my two-week notice."

"I think that's best for you." He put his hand over hers. "I'm going to pray that God brings the man He has for you into your life real soon."

As Janet left, Keith prayed for her. After praying, his thoughts went to Cynda.

When Cynda called him she'd forgotten to block her number, so he had the telephone number of the house where she was staying. He knew she was in a little town on the outskirts of Chicago. He was tempted to go up there and knock on every door until he found her.

Several hours later, Isaac stood in Keith's kitchen, trying to talk some sense into him. "Look, man, why don't you just call Officer Darryl? I bet he would be willing to help out."

Keith lowered his head. "I can't."

"Why not? He's a brother in Christ, isn't he?"

"Yeah, but I kind of used up all my favors a few months ago."

Isaac cocked his head and stared at him.

"Cynda stole my truck when she came home from the rehab, and I called on Darryl to help me get it back."

"After all you did for her, she ran again? I don't understand you, man. Why do you even bother?"

"I should be able to talk to you about this stuff, but if I can't discuss things like this with you, just let me know."

Isaac held up his hand. "Point taken. I'm here for you. I'm focused."

Keith sat down at his kitchen table. "You want to go over there with me? She's in a little town in Chicago."

They plotted and planned their sneak attack for hours. Isaac said, "It's not going to work, man."

"What do you mean?" Keith asked. "All we have to do is find the house she's in and bring her back home."

"Hear me out. The problem isn't finding Cynda. I don't even think we'd have too much of a problem dragging her out of that house if it came to that. The problem you're going to have is keeping her here once you bring her back."

"She'll stay. She loves me."

Isaac held up a hand. "But she doesn't *want* to love you. Nor does she want you wasting your life loving her, right?"

"That'll change. I just need more time with her."

"No." Isaac stood up and put on his jacket.

"What do you mean, no?"

"You're not going after her. I'm going."

Keith laughed. "She hates your guts."

"And that's why I should be the one to talk to her. I'm one of the people who didn't think she should be with you, remember?"

"Exactly. So how will your going to find her make her want to rush home to me?"

"Do I have to spell everything out to you? You rode the short yellow bus to school, didn't you?" Isaac laughed and picked his keys up off the table. "She needs to know that this thing between you and her can work and that she's not ruining your life by being with you. Since I'm the one who told her she has no business being with you, I think I should be the one to turn this thing around."

Keith twisted his lips. "I don't know."

Isaac put his hand on Keith's shoulder. "You've been there for me every time I needed a friend. Let me do this for you."

33

"Thou hast been a strength to the poor, a strength to the needy in his distress, a refuge from the storm, a shadow from the heat, when the blast of the terrible one is as a storm against the wall." Cynda stopped reading and put the Bible in her lap.

Ms. Dobbs glanced at her. "Well, say what's on your mind, beautiful one."

"This verse reminds me of a song I heard once," Cynda said, recalling the song that Keith played as they drove home from Dayton. "Do you think that God is really right in the middle of our pain and our problems?"

"I most certainly do. He's always been right here with me."

"Then why won't He do anything to help us, I mean, if this God really does exist? And okay, maybe the idea of a God in Heaven doesn't seem so far-fetched to me any more. But why does He seem to favor some and spit on others?"

"That's not God spitting on you, beautiful one. Man does the spitting, God's the one that cleans us up. But come to think of it, God uses man to do the cleaning also. Like when somebody speaks a kind word to you, that's God's sprinkler system."

"Or when someone loves you for no reason, not even caring if you love them back. You think that's God's sprinkler system too?"

"Yes, I do," she said softly. Ms. Dobbs touched Cynda's hand. "You miss him, don't you?"

"To tell you the truth, I don't know how I keep breathing. I hurt from missing him that bad. Didn't know I had it in me to feel this way about a man."

"Why don't you go back home? Why do you put yourself through this?"

She would never tell this woman what she used to be. She couldn't take seeing the disappointment in her eyes. She'd done enough by admitting that the baby she was carrying didn't belong to her husband. But she did want to help this nice lady understand. "I'm not right for Keith, ma'am. He's good and godly, and I am as unholy as you can get.

"So I'm willing to hurt and miss him for the rest of my life, if that means he'll find someone special. That's what I'd like God to do for him."

Ms. Dobbs stretched her hands out to Cynda. "So would you like to pray about it?"

Cynda started to decline, but this was for Keith. And she'd discovered that she was willing to do just about anything for the man that God sent to clean her up. "Yeah, let's pray for Keith. I'm all for that."

They clamped their hands together.

"Wait. How do we know that God will even hear my prayers?"

With a twinkle in her eyes, Ms. Dobbs smiled. "We don't, but I do know that He hears mine."

Isaac showed Cynda's picture door to door at coffee shops and the only barbershop in the small town. He went to the grocery store and on and on. Several of the town's people remembered Cynda.

"How could I forget a knockout like that?" one of the men he interviewed asked. But none knew where she was working. No one but the clerks at the grocery store had even seen her in the past week.

Isaac noticed a temp agency across the street from the grocery store. He couldn't remember if Cynda had ever done any clerical work, but he thought he'd give it a try anyway.

The lady at the temp agency asked, "Is her no-good husband looking for her?"

Isaac could only imagine the lies Cynda told these people. He was half-tempted to tell the woman the real deal.

"She tried to convince me that her husband was some kind of good guy. But what woman in her right mind would leave a good man with a kid on the way?" The woman sucked her teeth.

There it was. Cynda hadn't been down here bad-mouthing Keith to make herself look good. And here he was about to tell all of her business. Isaac looked to Heaven. *Lord, keep me near the cross.* He wanted to learn how to forgive so that a person's prior transgressions were completely washed away. He wanted to be able to see people as Jesus saw them. Completely washed in the blood. Would that ever happen for him?

His cell rang. The lovesick pup had called him three times in the last hour already, and he was tempted not to answer. But then again, he'd be climbing the walls if the shoe was on the other foot and Keith was out looking for Nina.

"What's up?"

"I've got an address for you," Keith said.

"How were you able to accomplish that?" Isaac asked, astonished.

"The favor of God, my friend." Keith laughed. "Actually, I googled it."

"You *what*?"

"I see you are as inept with computers as I am. I put the phone number through an Internet search and came up with the address." Keith gave the street address to Isaac along with driving directions.

That boy wanted his woman back, like right now.

When Isaac pulled up to the ranch-style house, he sat in his car contemplating his next move. Rubbing his thumb and index finger across his chin, he watched as Cynda opened the front door with broom in hand and began sweeping the porch and steps. Her long hair was pulled back in a pony-tail. Gone were the three- to four-inch signature heels. She had on a pair of simple black flat shoes. Isaac knew she was pregnant, but he still imagined her in something a bit flashier than black stretch pants and a big white T-shirt. This was not the Cynda he'd grown to know and hate. But maybe this was God's way of showing him something new?

See her differently, son.

"I'm trying, Lord. I'm really trying."

34

Isaac knocked on the door and waited as footsteps thudded toward him.

Cynda opened the door. "What do you want?"

Isaac reminded himself of Pastor Paul's message. *A godly man bridles his tongue.* "Your husband wants you home. He wants you to stop running away from him."

"Who's at the door?" a woman called from the back room.

"Nobody," Cynda yelled,

"I'm a friend of Cynda's husband. He's been looking for her."

"Oh my goodness, come in here. I need to see you," Ms. Dobbs said, anxiously moving around in her bed.

Cynda rolled her eyes as she shut the door behind Isaac and showed him to Ms. Dobbs's bedroom. The aged woman reached out her hands, and Isaac took them. "I'm Geraldine Dobbs, and you couldn't have come at a more opportune time," she said, all smiles.

"Why is that, ma'am?"

Still smiling, Ms. Dobbs said, "I've been laying here praying for my beautiful one." She looked at Cynda for a moment then turned back to Isaac. "She's hurting real bad. But I knew she would never go back to that man without some help. So I prayed and prayed that God would help him find her."

Isaac smiled now. "God *is* in the helping business."

Ms. Dobbs looked to Heaven and waved her hand. "Yes, He is." She then squeezed Isaac's hand. "Now you go talk some sense into that girl. Tell her to go home so that man of hers can help take care of that baby."

"I'll do my best." Isaac turned back to Cynda. "Can we go somewhere and talk?"

Her eyes rolled again as she walked out of the room, Isaac following. "I'll be on the porch if you need me, Ms. Dobbs," she said, while opening the front door. Cynda sat down on the porch swing as silence engulfed the space between them.

Finding his voice, Isaac told her, "Your husband needs you."

"Keith is better off without me. He just doesn't know it yet." She lifted her feet, so the swing could rock her. "Why don't you go tell him all the reasons I'm no good for him again? Maybe he'll listen this time. After all, I did prove you right on one point. I left him again, didn't I?"

"Yeah, but you proved me wrong on the other—You didn't go back to prostitution."

"Well, don't sing my praises. I was two seconds from going back on the street when this job fell in my lap."

"Do you really think you could've gone back to that lifestyle after coming so far away from it?"

She put her elbow on her thigh and her hand on her chin as she pondered his question. "I could have gone back."

"If you accepted a job like this, taking care of an elderly lady, basically being a recluse yourself, I don't think you would have gone back to prostitution."

"I would've gone back, but then I would've killed myself just so I wouldn't have to numb the feeling of guilt and shame."

* * *

He pictured her standing before him at the tent revival, accusing him of selling her into prostitution. Then he remembered the day he took her over to Spoony's and was disgusted with her. He'd wanted out of the relationship. And then he remembered Spoony saying, "Man, let me know when you are through with that."

"Do me that favor," he'd responded.

Spoony sat down and rubbed his hands. "How much you want for her? I know she's been running your stuff since Valerie died. I'm prepared to compensate you."

Laughing, he told Spoony, "Man, give me fifty cents. I don't care. Just take her off my hands."

All these years Isaac had been delivered from the game, delivered from running women, and he'd never even apologized to Cynda. He'd been too caught up in the things she'd done to him. But now as he chose to see it her way, he realized that he'd brought all that on himself. If he hadn't been so callous with her feelings, she wouldn't have snitched to the police on him, and he was sure she would have told him about his child.

"I'm sorry, Cynda. I have wronged you on so many levels." He closed his eyes. He reopened them and told her, "I wish to God I could take back what I—"

Raising her hand, she said, "Don't even sweat it. You were right about me."

Sitting down next to her, he lifted her face, forcing her to look at him. "No, I was wrong about you. Keith was right. From the moment he married you he loved and believed in you." He stretched forth his hands, sweeping them up and down her attire. "You're changing, Cynda. Day by day you are becoming the person Keith always believed you could be."

"His love has changed me. That's why I have got to love him enough to stay away."

Isaac put his finger over her lips, silencing her. "See it differently, Cynda. Love him enough to make him happy."

"I want him to be happy. That's why I left."

"*You* make him happy. If you don't go back, the man will die alone. You are the only one he wants."

"I don't want to hurt him anymore."

"Well, he's hurting right now." Isaac stood. "Our daughter misses you too, Cynda. She wants you in her life."

"Wait a minute. Did you just say *our* daughter?"

"That's what she is, right?"

She stood now. "Yeah, but ever since you found out about Iona, she's only been *your* daughter, like I had nothing to do with her."

"Okay, I can see that you're one of those people that don't forgive easily. You like to hold stuff over people's head, so I think you really need to go home, because you need Keith for things like this."

"And you need Nina."

"True, that. But I'm not a fool, Cynda. I'm going home to my wife. What about you?"

She stood up off the swing and slowly walked the length of the porch, clasping her hands together and then unclasping them. "And you promise that you won't give me any problems about seeing Iona?"

"We'll work something out. And I'll be reasonable."

"And you really don't think Keith will find someone else if I stay away a little longer?"

"No, Cynda. He only wants you."

A big grin covered her face. "Okay. Tell my husband that I'll be home as soon as I find someone to take over my responsibilities here."

"I don't think that's going to go over too well with him. Why don't you let me take you home today?"

"I can't do that, Isaac. Ms. Dobbs has been good to me.

She's bedridden, so I can't just leave her with no one to take care of her."

"Okay. I'll go tell your husband that he should expect you in a couple of days. Hopefully he won't punch me for botching the job he sent me to do." He massaged his jaw. "Your husband has a violent streak, you know that, right?"

Laughing, Cynda nudged him. "He was provoked. You just can't mess with the man's wife and expect to get away with it." She stopped laughing and pointed a finger at him. "And that's another thing, no more sermons about me."

"You should have been at the revival. The sermon was on me. And I didn't like it much either."

Isaac drove back to Keith's house without Cynda. With the traffic, it took him an hour to get back to Keith's house. When he arrived, Isaac gave his friend a play-by-play of the events.

Keith's eyes bulged. "She's not coming back until she finds a replacement?"

"Don't sweat it, man. The thing is, she wants to come home. She wasn't running game on me. She'll be here. Just be patient."

"All right. Thanks for your help, man. Can I take you to dinner or something?"

"Naw, I'm straight. I've got one more stop to make before I head home. I'll pick up something before I go there."

They hugged and said their goodbyes.

Thirty minutes later, Isaac found himself parked in front of his father's house, another person he'd figured God allowed him to hate, and to deny forgiveness. After all, the man had killed his mother. Subsequently, his little brother had also been murdered. He hated thinking about that thirteen-year-old boy that had become so lost. Hated going back to that awful time. But sitting in front of this house, there was nothing else he could do but remember.

* * *

When they'd arrived home from church that day, Isaac's usually wrong daddy started in on his mother. It was just barely one o'clock on a Sunday afternoon, but that no-job-having mug had a beer in his hand talkin' 'bout, "Where's my dinner? Do I have to do everything around here?"

How doing nothing but lying on your lazy behind had turned into "doing everything around here," Isaac didn't know. Nor did he have time to ponder it. He headed upstairs to change out of his Sunday best and get away from the drama. He opened his top drawer to put away his tie and socks. His thick red sock that held his money had been moved from its normal spot at the left corner of his drawer, and had less money than when he'd last checked it. "That bum robbed me again," thirteen-year-old Isaac said.

He heard his mother scream. Isaac swore under his breath and slammed his dresser drawer shut. "That's it. He is getting outta here." He opened his bedroom door and stormed down the stairs.

Slam! Boom! Crash!

By the time Isaac made it to the living room, Donavan was on the phone dialing 9-1-1. "Usually Wrong" was standing over his mama, yelling, "Get up, girl! Ain't nothing wrong with you."

Isaac looked at his mama stretched out on the floor, on top of the glass that used to be the coffee table. Blood was splattered all over the ugly orange carpet, and Mama wasn't moving. "What did you do to my Mama?" Isaac yelled.

"Boy, don't question me. Go on back upstairs."

"I said, what did you do to my Mama?"

Isaac's daddy turned to face him. "Oh, so you smelling yourself now, huh? You want a piece of me, boy?"

Isaac looked at the still form of his mother. His lip curled as he balled his fist. "Yeah, that's exactly what I want."

"Come on, Isaac," Donavan said, "don't do this. The ambulance is on its way."

Usually Wrong rubbed his fist in his palm. "Come on, boy. I'm gon' give you the whuppin' of your life."

A savage rage boiled in Isaac that he couldn't contain. When it exploded, his dad was pummeled with the residue of Isaac's violence, but he still didn't win. When the ambulance and police arrived on the scene, they carried his sweet mama out in a body bag. Usually Wrong went to the hospital, and Isaac went to juvie. He stopped believing in God when they sat him in the back seat of that police car.

Two years later, when his brother was in an alley shooting dice and a bullet exploded in his head, Isaac wished for the existence of God. He wanted to track God down, and curse Him to his ain't-never-looked-out-for-nobody face, but it was useless. Nobody was going to come out of the sky to see about him, to hear his cries. Only the rain came.

He was in his thirties before he stepped foot in church again. But it took prison, a trip to hell, and the events of September 11 before Isaac bowed his knee to God. Now he was finally ready to release the man that had caused him so much pain and, in the process, free them both.

When Isaac got out of the car and knocked on the door, his pudgy father opened the door and stood there with widening eyes. Isaac lifted a bucket of KFC and said, "I just left Keith's house. Thought I'd come by and check on you before I went home."

"Well, don't just stand on the porch letting the chicken get cold. Get on in here."

Isaac hadn't stepped a foot in this house since he was thirteen. He'd never wanted to see the spot where his mother took her last breath. But as he walked through the living room and noted that the bloody orange carpet had been replaced with tan carpet, and a wood table had replaced the glass one his mother fell through, he gently reminded himself to see it differently. His mother was already in Heaven.

It was high time he worked on getting his father there. If he could get his father to Heaven, maybe God would allow the man to meet up with his first wife and apologize to her, just as God had allowed Isaac to apologize for the wrong he'd done to Cynda.

As if reading his thoughts, his father said, "I'm glad you're here. I've been trying to read this Bible your wife gave me for Christmas, but I can't make sense of some of the passages."

"Let's eat this chicken, then we can go over some of those verses you're not understanding, okay."

"That'll be just fine, son. Just fine."

35

Determined not to wait another day, Keith went to Janet, hat in hand, and offered to double her salary if she would take on Cynda's responsibilities with Ms. Dobbs for the duration of her two-week notice. To his surprise, she told him, "I think getting away would do me some good right now. I'll do it."

Cynda was standing in the living room looking out the window when Keith and Janet pulled into Ms. Dobbs driveway. She felt her heart begin to race, and the palm of her hands became warm and sweaty. "Stop this. You're acting like a teenager." But in some ways she was like a teenager, feeling brand-new. She loved a man, and he loved her back, a first for her, something that should have happened to her years ago. But Keith had been worth the wait.

Cynda watched Keith and Janet come up the walkway. He waved at her. She smiled and returned the wave. Her feet, however, were still planted in front of that window, watching him come back into her life, just as he'd done so many times before.

Please, God, don't let me disappoint my husband again. Help me to love him the way he deserves to be loved. Cynda backed away from the window. She realized that she had actually uttered a prayer to God, something she had promised never to do. But her prayer was for Keith, and she could find no wrong in praying for her husband.

Cynda opened the door and fell into Keith's arms.

He'd heard Cynda utter the words the night she'd left him for the third time, but now he could feel the love she had for him by the way she held him. Tears of joy sprang to his eyes as he realized *This is it.* This is the love that God had in mind for Keith when He'd asked him to love Cynda, but Keith couldn't see it then. God had given him a gift, one that belonged to him alone.

Keith's gift from God hugged him so tight that he worried that the baby might get crushed. He moved her back a bit. That's when he saw that she was crying too.

"I prayed, Keith," Cynda told him excitedly. "I prayed that God would help me love you the way you deserve to be loved."

He smiled. "You already are, baby. I can feel your love."

Janet tapped Keith on the shoulder. "Can I come in, or are you paying me to stand on the porch?"

"Sorry about that." Keith stepped to the side and allowed her to walk into the house.

Cynda smiled and extended her hand. "Hello, Janet."

"Hello, Cynda." Janet briefly shook Cynda's hand.

"Thank you so much for taking my place here," Cynda told her. "You will love Ms. Dobbs. She's a very spiritual woman."

Janet didn't respond and just looked at every area in the living room so she could avoid eye contact with Cynda.

Keith gently rubbed his wife's stomach. "Is he moving yet?"

Cynda smacked his hand. "It might be a girl, you know."

Still rubbing her belly, he stood smiling at her. He liked

the way she was looking at him. Like she'd missed him more than simple words could say, a far cry from the way she'd looked at him when he married her. She moved his hand and put her arms around his neck and planted a kiss on his lips.

"You ready to go home, aren't you?"

"Sure am. I already talked with Ms. Dobbs's son, and he's okay with Janet working here while he finds a permanent replacement." Cynda turned back to Janet. "Let me introduce you to Ms. Dobbs."

They went into Ms. Dobbs's bedroom, and Cynda introduced Janet to her. She let the two have a quick conversation. Cynda put her hand on Keith's arm and told her employer, "Ms. Dobbs, this is Keith."

"I could tell that by the smile on your face. Come here, young man," Ms. Dobbs said. When Keith moved closer to her bed, she told him, "Don't let this one get away again, you hear me? Even if you have to put bars on the windows and chains on the doors." She winked at Keith. "It'll be for her own good. She's miserable without you."

Cynda smiled. "I'll thank you to not tell my business. Maybe I wanted him to think I was having the time of my life cleaning after you."

"You aren't fooling anybody, girl. I knew from the time you walked through my front door that your heart was aching. Now look at you. I think this is the first smile I've ever seen on your face."

Cynda linked arms with Keith. "That's because I got my man back."

"You go on home, beautiful one," Ms. Dobbs told her. "I'll be all right."

Keith smiled. "Beautiful one, huh?"

"Don't you think she's the most beautiful person you've ever seen?" Ms. Dobbs asked Keith.

"I sure do. And if you don't mind, I think I'll use that name for her myself."

Backing away, hands raised, Cynda said, "Careful, you two. I may be pretty on the outside, but my insides are still ugly."

"That's for God to work out." Ms. Dobbs kissed Cynda on the cheek. "Let Him do His work."

Before they left, Cynda gave Janet a tour of the house, showing her where the linens, medication, and cleaning supplies were kept. When she was finished, Cynda asked Janet if she had any questions.

They were standing in the kitchen, and Janet turned away from Cynda. "I'm sure I'll be fine. If I need anything, I'll ask Ms. Dobbs or her son."

Cynda got the message. Janet didn't want to be around her one second longer than was necessary. Cynda couldn't blame her. Truth be told, if she'd found Janet cheating on Keith, she wouldn't have wanted to be in the same room with her either. Cynda put her hand on Janet's shoulder and gently turned her around. "I'm sorry, Janet. I know I wasn't very nice to you that day you came to Keith's house."

"Do you think I care if you're nice to me?" Janet lifted her arm and pointed in the direction of Ms. Dobbs's room, where Keith was still holding court with the old woman. "It's Keith I'm worried about. You're going to go home with him today and then run off and break his heart all over again."

Cynda had no defense. All she could say to Janet was, "You were right when you told me that I didn't deserve his love."

"And you told me that you didn't want his love, and that you were getting out of his house the moment the getting was good. So why are you going back, pretending to love him now?"

Cynda pulled out a chair and sat down. "Keith made me love him. Don't you see, Janet, I didn't have a choice. He kept loving and forgiving and taking me back, no matter what I'd done to him." Cynda looked up, her eyes imploring Janet to understand. "How could I not love him?"

Janet had this dumbfounded look on her face. "So you're not just using him so you'll have a father for your baby?"

Cynda shook her head no.

"And you really do love him?"

Smiling, Cynda stood back up. "Yeah, I really love that big teddy bear."

Janet walked over to Cynda and put her arms around her. As they hugged, Janet said, "Don't ever let him go again, Cynda, not ever."

Cynda had a smile on her face the whole drive home. Keith held his wife's hand as he maneuvered through the traffic. When they walked through the front door, Cynda announced to the walls, "I'm home."

Keith pulled her into his arms. "For good this time, okay." He lifted her face with his index finger so he could look into her eyes. "I need you in my life, beautiful one."

"Where would I go? Nobody has ever loved me like you."

Keith wanted to tell her about the One who wanted to love her even more than he could, but she wasn't ready for that yet, so he'd love her the way God wanted and pray that would be enough to guide her.

Days turned to weeks, and the weeks flowed into months as Cynda and Keith adjusted to life together. He was still going to church alone, even though she'd asked him to read the Bible out loud to her at least a couple times a week. She decorated the house, always careful to ask if he liked the changes she wanted to make, and was careful with the budget they set.

One evening as they stood holding one another while

discussing plans for the baby's room, Keith said, "I don't care what you do to *Junior*'s room, just as long as you sit a bunch of teddy bears in there and paint the room blue or some other boyish color."

She moved away from him, walked over to the crib, and tossed the baby's pillow around.

He went to her, put his arms around her, and spread his hands around her belly. "What just happened, baby?"

"What are you talking about?" Cynda asked, puzzled.

"I was holding you over there. I thought we were having a moment, and you left me to come play with this pillow." He took the pillow out of her hand and turned her around to face him. "What's wrong?

"You keep calling the baby *Junior*." She ran her hands through her hair and took a step back, putting distance between them. "I don't want to name this baby after you. It wouldn't be fair. After I have this baby, I promise I'll keep having kids until we have *your* Junior, okay."

"And what will we tell our first son when he asks why his little brother is a Junior and he's not?" Keith shook his head. "No, Cynda, I won't have my son wondering if I love him less because he doesn't have my blood. This child will be named after me."

"I might be having a girl, Keith, and then this whole conversation is pointless."

"It's a boy." Keith smiled like a proud papa. "I can feel it."

"He won't look anything like you, Keith."

Keith smiled again. "You know what they say, if you feed 'em long enough they start to look like you, so I'll just have to overfeed this one."

She hugged him. "Keith Hosea Williams, you make it hard for a woman not to love you."

"You better love me, girl. I'm your baby's daddy."

36

Isaac and Cynda agreed that Iona would spend the summer with her, so as soon as school was out, Keith and Cynda went to pick her up. They'd gone to Dayton to visit on the weekend twice since the incident in the park, but this was different. Iona would be with her for a month and a half. Cynda was excited.

Cynda, now in her seventh month, struggled to get out of the car in the July heat, so Keith helped her out.

Nina opened the door to welcome them. "Dinner's almost ready. Just have a seat and I'll call you when I'm finished." Nina then yelled upstairs, "Iona, your mom is here."

Iona opened her door and came running down the stairs. "Mom, you're here, you're here!"

Cynda bent as best she could and wrapped her arms around her child. "I have missed you something awful."

Iona kissed her mother. "Look how big you've gotten." She pointed at her mother's stomach.

Nina walked to the kitchen, and Keith followed her. He washed his hands in the sink and started chopping cucumbers for the salad. "How've you been doing?" he asked Nina.

"I've been good."

"How are things with Iona?"

"It's been hard at times, but she's come around more in this last month than the entire time she's been with us."

"You think you'll miss her much this summer?"

She took the roast out of the oven then faced Keith with the truth. "It's funny the way things work, but I think I will. I'll probably cry myself to sleep the first few nights she's away. Isaac will probably harass you about bringing Iona home early, and then I'll adjust." She hunched her shoulders. "It's just the way life is."

"I just wish we didn't have to hurt you to be able to see her."

Nina gave him an adoring hug. "You're such a sweet man. I love you for thinking of me."

Isaac strolled into the kitchen. "Hey, get your hands off my woman."

"You just better be glad you saw her first," Keith said.

"Or what would have happened, Mr. Williams?" All eyes turned toward Cynda as she wobbled into the kitchen.

"I-I would've introduced her to Isaac, because I am a one-woman man." Keith went to Cynda and put his arms around her. "Ain't that right, baby?"

"It better be. You know I'm extra hormonal right now, so don't give me a reason to go off." She looked at Nina teasingly. "Like some too-cute-to-be-left-alone-with-my-man woman hugging on him."

"Girl, you don't have anything to worry about. The man I've got is a handful, so I sure don't want some other woman's untrained troubles."

Nina and Cynda both laughed.

Isaac looked to Keith. "I think we're being disrespected."

Keith grabbed Isaac's arm. "Let's go in the living room, so they can do this behind our backs."

Nina and Cynda worked in the kitchen getting the meal ready. Cynda turned to Nina and said, "Look, I'm not too good at admitting when I'm wrong or letting people know how sorry I am for stuff that should've never been done." Her lip quivered. "Iona has told me how much you've done for her since she's been here. I wish I could say I would've done the same for you, had the shoe been on the other foot, but I know I wouldn't have." Tears filled her eyes. "I'm just not good like you and Keith." She rubbed the small swell of her belly. "I still can't believe Keith wants to raise this child." She shuffled her feet. "Look, I'm going to get out of your way. I just wanted to thank you, that's all." Cynda turned to walk out the kitchen.

"Wait a minute."

She turned, and Nina pulled her into her arms. They held onto each other as they let go of the past and allowed themselves to move forward.

"See what I mean?" Cynda pulled away from Nina and wiped away her tears. "I never would've hugged you like that, not after all I've done to you."

Nina and Cynda then set the food on the dinning room table and yelled for their family to come eat. Donavan said grace, and the green beans, potato salad, corn on the cob, and roasted chicken disappeared within minutes.

Not much table conversation was going on while the food was being devoured, but once the dinner was in everyone's belly, questions about the baby came pouring out of Donavan and Iona.

Donavan asked Keith, "So is this going to be my god-brother or -sister, since you're my godfather?"

"You're right, Donavan. My child will be your god-brother or -sister."

"And even though we won't have the same father, he'll still be my brother, right, Mom?"

Cynda put her hand on Iona's hair. "That's right, baby." She looked around the table, amazed at how far they had come in the past few months. She and Isaac were behaving like adults, communicating with Iona's best interest at heart, laying aside their own selfish motives. She'd even granted Isaac an extra week with Iona. Isaac did baptisms at the church every second Sunday of the month, and Iona told her that she wanted to stay an extra week, to be baptized by her father.

Still seated at the dinning room table, Nina turned to Iona. "Are you excited about tomorrow, honey?"

Jumping in her seat, she responded, "You bet. I can't wait."

"What if Daddy drops you and you drown in that water? I bet that won't be so fun, huh."

"Shut up, boy." Isaac muffed Donavan on the back of his head then turned back to Iona. "Don't listen to your knuckle-head brother. I haven't dropped not one person in all the years I've been baptizing people. So do you think I'm going to slip up now when I've got my precious daughter in my arms?"

Iona started jumping again. "Nope, I sure don't." She licked her tongue at Donavan.

Cynda cautiously asked her daughter, "Do you think you're old enough to give yourself to God? Baptism is a serious thing."

Iona waved off her mother's concern. "I'm not getting saved tomorrow, Mom."

"You're not? So you changed your mind about getting baptized?"

"No, I am getting baptized tomorrow, but I got saved last month."

Eyebrow arched in confusion, Cynda asked, "Well, do you think you're too young to be getting saved?" She looked to Nina and Isaac. "Now, I understand that you will try to influence her in that direction. I just think she should be able to make up her own mind on this subject."

Iona held up her tiny hands. "Oh no, Mama, they didn't influence me on this. I just figured that since God's been loving me for almost eleven years, it was high time I started loving Him back."

Nina smiled but said nothing until she and Cynda were clearing the dishes and the rest of the family had moved into another room. "Did you understand what Iona was trying to tell you about the difference between baptism and salvation?"

Cynda sighed. "I had no idea, but I was too embarrassed to ask my own child to explain something like that to me."

"Well, what Iona was trying to tell you was, baptism is just an outward showing of a heart change that has already taken place on the inside of us. Make sense now?"

Cynda put the dishes on the counter. "Yeah, I think I get it. It's kind of like how I decided not to wear certain clothes, because to me those clothes represent who I was before I married Keith. So I tried to show him outwardly that I was different."

Close enough. Nina wasn't going to split hairs on an issue that Cynda would have to come to understand through a true heart change, which only God could give her. "So are you okay with going to church tomorrow? I know what happened the last time kind of made you back off of going to church."

"I had a talk with your husband about that. He knows better than to call me out in front of his congregation again."

"Good."

"Anyway," Cynda continued, "this is important to Iona, so I have to be there. I'm tired of missing out on special moments in my child's life."

Later that night, Cynda and Keith took the kids out for a movie, while Nina and Isaac stayed home.

"You hear that?" Isaac asked.

Nina furrowed her brows. "Hear what? I don't hear anything."

Isaac stretched out on the couch and pulled Nina down with him. "That's what I'm talking about—Peace and quiet. It's been a long time since we had any of that."

"Amen, Pastor Walker. Peace and quite is a good thing." She adjusted herself on the couch next to him then turned on the TV with the remote. "What do you want to watch on this Saturday evening?"

"I don't think there are any games on that I want to see, so you choose."

"Oh no. The last time I picked what we were going to watch you talked about me for a week."

Tickling her, he said, "That's because you picked a chick flick. Pick anything but a mushy love story."

"I like love stories."

Isaac frowned.

Nina turned off the TV. "Okay, then let's just talk."

"I like that idea, Mrs. Walker. Can you tell me something?"

Nina snuggled up closer to her man. "What?"

Isaac put his arms her. "Everybody seems to be doing better. I'm getting along with Cynda, you're getting along with Iona."

Nina arched her eyebrow.

"Most of the time."

"Okay."

"I know that you haven't conceived yet, so I was just wondering how you're doing. Are you okay with how things are?"

Nina smiled as she planted a kiss on her husband's forehead. "I'm okay. In fact, Mr. Walker, I figured something out."

"Well, don't keep me in suspense, woman. Enlighten me."

"You remember that my doctor told me he thought I was going into menopause the same day you brought Iona home?"

"Yeah, I remember."

"Well, I believe she was a gift to me. Iona coming to our house was God's way of telling me that He hasn't forgotten me, that I will have more children."

Isaac kissed her. "God can do it, baby. We've just got to trust Him."

"I know. Now I have a question for you."

"Shoot."

"Do you have your sermon ready for tomorrow?"

"Sure do. I finished it the other night."

Nina pointed her finger at him. "Nothing is in that sermon that will upset Cynda, right?"

"Stop worrying. I'm done with all that."

She leaned back against him. "Good. Did you call your father?"

Isaac and his dad had been having weekly talks since he arrived home from Chicago a couple months back. Nina didn't know what brought about this change in her husband, but she was appreciative of the fact that Isaac was changing, growing more in tune with God.

"Yeah, he's not going to be able to come for the baptism, though. He hasn't been feeling well lately. He's got a doctor's appointment on Monday morning, so we'll know more then."

"No sense waiting on the doctor's report when we can pray right now."

Isaac stood up, pulling Nina with him. "Let's do it. But since were praying, we might as well pray for Cynda too. That woman is still confused about God."

"Yeah, she is, but she's coming around."

37

The next day the Walker family got up early to have their last Sunday breakfast together before Iona left for the summer. They then went to church.

As Isaac baptized his only daughter, he felt a love for this child that was just as great as the love he felt for Donavan. *This is my child, Lord. I hope You are pleased with her. Take her and make her into what You desire her to be.*

He looked out into the midst of the congregation. Nina was smiling and crying at the same time. He had married a truly special woman. Iona may have given her heart to the Lord, but she was still giving Nina the blues. That his wife could be happy for Iona was a true testament to her walk with God. *Lord, do something miraculous for Nina. Give her the desires of her heart.*

When he stood behind the pulpit and preached, he felt compelled not to use the message he'd worked on all week, but the Holy Spirit had redirected him to preach the word God had given him during the revival. The word Isaac had ignored in favor of his own agenda. He wasn't ignoring God today. So he opened his Bible and preached a message of love.

Cynda sat next to Keith and Iona. Her daughter was glowing with the love of Christ, and so too was her husband. As Isaac preached, Cynda looked around at the congregation and noticed how willingly they accepted the knowledge that God could love them so much that he was willing to give up His only begotten son. She also began to understand Keith better when Isaac said that it was God's loving kindness that drew people to Him.

Keith had loved her with kindness. The more patient and loving he was toward her, the more he kept drawing her back into his arms. Keith loved her like God loves His people. Right then and there Cynda stopped worrying about her past issues with God and closed her eyes, willing herself to feel His presence. She told herself, *If I can feel His presence, then I'll give Him my heart.*

Keith leaned over and put his arms around her, causing her insides to flutter.

"What was that for?"

"I just could tell that you needed to feel something, so I hugged you."

Keith had once read her a passage out of the Bible where Jesus told a group of people who asked to see God, "When you see me, you've seen the Father." So maybe when she felt Keith's love, that was God's way of showing His love for her also.

"Dear Lord, You have been here for me, haven't You?" Cynda asked.

"What?" Keith asked.

Cynda shushed him and continued to listen to the message. When Isaac finished and gave an altar call for those who wanted a personal relationship with Jesus, Cynda squeezed Keith's and Iona's hand, then stood in the middle of the aisle. She saw tears cascade down Keith's boyish face, but she couldn't move. Her feet felt as if they were stuck to the blue-carpeted floor. But then her eyes were drawn to the altar.

A man clothed in a brilliant white robe beckoned her with outstretched hands. A rainbow was upon his head, and his face shone like the sun. His feet were like pillars of fire. It was the same man who'd helped her when she was nine years old and had gotten lost. The same man who blew the breath of life into her and wiped away her sweat and tears while she lay disoriented and confused at that rehab. He was waiting for her. She couldn't wait to get to him. She had to tell him he was right. The Good Shepherd had followed her all the days of her life until she finally relented and allowed His love to guide her home.

As Cynda bowed before the altar, the sweet love that God had long desired to bestow on her now flowed into her heart, dissolving all worries of going back to prostitution and not being good enough for her husband. She would be all right now, for God loved her, and she loved Him right back.

A woman dressed in a white button-down shirt and black skirt touched her shoulders. "Would you like me to pray with you?" she asked Cynda.

Head still bowed, Cynda pointed to her friend. "I want to pray with him."

The lady whispered in her ear. "No one is over there."

Cynda smiled as she allowed the woman to help her up. "Yes, I'd like prayer very much."

When they were in the car getting ready to head back to Chicago, Cynda asked Keith if he could stop at West Memory Garden Cemetery. On their way, Keith saw a man standing on the side of the road selling flowers. He pulled over and bought a dozen carnations and handed them to Cynda, saying, "I figured you might want these for your visit."

Cynda leaned over and kissed him. "You think of everything. Thank you."

As they pulled up to the grounds, Keith asked, "Do you want me and Iona to walk through the cemetery with you?"

"No, baby. I need to do this on my own."

Iona leaned up from the back seat. "Are you sure, Mama? You don't walk so good on your own."

"I'll make it, honey. Don't worry about me."

Keith helped Cynda out of the car. "Do you have your cell phone in your purse?" he asked.

"Yeah."

"Call me if you need help getting back."

She assured them that she was no fool and headed up the road toward her family's plot. Even though she hadn't been to this place since she'd buried her grandmother over a decade ago, not much had changed. The caretakers had done regular maintenance, the grass was mowed, and the weeds cut down. The mammoth-sized headstones and smaller marble headstones jutted up from the ground, outshining her family's ground-level brass plates. Her family probably hadn't received any special care since their bodies had been laid in this plot.

Cynda put six of the carnations on her grandmother's side. Smiling, she stepped back and told her grandmother, "I know you spent a lot of nights praying for me, Grammy, so I came here today to let you know that I'm okay. I did get lost again." She turned toward the parking area and saw Keith leaning against their car. She then turned back to her Grammy, "But this nice man helped me find my way back." A tear trickled down her lovely face. "I accepted Christ into my life, Grammy. Isn't that wonderful?"

Cynda turned toward her mother's grave and paused for a moment. She'd carried a lot of hatred for this woman and felt justified in blaming her for everything that went wrong in her life. Cynda had always justified her man-hopping ways by saying, "What do you expect? My mother was a whore." She'd justified taking drugs because she needed to forget the stuff her mother allowed her pimp to do to her. But the truth of the whole matter was, she had stood by and numbly participated in everything that happened to her in her adult life.

"I hated you for so long, Mama, blamed you for everything." Her eyes misted over with tears that cascaded down her face. Wiping the tears away, she said, "It's time I take some blame on my own shoulders. Time for me to let you rest in peace."

Cynda took the remaining six carnations and placed them one by one on her mother's grave until they formed a perfect heart. "I have a husband now and a daughter." She patted her stomach. "Oh yeah, we have a child on the way also. I'm going to tell my children about the good things you and I did together. Like the many presents you used to give me on my birthday and Christmas. Good memories, that's what I'm going to give them." And as she thought on those things, it didn't hurt so much to think of her mother.

A couple of fat raindrops plopped on her forehead, the beginning of the forecasted rain storm.

"Cynda."

She turned to see Keith waving her toward him.

"I've got to go," Cynda said as she turned back to her grandmother's grave. "In case I never told you when I was little, I love you, Grammy." She looked at her mother's grave, hesitated a moment, then with one long-suffering sigh and another plop of rain on her head, she gave her gripes with her mother over to God and said, "I love you, Mama. Wish I could have spent more time with you."

Keith kept glancing at the sky as she walked toward him. She saw the worry lines etched on his face. She wasn't worried though. No harm could come to her underneath God's sprinkler system, only cleansing.

Epilogue

Keith Hosea Williams, Jr. was born on a Sunday afternoon in mid-September, four hours after service ended and three weeks after Cynda and Keith had taken Iona back home. Cynda felt the pains all during service, but she was having such a good time in praise and worship, and then the pastor preached such a mighty word, that she couldn't bring herself to tell Keith she was in pain. When her water broke, she tapped him on the shoulder. "I think you'd better take me to the hospital."

"What? Is it the baby?" Keith stood up just as pastor Norton was making his altar call. "Let me help you up."

Taking hold of her arm, Keith pulled her out of her seat as men and women were walking down to the altar. "Did you pee on yourself?" he asked as he viewed the puddle in the seat Cynda had just vacated.

"No, baby," she whispered. "My water broke."

"Your water broke!" he yelled loud enough for the entire congregation to hear.

Janet sat three pews in front of them, next to Harold Dobbs. She had a 3-carat diamond ring on her engagement finger and an endearing smile on her face. She turned in Cynda's direction. "Congratulations."

Pastor Norton said, "Congratulations, and a safe arrive to the little one." He waved them off and continued to minister to his congregation.

The baby was now in Keith's arm. Cynda saw the tears at the corner of his eyes as he cooed and made faces over the baby. When he looked at her, the tears cascaded down his face. "Thank you for my son."

A twinge of guilt kicked at her heart, and she almost opened her mouth to remind him that the child wasn't his, but then she thought of how his love had opened up a whole new world for her, caused her to see and feel things in a manner that she would never have thought possible before he came along.

Tears of joy filled her eyes as she bent over and kissed her son and his father. She looked to Heaven and silently said, *Thank you, Lord, for loving me, even when I was unlovable.*

Two angels stood outside the most magnificent pearl-laden gates shouting, "Behold the glory of God!"

Directly behind the pearly gates was a massive space, where a cushion of snowy white clouds caressed the feet of its occupants. The tree of life, its leaves a heavenly green, and its fruit succulent and enjoyed by all, stood bold and beautiful in the middle of the outer court. Sweet, blissful music could be heard throughout the great expanse of Heaven. It was the harp, but it was better than any harp on earth; it was the guitar, but it was better than any guitar on earth.

Clothed in glistening white robes, and bare feet, thousands upon thousands of saints moved through the joys of Heaven. Many had crowns on their heads with various types of jewels embedded in them. Several occupants stood, surrounded by the most beautiful array of flowers, some of which had colors out of this world. Heaven was the great garden of love, so these flowerbeds could be found all over this glorious place.

On the opposite side of the outer court stood a great multitude of warrior angels in all their beauty and majesty, protecting the saints of God. They wore white radiant garments with gold-edged trim that embellished the front of the garment. At their waist hung a huge golden sword, and large white wings flapped from behind.

The outer court was like a waiting room. The saints were waiting to be admitted into the inner court, and some, the holy of holies. The warrior angels waited for their next assignments.

Right now, a great commotion was going on amongst the angels. They were anxious to know their next assignment. Some had been waiting hundreds of years to do what they were designed to do. The captain of these angels lifted his hands to silence them. "Brothers," he said, "I will have news for you momentarily. I am on my way to meet with the General now."

"Captain Aaron," a familiar voice among the angels called out to him.

"Yes, Arnoth?"

"I have completed my mission."

"And well you have. I will talk to the General about your wings."

Arnoth bowed. "Thank you, sir."

Aaron disappeared from the heavenly hosts in the outer court and walked through the inner court, with its unnumbered mansions and room enough for everyone, on his way to the Holy Place. Sadly enough, the beauty and splendor of Heaven would only be enjoyed by the few that served God. As he passed by the room of tears, he glanced in and shook his head in wonderment. It still amazed him that humans had tears so precious that God would bottle and preserve them in a room as glorious as this.

He opened the door of the Holy Place and stood in the back, as he heard the voice of thunder and lightning. He then heard a multitude of praises. As the voices became thunderous, Aaron also joined them. In this place, where God sits high and is lifted up, praises are sung to Him forever. His glory lovingly fills the atmosphere, spreading joy throughout His Heavenly court.

His omnipotence glistened through the emerald rainbow arched above the magnificent throne. The twenty-four elders surrounding Him were also seated on thrones, and clothed in white radiant robes, crowns of gold on their heads.

Seven lamps of fire were burning and a sea of crystal lay at the Master's feet. In the midst of the throne and around it, were four living creatures with eyes covering their entire body. The first living creature was like a lion, the second, a calf, the third, a man, and the fourth, a flying eagle. Each of the creatures had six massive wings, enabling them to soar high above the thrones, and didn't rest by day or night. Generating cool winds throughout Heaven, they bellowed to their King, "Holy, holy, holy, Lord, God Almighty, who was, and is, and is to come!"

The twenty-four elders fell down before Him and worshipped, saying, "You are worthy, O Lord, to receive glory and honor and power, for You created all things, and by Your will they exist." They threw their crowns before the throne in adoration.

Thunder and lightning sparkled from the throne of grace once more. Then Michael's glorious nine-foot form stood, his colorful wings glistening as they flapped in the air. "Yes, my Lord," he said, as he took the scrolls from the Omnipotent hand that held it.

Michael, whose sword was longer and heavier than the other angels, stood in front of Aaron. Jewels were embedded throughout the handle of his sword, and symbolized his many victories. The belt that held his sword sparkled with the gold of Heaven. Michael had defeated the Prince of Persia more times than he cared to remember, but the enemy was getting stronger as his time drew near. Michael eagerly awaited their next meeting. It would be their last. "Here is your assignment."

Aaron took the scrolls. "My General, my Prince, Arnoth has completed his mission."

Michael smiled. "And so he has."

"Will he be knighted today, sir?"

"Let's get it done."

They left the holy of holies and entered the inner court. The angels got excited at the sight of their general, the one angel who could stand against Lucifer time and time again and come out the victor. After all these years he still amazed them.

Captain Aaron raised his right hand, and the angels fell silent again. He passed out the assignments and sent several thousand angels on their way. Then he said, "Arnoth, come forth."

As a sea of angels parted, Arnoth made his way to the front. He kept his head down, ashamed of the tattered condition of his wings, now torn and shredded in places. His beautiful white wings no longer flapped in the wind, but drooped against his body.

"The battle was fierce," Michael said, as Arnoth stood before him.

Arnoth's head was still bowed low, as he wiped the sweat from his brow. His charge had finally come to the Lord. He'd fought against legions of demons that tried to keep Cynda bound, but those demons didn't prevail. He told his general, "I'm just thankful that God still has some praying saints out there."

"Amen to that," Captain Aaron said.

Michael unsheathed his sword and pronounced over Arnoth, "May the Lord strengthen you to do battle with the forces of darkness until the evil one is shackled." Then he touched both of Arnoth's wings with his sword, and they stretched forth as the wings on an airplane. And as his wings flapped in the air, they became glorious again, showing no sign of the fierce battle he endured to bring one wayward soul back to God.

A Reading Group Guide

1. Although God never stopped loving Cynda, the Lord abhorred her sins. What does the Word tell us about God's view of sin?

2. Until Cynda met Keith, she could not conceive of God's unconditional love for her. If you displayed this kind of love, do you believe that you could win more people to the Lord?

3. Has God ever called you to love a family member or friend unconditionally? Were you able to handle this call from God? Why or why not?

4. From her childhood, Cynda had an angel dispatched to protect and guide her back to her first love. Give biblical examples of Heaven's angels ministering to God's people.

5'.   Throughout the Scriptures, the Lord used wanton-
     ness, particularly in women, to fulfill His purpose. Re-
     view these examples and discuss.

     Old Testament   New Testament
     Genesis 38   John 4:1-30
     Joshua 2; 6:16-27   John 8:1-11
     I Kings 3:16-28   Hebrews 11:31; James 2:25

6.   Keith's love for Cynda was unconditional, but in
     truth, only God loves us unconditionally. How does
     that make you feel to know that God is willing to love
     you right where you are, and love you into repen-
     tance?

7.   During hard times with Cynda, Keith prayed and
     fasted for her deliverance. A regular fast occurs when
     an individual denies food for a certain amount of days
     and only drinks water. However, sometimes individu-
     als fast for only a certain amount of hours per day or
     from certain foods. Can you think of someone that
     you would be willing to fast and pray for?

8.   Isaac's brawl with Keith and Cynda could have ended
     his ministry. Isaac often let the cares of life force his
     spirit man into hibernation. If you find yourself in a
     position like that, how can you get back to right
     standing with God?

9.   Isaac felt his lack of forgiveness toward Cynda and his
     father was justified. But God's word tells us that if we
     do not forgive others then God will not forgive us.
     Why do you suppose God feels so strongly about for-
     giveness?

10. Although Nina's heart broke at the thought of not being able to have another child, she somehow found the strength to open her heart to Iona. Why do you think that was? Do you believe Nina's actions had anything to do with her love for God?

11. If being a Christian means being Christ-like, how do you explain the fact that most Christians do not display unconditional love for their fellowman?